LILY IN BLOOM

BY

T.J. BURTON

Teresa,

Happy reading! Thanks for reading what I hope is is the first of many.

Fondly,

Tammy

2012
Charles Towne Publishing
Charleston, South Carolina

Charles Towne Publishing

Charles Towne Publishing
Charleston, South Carolina 29401
www.charlestownepublish.com

ISBN-13: **978-0615643632**
ISBN-10: **0615643639**

First Charles Towne Publishing edition September 2012

Manufactured in the United States of America

For information regarding special discounts on bulk purchases, please contact Charles Towne Publishing at
accounts@charlestownepublish.com

LILY IN BLOOM

"To my mother. Thank you for your love, support, and inspiration."

Chapter 1

"This color would look lovely on you darling! It is the perfect shade of blue for your eyes." The dressmaker gushed over a bolt of fabric as she held it up under Lillian Carter's chin.

Lily smiled weakly and looked over at her brother, James. She knew that they couldn't afford custom dresses and that was why she hadn't wanted to come to the dress shop at all but her brother had insisted. He wanted her to have new clothes for the upcoming spring season in Boston.

"That's perfect, we'll take it." James said with a stubborn set to his jaw.

"You look like you just swallowed sour milk!" Lily said to her brother with a laugh. James scowled more deeply and gave his sister a hard look. Undeterred, she stopped laughing but continued to smile. "We don't need to buy dresses James. I am sure I can make do with what I have. I can always rework them to be more in fashion."

"Absolutely not. With Tom's wedding happening this season you'll need clothes for all the events we'll be attending. It will be the perfect opportunity for you to be introduced to perspective suitors." James' face remained set.

Lily's smile slipped from her face but she said nothing and James did not notice because his wife had emerged from the dressing room. Elise stood before them in a beautiful pink evening dress. She pirouetted and then stepped in front of the mirror.

"What do you think?" Elise asked with a smile. Her dark hair and eyes were set off beautifully by the fabric, which came off the shoulder and hugged her supple curves.

"You look beautiful." Lily said, with a smile, to her sister-in-law.

James moved closer to inspect his wife and the two shared a look that made Lily turn away with a slight blush on her face. Her brother and Elise had fallen madly in love six years ago and had been married for the past five. They seemed just as passionate about each other now as they had then. Lily hoped for the opportunity to find that for herself someday but her time was running out.

"Miss Carter, why don't you step into the dressing room, I have some dresses made up in that blue silk." The dressmaker discreetly led Lily out of sight of the couple.

As Lily emerged from the dressing room a few minutes later, in a fitted gown with a low neckline currently in fashion, she was glad that James had taken her to buy new dresses. Her current wardrobe had been purchased four years ago when she was fifteen and was far to girlish for a woman almost twenty.

"Lily, it is positively gorgeous! My god, when did you become so stunning!" Elise gushed as she saw the figure Lily posed in the mirror.

Lily looked at her reflection and was taken aback by what she saw. The women in the shop had piled her honey colored hair on top of her head and let a few tendrils fall around her face. The natural curls complimented her high cheek bones and full lips. The color of the dress accentuated the shade of her eyes and made their exotic slant even more noticeable. The dress hugged her curves and made her waist appear non-existent compared to her hips and bosom. She felt like she was seeing herself for the first time.

James positively scowled and turned to his wife. "I have changed my mind. We're not buying these for Lily, men will be crawling over themselves…"

"Too late." Elise cut him off. "This gorgeous creature is about to be unleashed on Boston society. God help them all!"

Their purchasing done, the Carter's left the dress shop to return to their Commonwealth Avenue home. James stepped away to retrieve their carriage while Elise and Lily waited.

Lily took a deep breath of the fresh spring air and looked around. The dressmaker had a dress that fit her almost perfectly and had allowed her to wear it out of the shop. It felt wonderful to be in new clothing. A nearby dogwood was putting out its blooms. By the beginning of May large flowers would cover the tree. It would be wonderful to see greenery again after a long cold winter in Maine. She began to day dream of flower gardens at home and lost herself in the thought. She was so caught up that she did not notice the two boys or the ball that were heading straight for her.

"Toby, look out!" A deep voice pulled her out of her reverie but not in time. A boy of four or five came barreling into her, causing her to lose her balance. As she tried to right herself, she took a step back. Unfortunately, Elise had set down the hat boxes there and she tripped, tumbling to the ground. She felt her head bang an iron fence behind her and pain shot through her body. She saw stars but somehow maintained consciousness.

"Toby! What did I tell you about running when you're not looking!" She heard a sharp male voice.

"I was looking. I was looking at the ball." The little boy responded. If her head hadn't been swimming, she would have laughed.

"Are you alright?" His deep voice pierced through her haze but it took Lily a moment to realize that the question had been directed at her. As she forced her eyes to focus she saw Elise bent down above her. Next to her was the boy who had run into her a moment before. He looked very frightened. She tried to speak but somehow couldn't form the words.

"It's alright. Don't try to talk, just rest for a second." Lily turned to the baritone voice that was coming from her right. Her breath stopped in her throat. Above her was the most gorgeous man she had ever met, Eric Sampson. She had met Eric five years earlier on her first trip to Boston with her brother. Strong hands reached down and slid under her back. Shivers raced up and down her spine that had nothing to do with her fall.

At fourteen, he was the first man that had awoken her to the womanly feelings other girls her age had been talking about. He had wavy dark hair and eyes that seemed to look right through you. A straight nose and strong jaw made his face extremely handsome and his broad shoulders and muscular body had women falling all over themselves to talk to him. He had been charming and witty and Lily had thought of nothing but him the entire season they had spent in Boston.

Eric gently lifted her into the sitting position and her head swam. Lily swallowed hard and forced the butterflies in her stomach down. How could she still react this way after five years? She looked at the only man she had ever desired in her life. He was still amazingly handsome but he seemed older or harder. She wasn't sure what it was but he looked different. No less attractive, but not the rake she had met. As she was about to speak Toby jumped in.

"I'm real sorry I ran into you like that." He looked down at the ground.

Finally, her voice returned to her. She could not stand to see this little boy look so sad over an accident.

"Apology accepted. Accidents happen to everyone." She smiled at him as he looked at her in surprise.

"Do you mean it?" He returned her smile, clearly looking relieved.

"Don't look too happy, Toby. I have not forgiven you and you will be in trouble when we get home." Eric spoke sternly to his son but the man turned and smiled his thanks to her.

"Are you ready to get to your feet?" Eric once again looked at Lily and the butterflies flew up in her chest but she nodded her head. He slowly lifted her from the ground as if she weigh no more than a feather and lightly set her on her feet. She felt slightly dizzy but was afraid to speak. What was happening to her?

As he removed his hands, she began to sway and he once again placed his arms around her, pulling her closer to steady her. She felt hot and her body was tingling everywhere it was touching his, which only made her head swim more. She could not help herself, she tilted her head back looked up into his handsome face.

Recognition and what Lily thought might be desire crossed over Eric's face as he looked down at her and Lily almost forgot to breath. She felt her arms traveling up around his neck and she had no power to stop them. His face seemed to be moving closer to hers, slowly but surely and Lily felt her eyes flutter closed.

"What the devil is going on here?" An angry voice interrupted the moment and Eric's head snapped up. Lily turned to see her brother striding towards them.

James approached the group on the sidewalk. He looked spitting mad. " I knew I should not have allowed you to buy those dresses. Five minutes in one of them…"

"James, calm down." Elise stepped between James and Eric. "Lily fell and hit her head. This man was only helping her."

James stopped abruptly. His look turned from anger to concern. "Are you alright? Should I call a doctor?"

"I'm fine. Just a little dizzy." Lily tried to speak normally but Eric was still holding her and she was having trouble concentrating.

"Perhaps we should see if you can stand on your own now." Eric slowly let her go and Lily managed to steady herself on her feet. She still felt dizzy but now that she wasn't so close to Eric she felt like she could breathe again. A slow throb was building in the back of her head and working its way to her temples.

"Thank you for your help. I'm James Carter, this is my wife Elise and my sister Lillian. We are in your debt."

"Eric Sampson, I believe we have met. This is my son Toby. I am afraid that I can take no such offer since it was my son that knocked her over in the first place. Your sister was most gracious. I would like to make this up to you in some way."

"Eric Sampson? Of course. You own a few of our ships." James seemed delighted now, his anger completely forgotten.

"Your ships were of excellent quality. We are still using them. I have been planning on contacting you for a new contract. Would you consider coming to my home this Friday for dinner. I would like to show Miss Carter my gratitude and perhaps discuss some business with you." Eric smiled and Lily felt her head throb again.

James smiled back, looking ecstatic. "We would be delighted. Tell your wife we look forward to seeing her again as well."

"Thank you for the thought but my wife passed away two years ago." Eric looked at his feet his face tightening.

"How horrible." Elise nodded sympathetically.

Lily who had been focusing all of her energy on remaining standing looked up suddenly. The movement caused the blood to rush from her head; the world began to go dark. She tried to grab at air but she couldn't seem to balance. For the second time in minutes, she fell to towards the ground.

Chapter 2

Lillian opened her eyes to the sight of blue sky before her and tried to puzzle out why on earth she would be looking at the sky in the middle of the day. Slowly, the sounds around her began to penetrate her mind.

"Lily…Lily can you hear me?" Lillian turned to see the faces of her brother and sister-in-law staring down at her.

"What?" Was all she could answer.

"James, I will get her into a carriage, you go fetch the doctor with ours. She must have hit her head worse than we thought."

"Did I hit my head again?" Lily asked feeling very confused.

"No honey, I caught you this time." A voice whispered in her ear.

"Mr. Sampson, would you be so kind as to help me get her into the buggy?" Elise hailed the carriage over as Eric gently lifted her into his arms.

The driver got down off the seat to open the door as Eric carried her over.

"Where can I take you folks?" He asked with concern.

"820 Commonwealth Avenue please." Elise stepped out of the way as Eric climbed in and set Lily down on one of the seats then stepped back out.

"I can follow you to help you when you arrive home." Eric offered to Elise as she climbed in.

"Thank you but we should be fine. It was nice to meet you. We look forward to seeing on Friday." Elise motioned to the driver and Lily lifted her head briefly to see Eric, holding his son, watching the carriage drive away.

"Well, there doesn't seem to be anything wrong with her that some rest won't cure. She may experience some nausea, just try to keep her hydrated. Call me if you need me." The doctor told James and Elise as he walked out the door.

"Is Aunt Lily alright?" Emma, James and Elise's oldest child, asked as she looked up at her parents.

"She is fine. She is just going to be sick for a few days." James assured his three-year-old daughter as he touched her hair gently.

"I see flower?" Little Jamie asked in response, using his pet name for his aunt. He was two and his aunt was his favorite person in the whole world who wasn't his parent.

"Not now sweetie." Elise picked up her son. "We need to give your flower time to recover. But you will see her soon enough."

Lily lay in bed listening to her family. She loved her niece and nephew dearly but was glad that she had been awarded some peace and quiet. She needed to piece together the day's events.

She thought back to her first meeting with Eric Sampson. He had been, and still was, the most handsome man she had ever seen. They had been at a party given by a well to do merchant when Eric had been introduced through common acquaintances to her brother. Lily had never, before that moment, understood why girls got so silly around men. She thought many good looking or enjoyable to talk to but did not feel the need to act like a complete fool to gain their attention. One look into the dark pools of his eyes made her tingle all over. When her brother introduced her, Eric gave her a small half smile that reached his eyes and made him even more handsome. She had become completely tongue tied as his much larger hand enveloped hers and she watched the muscles of his arms ripple as he bent down to kiss her outstretched hand. She wanted to profess her undying love right then and there.

Before Lily had been able to recover, a gorgeous red haired woman had slid next to Eric and was introduced as Eric's wife.

Lily felt crushed in an instant. She had never been so elated and so deflated in a matter of seconds. Caitlin Sampson was everything Lily could imagine the wife of a man so handsome and dashing should be. As Lily watched Caitlin mingle during the party she was struck by the other woman's seeming perfection. Caitlin was tall and, with her red hair, had a commanding physical presence. Beyond that, however, she seemed to be the life of the party. Caitlin knew everyone there and seemed at ease in any conversation. She subtly flirted with the men and conspired with the women. Lily felt her first stabs of jealousy.

At home that night she realized what a fool she had been at the party. Eric had to be much older than her and would not have been interested in her even if he wasn't married. Besides, Caitlin seemed larger than life. Lily enjoyed outings but loved her quiet time with her family even more. To Eric, she would seem dull and drab.

That had not changed. Even though he was a widower, she was not the exciting woman he would be looking for. The trouble was, she had not met a man who made her feel the way he did.

The week passed without much event and Lily felt anticipation growing inside her as Friday night approached. She told herself that she should not get excited that Eric was not interested in her and he had just invited them as a token of his appreciation. But a hope was creeping into her thoughts that he might share the same attraction for her that that she did for him. She shook her head. She was acting like she was fourteen again. She barely knew the man and she was not going to let her feelings run away with her again.

A knock at her bedroom door interrupted her thoughts and Elise entered with one of the maids, May.

"A few of the dresses have come in! I thought you might you want to take a look and see if there was anything suitable for dinner tonight." Elise smiled as the boxes were brought into the room and Lily couldn't help but share her enthusiasm. She did not normally spend a great deal of time picking out clothes but she couldn't help herself today.

Forty-five minutes later the two women stood in front of the mirror, holding up dresses to themselves.

"I definitely think you should wear the burgundy gown. It is perfect for your complexion." Lily told Elise as she debated between two dresses.

I think you're right. Besides I'll have lots of opportunities to wear the other. This is so exciting. Having a full season again! Which gown are you going to wear?"

"The dark blue I think." Lily inspected her reflection one last time.

"Hmmm." Elise stood behind her in the mirror. "Yes, dark blue is the way to go. It darkens your eyes and adds mystery. Men love mystery, especially when they are as handsome as Mr. Sampson." Elise made the comment casually but Lily caught her looking at her from the corner of her eye and Lily blushed despite herself.

"I hadn't noticed." She managed to stutter out, avoiding any further contact with Elise's gaze.   "Don't be absurd. I saw the two of you ogling each other. Of course you noticed and he noticed too." Elise began to remove the dresses from the bed but Lily stopped her.

"Oh Elise, do you think?" Lily couldn't contain her excitement.

"I knew it!" Elise said with a laugh. "This is wonderful. I know that James said he could make it work if you didn't get married but if you have found someone, then all of our worries would be over!"

Lily felt a great deal of the excitement drain from her body. She let go of Elise's hands and sat down on the bed. She wanted to explore her feelings for the man, go on a carriage ride or take a walk on the Common. She wanted to do what other people her age did. But, now she had a perspective marriage looming in her future. How could her parents have done this to her and her brother?

"I'm sorry Lily, I didn't mean... I know you hardly...I..." Elise fumbled for what to say.

"It's alright. I am sure I will meet the perfect man and all of this will work out just as you said. I am nineteen. It's time I settled down with my own family. A few more years and I'll be an old maid." Lily took Elise's hands again and smiled. She didn't want Elise to feel badly. It was her problem to deal with.

The carriage pulled to a stop in front of the Sampson residence and Lily stepped out of the carriage immediately struck by the beauty of the building. It was a large brownstone that spoke of affluence and prestige. The butterflies that had been flying around her stomach all day began to beat faster.

As casually as she could manage, Lily turned to her brother "What is it that Mr. Sampson does?"

"I know, it's an impressive home. He owns and runs a very large shipping company. We have sold him a few ships in the past but I am hoping this new schooner will be of interest to him. I am hoping to gain a contract for them."

Lily nodded her head. The boats built by her father were excellent ships but were about to be replaced by a newer, faster model. James had shut down part of the company to build a new model, the three masted schooner. It had almost put them out of business but if James could get some contracts for this new boat, Lily would only have to marry to save them from financial ruin.

"Please come right this way." A butler escorted them from the front door into the parlor. "Mr. Sampson will be with you momentarily. Please help yourselves to any refreshments you desire."

As the butler turned to leave a streak of movement came dashing into the room, stopping in front of Lily.

"I was looking where I was running this time." Toby gave Lily a big smile. "Dad said I couldn't be at dinner but I could come visit you before I went to bed. Are you feeling better?"

"Much better, thank you." Lily patted Toby on the head and he bent it down sheepishly.

"That's good. I was worried."

Lily bent down next to his ear and whispered. "That is awfully kind of you. What a nice boy you are." She pulled herself back up and the two shared a smile. Unexpectedly, Toby leaned over and hugged her.

"Thank you." He whispered back.

"Time for bed Toby." Eric's voice came from the door.

Lily did not know how long he had been standing there but she felt a slow blush creeping up her cheeks.

"Aw dad, do I have to?" Toby stood next to Lily stubbornly crossing his arms. "I want to stay and talk to Miss Carter more."

"You know our agreement, up to bed." Eric bent down and kissed his son goodnight and then watched as Toby made his way up the stairs.

Finally, he turned back to his guests. "Thank you so much for coming." Eric shook hands with James and kissed Elise on the hand. He turned towards Lily.

"I hope that you are feeling recovered?" He bent down and kissed her hand as well, politely smiling as he let it go.

She smiled back but his eyes had left her face and had turned towards the bar. Disappointment coursed through her. "I am. Thank you." She answered his question in a quiet voice.

"Excellent, what can I get all of you to drink?" Eric moved away from her and began to pull out glasses. "How about a brandy?" He turned to James.

James nodded his head Eric poured out the drinks.

"You have a lovely home." Lily attempted polite conversation but she sounded strange to her own ears. She wondered how she could have allowed herself to get so excited about seeing him again. It was clear that her instincts were correct. She was not a woman Eric Sampson would be interested in.

"Thank you, I live here as business requires but Toby and I are in search of a quieter home for him to really stretch his legs."

16

Elise piped in. "You should consider Maine. I know it seems far but it is an easy ferry ride and the coast is so beautiful."

"Seacoast Shipping Company is based in Kennebunk?" Elise nodded. "How far from Boston is it?"

"I believe it is about 120 miles over land but takes no more than three or four hours by sea." James filled in.

"It is a pleasant amount of time to be on the ocean." Elise continued. "It feels adventurous rather than tedious. You should come visit sometime."

Lily's head shot up and she looked over at Elise who appeared be smiling serenely. Elise turned to her.

"Don't you think Lily?" Elise's smile broadened and Lily stared at her dumbfounded. She did not know what to say. Luckily she was spared answering as the butler returned to announce dinner.

"James, tell me about this new ship you are building." Eric turned towards his guest as they sat down to begin their meal.

"It is a newer model schooner that would be far better suited to trans-continental travel because of its speed. It has an added third mast." James stopped as the first coarse was set in front of him.

"What is the difference in speed?" Eric asked

"Well depending on the wind of course, it could be up to twice as fast. But even without a great deal of wind, this new schooner easily outstrips older models. I have some numbers I can show you sometime next week if you're interested."

"Excellent, how about Thursday, 1:00 o'clock?" James nodded to Eric. "What made you decide to make this change? I am assuming most companies in you area focus on the fishing industry."

"Yes, although a great deal build ships for uses like yours, transporting goods on the east coast. That is the main reason, actually, that we are going with a newer model, to bring in new business. Although the high quality of our product has always kept us in business. But I felt that by taking this risk, I had the potential to make a move ahead of the other builders and independently provide for my family. I believe in this ship so I hope it is a risk that has great rewards."

"We all believe in it." Elise piped in. "It has been a family adventure! One that we all take pride in."

"I am sure Mr. Sampson does not want to hear about our family adventures." Lily was desperate for the subject to change. She was not sure why but she felt extremely vulnerable. She did not want Elise divulging personal information. Especially now that Eric seemed so disinterested.

"On the contrary," Eric turned to her for the first time since asking about her health. "I would love to know about your family adventures."

"We have had to cut back on expenditures, and trips. I am an old married woman so it does not matter to me but poor Lillian has had to miss out on four years of the Boston social scene."

Eric smiled. "How have you survived Miss Carter?"

"It has been quite easy actually. My family is wonderful company and, as Elise said, the coast of Maine is beautiful.   I haven't missed society at all." Lily felt her spine stiffening with every word. She spoke the truth but she knew just how boring the truth sounded. To Eric, she must seem even less interesting than she did before.

"My sister has been a huge support in this process. How many young women do you know that would miss out on dresses and parties for ships and sails without complaint?"

"You're very lucky." Eric looked down the table at Lily. Lily felt herself blushing but his eyes seemed only to hold admiration not disapproval.

"This lamb is delicious." Elise deftly changed the subject as the meal continued.

Lily was glad for the reprise and took a moment to sneak another look at Eric. As she did, she found that he was still looking at her as if studying her and she quickly looked away again.

The rest of dinner past without much event and Lily did not feel Eric's eyes on her again. She was disappointed and wondered if she had any hope of attracting him. If she did, she was going to have to stop being so mousy and start acting more boldly. Her cousin, Amelia, always told her you have to leave a man an invitation big enough for him to read.

As they retired for after dinner drinks James escorted Elise and Eric offered Lily his arm. For a second hope fluttered in her chest but he did not meet her look as she looked up at him and it was quickly dashed.

"Eric," Elise called from behind them. "Will you be attending the picnic on the common on Sunday?"

"Yes, Toby would not miss it for the world." Eric rolled his eyes slightly but there was a smile on his face.

"Perhaps we will see you there." Elise replied and Eric nodded his head. Lily felt another shiver of excitement at the thought of seeing him so soon.

"Perhaps we will." Eric smiled and nodded politely but Lily could catch no promise in his statement and she again felt disappointed. She thought that she had felt a spark between them, what had changed?

James and Eric shared a glass of port and then James excused them for the night. Lily sat in the carriage as they pulled away from his Beacon Hill home hoping that Sunday held the promise that today had not.

Chapter 3

Sunday dawned bright and sunny and Lily felt her spirits rise with them. Today was the perfect day for a picnic.

As they entered the Common, Lily saw all of the families that had already arrived and felt a ripple of excitement. She was wearing one of her new dresses, a cream-colored muslin gown that came off the shoulder, showing a good expanse of her skin. The corset made her already slim waist appear no bigger than the expanse of one hand and her bosom to plump nicely. With her hair pulled up, she was the picture of femininity and she felt it. As they searched for a place on the Common to seat themselves, Lillian waved hello to many of her acquaintances. She noticed many men giving her discreet stares and she smiled shyly to herself. Today was the perfect day to try to convince Eric Sampson to court her. Her cousin Amelia routinely brought men to their knees with just a look. Today, for the first time in her life, she would attempt to do the same.

As the Carters settled in to their picnic area another party approached them. The Johnsons were old family acquaintances of the Carters but the two families had never been close. As a child she had played with the Johnson's daughter Isabelle while her father had conducted business with Harold Johnson. Isabelle had been very bossy as a child prone to fits when she did not get her way. Lily had dreaded the visits then and did so now.

As she looked to Isabelle's right she noticed that two others were approaching with the party, Eric and Toby Sampson. Lily felt her insides drop. As Isabelle noticed Lily looking she placed her arm through Eric's and her smiled broadened. Lily did not flinch but inside she gritted her teeth. She felt jealousy rising up inside of her but she did not let it boil to the surface.

"Lily, how are you? This is my escort for the day, Eric Sampson." Isabelle positively beamed as Lillian stood to greet them.

"We've met." Eric cut in. As Lily stood he took her hand and kissed it. Lily felt her heart flutter and she cursed it for responding to man who was obviously courting another woman. She desperately wanted to ask what Isabella might have that she did not but she understood the absurdity of even thinking the question. He had done almost nothing to encourage her and she had to stop reacting to him this way. She suddenly realized, however, that they were still holding hands.

Isabelle's look soured at Eric's response but she was not at a loss. She once again thread her arm through Eric's and asked him to help her be seated.

Lily sat herself and placed, what she hoped, was a smile on her face. She felt like doing anything but smiling politely. She gritted her teeth, to think just moments ago that she had been trying to figure out how to get Eric to court her. Apparently, Isabelle had already figured it out.

"Hi Miss Carter. I'm sure glad I get to see you today since I didn't really get see you at all on Friday night." Toby smiled and leaned towards her. "Can I give you a hug?" he whispered.

Lily felt her spirits lift slightly at this boy's adorable antics and nodded as she held out her arms to him. Once he had finished hugging her she turned towards her niece. "This is my niece Emma and my nephew Jamie. They could not wait to meet you after hearing about our adventure."

"What adventure is that?" Isabelle could not keep the contempt out of her voice as she asked the questions.

"It was nothing." Eric interjected. "Toby I think I see a patch of daisy's over there. Perhaps you could pick some for the ladies."

Toby, clearly enthused by the idea, left with Jamie and Emma as the Lily and Elise began unpacking the picnic basket along with Mrs. Johnson. Isabelle, still pouting did nothing to help.

Lily concentrated on unwrapping the chicken that their cook had packed. She looked up briefly to see Isabelle gently place her hand on Eric's arm and smile coyly into his eyes. Lily felt her heart skip a beat and she felt slightly sick to her stomach. Isabelle was clearly a practiced flirt.

Just then Lily's brother rose from his seat and moved towards a uniformed man. The two embraced and Lily looked up to see the Carter's childhood friend Mark Summers standing before them. Lily rose and looked at the man before her. With sandy colored hair and golden eyes that danced, he had always been a handsome man. His time in the army had made him even more broad and dashing.

"It is wonderful to see you again!" Lily heard James remark. "Tom is going to be so thrilled that you have come. This wedding is turning out to be the event of the century." James moved out of the way and introduced his wife and children.

Lily smiled as she moved forward to greet him. The Summers had lived next door to the Carter's for as long as Lily could remember and she had grown up tagging after James and Mark. They had not liked it one bit. They barely tolerated Tom, who was two years younger. To have a small girl at their heels was a bother they were constantly trying to shake. She had tried her best though to keep up.

"Hello Mark." She smiled devilishly thinking of all the times she had imposed herself upon them.

Mark stared at her for a full ten seconds and Lily's smile began to fade. Finally he spoke.

"Well, I'll be damned. The little sprout has grown into a flower. And a beautiful one at that." He reached for her hand and kissed it, a kiss that lingered longer than was necessary.

Lily felt herself blushing from his comments or, at least, the audience who had witnessed it. She looked down at the ground and then up through her lashes. She was completely unaware of the fetching picture she posed.

It did not seem to be lost on Mark who continued to stare at her as though he could not believe what he was seeing.

"How could you be the girl who pestered us constantly?" He asked with a laugh as he finally released her hand.

James stepped forward again and introduced Mark to the rest of the party.

Eric turned to Mark, glad for the distraction away from Isabelle. "So Mr. Summers, are you on leave from the army?"

"No actually, I served two terms, and I am retiring. I wanted to see the west and I have certainly achieved that goal. Besides, there are a lot of rumblings about relations between the North and South and I think it could get ugly before it's all over. After battling Indians for eight years in the name of America, I am not sure I can battle my own countrymen." His faced tightened but he did not elaborate any more than that.

"Well, it must feel good to be back among friends." Eric replied.

"It is indeed." Marks smiled returned. "Right before I left, I had to fish Lily out a river. She had tried, yet again, to follow us and almost drowned herself. At the time, I had been annoyed as all get out but I sure am glad now I was able to save her. It was well worth the effort." Mark smiled at her and Lily again felt herself blush. Out of the corner of her eye, she saw Eric grimace slightly and hoped he was just a little jealous.

Harold Johnson turned to James and began to ask him about his latest business venture and Eric and Mark joined in, easing the tension in the group.

"It sounds interesting, I think you might have landed on something." Harold nodded approvingly.

As the men continued talking, a wagon pulled up. It was meant to give the children rides around the common for additional entertainment. Emma and Jamie came running over and Elise quickly agreed to accompany them. Toby joined the two and asked his father if he too could go.

"I'm sorry little guy, I have to finish this conversation

but maybe the next time the wagon makes the trip down the Charles, we can take a ride."

Toby looked on the verge of mutiny when Elise suggested that he ride with her and the children. "Lily can accompany us to sit with Toby."

"I'll accompany him!" Isabelle, seeing her opportunity, rushed in.

Eric looked unsure of what to say when Lily interjected into the conversation. "Why don't we all go? It sounds like fun and the men can finish their discussion."

Isabelle looked put out but did not openly disagree. Lily, Toby, and Isabelle made their way to the wagon, Elise and her two children just behind. The driver smiled and began helping them up into the wagon. Toby was first aboard and Lily began to follow. As she stepped her left foot into the bed of the wagon, Isabelle began her ascent. Lily was pulling her second foot over the side when the wagon gave a quick jolt. In sickening slow motion, she looked at the driver and saw a look of horror on his face and then at Isabelle lying on the ground. She was not able to recover herself before the wagon, very light without many passengers or a driver, took off down the river path.

Toby fell into her body and both went crashing to the floor of the wagon bed. It was by sheer force of muscle and will on Lily's part that they did not fall out of the back. Lily attempted to regain a sitting a position, with Toby in her arms, but was sent crashing back down to the floor. As the wagon bounced along at a dizzying speed, Lily felt herself being smacked over and over into hard wood. She had to protect Toby.

"Tuck your arms and head into my chest!" She called to him as they careened down the path gaining speed. He obediently responded and she rolled onto her back to protect his body. She tried to keep her head up and keep it from hitting the bottom but her back was getting the full force of the blows. She could feel sharp shooting pains running up her spine but there was nothing she could do. She held onto Toby tighter and tried to keep them from moving too much.

Just then the horses veered from the path and wagon gave a sick lurch and came up on two wheels. The two of them, locked together, went sliding from one side of the wagon to the other and for a dizzying second, Lily thought they were going to fall out. The wagon righted itself and slammed them back into the center of the floor. Lily began to wonder how this ride would end. She could feel herself weakening from the exertion but kept her muscles taut so as to protect Toby. She became aware that she had been muttering words of comfort into his ear as they bounced along. She felt her neck giving and wasn't sure if she could hold it up any longer.

Just as Lily was feeling she couldn't last another second, she saw a rider pull up to the side of the carriage and then another came up the other side. Relief rushed through her body and she suddenly found the strength to keep Toby and her from being thrown against the bottom.

"Hang in there." A voice called and she recognized the face of Eric riding next to the carriage. She looked over but the other rider was gone. Where was he, she thought desperately, but even at this thought, the carriage began to slow down and a second rider caught up to the wagon.

As the wagon came to a halt, Lily laid her head down for the first time in what felt like hours, and took a deep breath. She thought she should let go of Toby but could not make her arms work. He did not try to move, and Lily had a sudden rush of fear, was he all right?

"Toby are you ok? Are you all right? Toby can you hear me." Lily voice was growing hysterical but she didn't notice.

Toby picked up his head and looked at her with big eyes. "Boy, am I glad that's over!" He gave her a small grin.

She returned the smile and suddenly broke into tears.

"What'd I say?" Toby looked at his father who had climbed into the wagon.

"Nothing son, Lily was just scared for you, that's all." With those words, he picked up Lily, who was still holding Toby, and held her as she cried.

"Are you hurt?" He asked her softly.

"I don't think so." Lily sniffled into his shirt. She became aware that she must look positively frightening. Her hair had come undone and was now hanging down her back. Her clothing had ripped in several places and her skirt was twisted around her and Toby. James climbed into the carriage and began to pry Lily's arms apart to free Toby and then help his sister to stand. As he pulled, Eric pushed and together they got her into a standing position. Her legs felt wobbly but she was able to support her weight. She turned to Eric.

"What you must think of me, Mr. Sampson, first fainting and now crying."

"I think you are very brave and that Toby and I may be a plague on you." He smiled at her as he picked Toby up and held him in his arms. "I don't know what would have happened to my son if it had not been you in the carriage with him? Toby seems completely unharmed." He lightly touched her arm and she felt her pulse race.

"Anyone would have done the same." She could feel herself blushing again.

"I'm not sure that is true. Thank you." He looked in her eyes and an understanding passed between them. She knew how grateful he was and he knew that she had done it without a thought to herself.

A third rider pulled up to the scene. "Sorry I am late, apparently I wasn't your rescuer this time." Mark pulled up with a devilish smile on his face.

Lily turned to him and he swooped off his horse to take her hand.

Lily smiled weakly at him. She had the vague sensation that it was Eric who should be holding her hand.

Chapter 4

Lily walked gingerly to James' horse. She felt sure she never wanted to look at a wagon again. Mark tied his mount to the back of the wagon and climbed into the driver's seat while Eric and Toby mounted together.

As Lily looked at the horse she was about to mount it occurred to her that they hadn't arrived at the picnic on horseback.

"Where did you get the horses? I don't remember seeing a stable." Lily asked the group at large.

James looked slightly sheepish, but answered "We, ahhh, borrowed them from a few passersby."

"More like commandeered" Mark added with a grin.

Lily smiled at him. "Well, I appreciate you acquiring these fine animals when you did. A few more minutes and I would have turned to jelly."

"Thank goodness you didn't." James squeezed her shoulder with a smile. "The good doctor will still be making a return trip to the house tonight. We may as well have him move in!"

Lily laughed and then felt a sharp pain in her side. She gritted her teeth but her sudden silence caught the attention of all three men.

"Is everything alright?" Mark asked, his voice full of concern as he jumped into the seat of the wagon.

"Fine. Just a little pain in my side." Lily waived them off

but the group did not resume.

"Perhaps you should ride in the back of the wagon, rather than sitting up on the horse." James said looking concerned.

"I would rather die, than step back into that wagon." Lily sat more erectly on the horse to show them she was fine.

Eric chuckled. "I admire your strength but your brother is right. I am sure you will be fine in the wagon, perhaps you should…"

"I am not arriving at the picnic in the back of that wagon. It will make the situation look much worse than it is and I am already going to be on the tongue of every gossip in town. Laid out in a wagon, they will be singing my death march.

"Lily don't be stubborn, it would be best…" James did not get a chance to finish.

"I am either riding on this horse or walking. I will not step into that wagon."

"You are as stubborn as I am, you know that." James smiled at his sister.

Mark again started the team of horses moving and Eric and James followed suit.

Mark leaned over to Lily and smiled. "I don't know when I have ever seen a woman look more beautiful than you do right now."

"Oh Mark, you must be joking, I am a mess." Lily laughed a little nervously.

"I have to agree with you on this one Mr. Summers." Eric called from the back of the group and Lily blushed again.

As they pulled up to the picnickers a crowd of people rushed around them all firing questions.

"What happened?"

"Were you hurt?"

"Where did you go?"

Lily felt her head begin to pound. James dismounted and began to disassemble the crowd as Mark returned the wagon to its driver. Elise came running over, Isabelle hot on her heels.

"I can't believe you are alright! You are alright aren't

you?" Elise began touching her legs to feel for breaks as Lily still sat on the horse.

"Can't you see she is fine?" Isabelle added in a huff. "I am the one that was thrown to the ground. Why is everyone so concerned about her?" Isabelle took a breath and looked ready to continue when Eric broke in.

"I have your sister-in-law to once again thank for Toby's safety. If you need anything at all, please contact me. I wish I could stay and help you more but I must return home and have Toby examined."

"Of course." Elise understood his desire to look after his child.

"Ah Dad, I'm fine. I told you Miss Carter kept me safe. I want to go with them and make sure she's ok." Toby stared up to his dad with a determined look.

"Toby, Miss Carter needs to rest and so do you." Eric took the boy's hand.

"Can we go visit her soon?" Toby pleaded with his dad.

Eric stopped and turned to his son. "If Miss Carter is amenable to it…"

"I would be delighted." Lily gave Toby a winning smile and Eric kissed her hand in farewell then father and son departed.

The Carter family followed suit.

Chapter 5

The doctor had told her that she had bruised some ribs and was going to be very sore the next day but when Lily woke up she felt like she would never move again. Elise came in, followed by May.

"Should we bring breakfast up for you?" Elise asked with a smile.

"That would be lovely." Lily returned the grin. She hadn't felt like eating the night before and was absolutely famished. She was not quite sure how she was going to get the spoon to her mouth but at this point she did not care.

"Wonderful. After breakfast, we are going to get you up and dressed for a short visit." Elise plumped the pillows on a chair while she talked.

"Elise, you can't be serious. I cannot move from this bed. I can barely lift a finger."

"It is important not to allow yourself to stiffen up any further and besides, you wouldn't want to miss the dashing Mark Summers would you?"

Lily found herself slightly disappointed that it was Mark and not Eric coming to see her. Then she chastised herself. Mark would be excellent company and it would be wonderful to catch up. Besides, she had to start seriously considering other men. She could not spend her life pining for a man that she knew couldn't possibly be interested in her.

As Lily ate her breakfast she called May back to help her

dress her hair. Normally she would have done it herself, but she was just too sore. Then she pulled out one of her older day dresses. It was still in good condition and was very flattering to her figure. She had considered wearing a new gown but had rejected the idea. Those must be saved for larger social gatherings.

Within the hour May had her out of bed and ready to go and, Elise had been right, she felt better as she slowly moved. Her ribs were still extremely sore but they would heal.

"I thought I would help you downstairs." Lily accepted Elise's arm gratefully and the two made their way down the steps.

"I wanted to tell you that your cousin Amelia and Aunt Caroline are arriving in a few days with Tom. We are going to have a house full before you know it."

"How wonderful!" Lily could not wait for her cousin to arrive. Her Aunt Caroline and her mother had been sisters and looked very much alike. As a result, she and Amelia shared an amazing number of features, most notably their eyes. While their coloring was completely different, Amelia had her father's dark hair with a golden complexion, both women had an exotic quality to the shape of their eyes with a vibrant blue color that seemed to attract men. The difference was, Amelia was far more adept at flirting with men and keeping their attention after the initial attraction. It had been something that Lily had never been particularly interested in but now she wondered if her cousin couldn't give her some solid advice.

As they reached the bottom the stairs, Mark came out of the sitting room and took Lily's arm from Elise.

Elise followed the two of them into the sitting room and picked up her embroidery bag. She would be chaperoning the visit but tried to make herself inconspicuous.

Lily smiled at her old friend glad to have him back with her family. He had been much like a brother to her. "Thank you for coming to keep me company. It is wonderful to have you back in town."

"You are quite welcome." Mark replied. "How are you feeling?"

"A little sore but I'll be fine. Thank you for asking. How are you after all of our time away? Tell me about life in the army."

As Mark began to give Lily details about the campaign in the west, Lily leaned forward listening intently. She found what Mark was saying fascinating. He told her of the difficulties with Indians or the Indian difficulties with the whites. He told of her of the hardships of the settlers and she asked him question upon question.

The two talked for over two hours and Lily enjoyed every minute of he conversation but she found herself slumping back slightly in her chair.

"You are exhausted you poor thing, why didn't you say something? You didn't have to let me keep prattling on!" Mark rose to help Lily out of her chair.

"Oh, it was a pleasure to hear you speak. What an exciting and heartbreaking experience. Will you be returning to the west after the wedding?"

Mark lead her slowly back to Elise and smiled as he answered her question. "No, I don't think I will. I am almost finished my tour of duty and I think I am ready to come home and settle down a bit more."

"Will you come back to Maine?" Lily asked curious to hear the answer.

"Yes, I think I will be. Although your brother is one of the only employers in the area so it will depend on whether he is willing to give me a job."

"I can't imagine he'll refuse you. It would be wonderful to have you in Kennebunk again." Lily fluttered her lashes in an attempt to flirt and the attempt was not lost on Mark. He gave her a surprised look and then smiled. Lily immediately felt a wave of guilt wash over her but she pushed it back down. There was nothing wrong with flirting with handsome, available men, she told herself. But she couldn't help feeling she was misleading the man.

"It would be wonderful to be back." And he kissed her hand in farewell.

Elise looked up from where she sat in the corner but said nothing as Mark left the room. As Elise's gaze turned to Lily, Lillian felt herself reddening with embarrassment but placed a false smile on her face. She did not want to talk about Mark with Elise or her actions of the past few days. And although Elise's gaze was filled with question, she said nothing.

Lily suddenly felt exhausted. "Elise, would you mind helping me back upstairs, I think I need to rest."

"Of course, dear. You must be tired." Elise took Lily's arm and began guiding her back to her room.

Chapter 6

The next morning Lily woke and stretched in bed. Once again, she felt as though her body was lying on a bed of needles. On top of this she had a knot in the pit of her stomach that something was wrong. She remembered her meeting with Mark yesterday and groaned. It wasn't that she had done anything wrong. It was just that Elise would be full of questions to which she would have to come up with answers. While most girls probably flirted with multiple men, she was not one of them and her family would want to know her intentions.

Reluctantly, she pulled herself out of bed and began the agonizing process of dressing. She thought back to her meeting yesterday with Mark. Why had she begun flirting with him? If she were honest with herself, it was nice to feel that a man was interested in her. Perhaps her instincts yesterday had been correct. She should be flirting with Mark and other men as well. She had to keep her options open. If she was going to find a husband this season then she was going to have to start gaining the interest of men.

Her body felt more limber and her mind clear as she headed downstairs for breakfast. Ready to face the firing squad, she was surprised when her brother only smiled cordially and Elise began to discuss wedding plans. Tom was due into town in two days and the social events surrounding the wedding would begin. Lily felt the tension in her body ease as she enjoyed the meal with her family. As she began to think about what she would do with her day, her brother looked up at her.

"How are you feeling this morning?" He asked pleasantly.

"Better thank you." Lily stirred her tea. Perhaps she would take a walk in the gardens after she helped out in the kitchen.

"Remember, nothing strenuous today. The Sampsons are calling at noon. I have a meeting with Mr. Sampson at one but they would like to check in with you first."

The spoon Lily had been holding clattered onto her saucer as tea slouched out of her cup. Her brother's eyes narrowed but she set the cup down and nodded. Damn that man! It was annoying that the mention of his name could shake her so!

An hour and a half later, Lily waited in the sitting room for her visitors. She had been unable to help in the kitchen as she had had to go upstairs and change. Instead she sat attempting to embroider with Elise but she could not concentrate on her stitches. She had never enjoyed such tasks to begin with and with her nerves so jumpy, her work looked like a disaster.

"How can you tolerate such mundane activity?" Lily huffed, her nerves raw.

"I don't know, I kind of like it. We are usually so busy cleaning and shopping and playing with the children it feels like a luxury to just sit and stitch." Elise continued to work a small smile on her face.

Lily felt a stab of guilt at her sharp words. "I'm sorry Elise. I don't mean to be so abrupt. I am just unused to all this entertaining."

"We entertain all the time at home." Elise's smile broadened.

"Elouise Parker and Mabel Grey are not the same thing as gentlemen callers and you know it. We do not dress in our finest and sit around waiting for the ladies of Kennebunk to come calling." Lily felt herself relaxing and laughed along with Elise.

"You're right. But you sure do make a pretty picture sitting there." The soft pink dress brought out the honey of her hair and creaminess of her skin. It hugged her curves and accentuated her figure.

"Elise, you haven't asked me about Mark yesterday or Eric today." Lily made the statement even though she had been dreading the conversation. It was better to just get it over with.

Elise took her hand. "Lily, enjoy this part of your life and by all means, keep your options open until you are sure about one man. Your brother had to do a great deal of convincing for me to decide he was the man I would marry." Elise gave her hand a squeeze. "When you decide you've met someone special, tell me and then we will share with your brother."

Lily leaned over and hugged her sister-in-law, thankful to have her in her life. As she pulled away, the front bell rang signaling the arrival of the Sampsons.

As their butler showed Eric and Toby into the door, Toby smiled at her and pulled from behind his back a bouquet of wild flowers. "These are for you."

"Thank you so much. Could I get a vase to arrange them in?" Elise nodded and left to fetch a vase.

"Thank you." Eric kissed her hand. A shiver ran up her arm and for a moment she held her breath. All of her convictions to forget Eric Sampson flew from her head. Then Eric let her hand go. "Toby barely has a scratch and we have you to thank for that. I hope you have fared as well?"

"I have a few bumps and bruises but nothing serious. After a few weeks of moderated activity, I will be back to my usual self." Lily felt her heart beating quickly but tried to keep her voice calm and steady.

Eric reached for her hand again, holding it in his own. "I am sorry you were hurt even that much." The two stared at each other for a few moments not saying a word. Inexplicably, Lily felt herself leaning towards him as he held her hand and her eyes fluttered towards their hands then back to his face and then began to close. She felt her whole body heating up and excitement coursed through her.

She heard Elise's voice as she entered the room. "Do you think this vase is large enough?"

Eric let go of Lillian's hand and Lily felt her world tilt as she tried to concentrate. "Ah, fine." Was all she could say as she hurriedly stood and began to arrange the flowers.

Elise's eyebrows shot up but she remained silent. Instead she turned to Toby. "My son and daughter would love your company if you would like to join them outside. They are looking at flowers in the garden."

"That would be great!" Toby bounced on the balls of his feet as Elise rang for May to escort the boy.

"He's welcome to stay with the children and their nanny until you are finished your meeting with James." Eric nodded his thanks and Elise once again assumed her position in the corner.

Lily felt a knot of tension in her stomach at the prospect of uninterrupted conversation with this man. "Well, we have told you all about Kennebunk. Where is it you are from?"

Eric laughed and began to tell her about his home in New York. He had two brothers, he was the oldest, and his father had passed away some years ago but his mother had raised three teenage boys with an iron will. He chuckled as he told her about a time that her brothers had tried to swipe horses from a neighbor's stable for fun. His mother had made them clean the stable every morning for a month. "It was the cleanest stable for miles."

In turn he asked her about her childhood and she told him stories about growing up on the ocean and her many attempts to chase after her brothers.

"When did you stop chasing them?" He asked with a laugh.

"Well, Mark left for the army and my older brother for Harvard. I was ten or eleven and my father decided it was time for me to start pursuing more ladylike endeavors. I did what was asked of me grudgingly. When my parents died, I had to become the lady of the house. It left little time to continue exploring outside."

"It must have been difficult." Eric voice was sympathetic.

"It was the most difficult time of my life. But, I had my brothers and soon Elise. I am lucky to have them."

Eric reached for her hand a third time and gave it a small squeeze. He let go quickly this time and was about to ask her more about her childhood when Elise interrupted.

"Mr. Sampson, it is one o'clock."

"Thank you Mrs. Carter. Miss Carter, it was wonderful to see you again." He kissed her hand in farewell. She once again felt the excitement inside her at his touch. Elise rose to escort him to James' office and he left the room with a final smile. Lily did not want to see him go but could not help herself from smiling at the thought of his visit. When would she see him again?

Chapter 7

Elise stepped out of the room behind him and smiled as she lead the way to James' office. The door was open and Elise and Eric could hear James talking.

"As soon as the wedding is over we will get you settled into your new position and start training you for the job. I really think you are going to enjoy working at the shipping company."

"I know that I will, it will be wonderful to be among friends and family again." Eric recognized the voice of Mark Summers although he could not see him.

"We are thrilled to have you back. I have something else I want to discuss with you that is a delicate matter. Please don't answer today but take some time to think about it."

"Alright, this sounds serious."

James sighed then began to speak. "Tom has met a woman that he truly cares about which thrills us all but that is not the only reason he is getting married. Our parents, not realizing they would pass away together, tied up a great deal of our family's money by stipulating in their will that we would not receive our inheritances until after we were married. I am sure they wanted to avoid any of us getting the money too young or when we hadn't settled down yet. Because the business is part of our inheritance, I have had to run and develop it with a third of the assets available to my father. We have reached the end of our funds this year and the new ships are just not ready for sale. I have a number of contracts lined up but I need more money to complete them. Tom is marrying to free up his inheritance."

There was a pause and them Mark spoke. "I see, what does this have to do with me?"

"I need Lily's part of the inheritance as well, if the business is going to survive the next six months. After that, the contracts will begin paying out and we should be making more money than we ever have before. I have tried going to several banks but the company is too mortgaged to borrow. I have had to wheel and deal to get it this far. Lily knows that she has to find a suitor this season to save the business although I am worried about her. I don't want to force her into a loveless marriage for the sake of the rest of us. It isn't fair. But I don't know what would happen to my life or Tom's for that matter if it does."

"Are you asking me to marry Lily?" Mark sounded a bit stunned.

"Like I said, don't answer today but think about it. Get to know her again, the two of you seemed to get along very well at the picnic and, unlike many arranged marriages, I know I can trust you with her happiness. I know it's a lot to take in but give it some thought."

Mark could not answer because Elise pushed open the door and stood in the doorway staring at her husband. "Could I speak with you please?" Her tone was stiff and Eric could tell, even from behind her that her mouth was drawn in a straight line.

Mark shook hands with James then walked out the door as Elise closed it behind him. Mark gave Eric a small grin then shrugged." It is not every day that you get offered the hand of such a beautiful woman. I should consider myself lucky."

"Indeed, you should. She is the most beautiful woman I have seen for a long time. You would be a lucky man." Eric stated flatly. With that, Elise stepped out and Eric went in to speak with James.

Elise returned to the morning room fifteen minutes later looking very upset and Lily was surprised and curious as to what had happened. She expected Elise to return immediately to discuss the details of her meeting with Eric Sampson. Even now that she was back, Elise sat silently in her chair stabbing at her embroidery. Lily almost asked but decided that Elise would share when she was ready so she too picked up her embroidery with a sigh. Gossiping would have been much more fun.

Finally, Elise tossed what she was working on down and let out an exasperated sigh. "Your brother can be the most infuriating man! Sometimes I don't know what to do with him!"

Lily smiled but said nothing. Her brother and sister-in-law had gotten into more than one fight and she stayed out of it whenever possible. Things usually smoothed over in a day or two.

"How do you think you feel about Eric Sampson?" Elise's question took her off guard.

"I am not sure. I mean, I haven't had time to…I thought you just said we wouldn't talk about this until I was ready?" Lily stared her sister wondering what had caused this sudden change.

Elise ignored the question and continued, "When he was here just now how did you feel?"

Lily blinked and then smiled. "I feel like I can barely think or breathe, like we are the only two people in the world. I feel like I want him to kiss me." Lily blushed at her own words but she wanted to share. It felt good to say them out loud and admit her feelings.

Elise took a long deep breath and stared at Lily, then she spoke. "Then I am going to help you. It is clear that he is interested in you as well though he is resisting. I am not sure why but we are going to have to do some digging to find out. In the meantime, I think it is time you had a crash course on how to make a man beg for mercy."

"Elise, I am not Amelia, I have tried to employ her techniques, I just am no good at them. Besides, I don't see why we need to rush…"

"I don't want you to be Amelia. I am sure part of the reason he likes you is because of your straight forward personality, your gentleness, I could see it at dinner. No, we need to teach you how to be you only in a way that brings more attention to yourself. And if we don't do it soon, you may lose

Mr. Sampson. Tom will be arriving tomorrow with you Aunt Clarisse and Amelia. She can give you some additional pointers but you and I are starting right now. I am sure he will be at the Winchester's ball on Friday night." Elise sat up straight in her chair. "Lily, there are many men out there who are more infatuated with you then with Amelia. You just never give them any encouragement so they think they don't have a chance. Now here is the first thing I want you to do…"

"Elise, men do not find me more attractive than Amelia." Lily looked at her sister-in-law stunned.

"Don't be ridiculous, of course they do. Alright. The first thing you have to do is laugh when they talk, act interested. It does not have to be a laugh that attracts the whole room…"

"Like Amelia." The two women smiled at each other.

"Exactly, just enough that he thinks you think he is the most fascinating man on the planet. Like this…" Elise looked up through her lashes and laugh softly, looked adoringly into space.

Lily knew exactly what she meant. Elise did not attract attention from the whole room but would make whomever she was speaking to feel incredibly desired. She leaned forward listening to every word Elise said.

For the next two hours, Elise explained and demonstrated and series of conversation starters then moved on to phrases and movements to make a man feel special and to quietly attract attention. For the first time in Lily's life she felt like she understood what attracted a man besides a pretty face. She supposed, if she had a mother around when she had become interested in men she would have observed these things but after her parents died, she avoided as many social engagements as possible.

"Now here is the last thing that I am going to tell you about today and probably the most important. Men, for whatever reason, like a woman who is a bit of a challenge. If she is too accessible, he finds it boring. Don't be afraid to say no if he asks you to dance or if he tries to kiss you. It only makes him want you that much more."

Lily looked doubtfully at Elise. After all the advice on how to attract a man, now she was supposed to push him away?

"Believe me, I am married to your brother because I made him work to win my love. Besides, Mr. Sampson seems to be very good at pulling himself away and it doesn't seem to have deterred you now does it?"

Lillian's mouth dropped open and then she laughed. Was Eric just playing hard to get? No, she thought sadly, he just wasn't interested but she would see if any of Elise's strategies could change his mind.

Chapter 8

"Darling, you are glowing. Society certainly agrees with you!" Amelia rushed up to Lily embracing her as only Amelia could. Her brother Tom and Aunt Clarisse, her mother's sister, followed behind.

"I have missed you." Lily hugged her cousin back, glad for her presence. Amelia brought such energy and enthusiasm to life.

"I've missed you as well. As soon as we get all of the bags in, you must tell me all about your time in Boston."

As Amelia moved to hug Elise, Lily clasped her brother's hands. It was wonderful to see him again. Her brother Tom was much more like their mother in personality than either she or James. He was exuberant and full of life like Amelia. While Lily looked like her mother, she had always resembled her father in manner. The two had been a perfect complement to one another in marriage and that is what Tom had found in his bride to be. Danielle was quiet and subdued but somehow seemed to fit Tom perfectly. "How have you been?" She gave her brother a hug.

His smile was strained as he spoke. "Glad to be here." He said as he released her.

"Is everything alright with Seacoast?" Lily knew that the business' position was precarious, but she had hoped things were on the upswing.

"Fine, fine, we will talk about it later." The drawn look to Tom's mouth did not go away and Lillian wondered what was wrong but kept quiet. Tom was right, now was not the time to talk.

The party moved to the parlor and refreshments were brought for the travelers. As they sipped tea, Amelia spoke.

"So you must tell me what has been happening, cousin." She turned to Lily.

"Not all that much. I have missed most of the parties and dances because of various afflictions but…"

Elise piped in, "Please, wait until you hear about her afflictions!" and began to recount all the events that had unfolded in Lily's life for the past two weeks.

Amelia, Tom and Aunt Clarisse listened and laughed as Elise regaled them with stories. As she finished, Amelia spoke. "Well, cousin, you have done well. Eric Sampson is a handsome man and rich. I am jealous."

Lily smiled and it was her turn to look drawn. "Well, don't be. He is not actually a suitor of mine. We have just had a few chance encounters."

Amelia gave her a knowing look but said nothing and Lily was grateful. She hoped there was more to their relationship but she did not want to admit it to anyone but Elise yet. If she was going to be rejected, it needn't be in front of her entire family.

Tom seemed more relaxed as well and laughed with the rest of the family. "As beautiful as you are, I don't see how he could resist you." He said with gusto. "Tell me that James has properly outfitted you for the season."

"Of course I have." James entered the room accompanied by Mark. As James hugged everyone hello, Mark stood away from the family.

Lily looked over and smiled at him and he approached her. "I am sorry to be intruding upon your family's reunion."

"Don't be ridiculous, you practically are family. Tom, Mark has completed his second term in the army and has returned in time for your wedding, isn't that wonderful!"

Tom turned to his childhood friend and the two

embraced. As the two separated, Amelia stepped forward.

"Well, hello there." She smiled seductively and held out her hand as Mark bent down to kiss it.

"It's astonishing. You and Lily have identical eyes." Mark stared in disbelief.

"Yes we do. That is where the similarities end however, although my mother wishes it were otherwise." Her hand subtly brushed his coat sleeve as she turned to sit down. "Now tell me, where have they been hiding you?"

Mark laughed and began to tell her about his experiences in the army. Lily realized that Amelia had not known Mark as her and her mother had not come to live in Kennebunk with them until after the death of Amelia's father.

James interrupted the group's conversation as a bottle of champagne arrived. "I would like to make a toast." He smiled. "To family and friends and the success of Seacoast Shipping!"

Everyone toasted and Lily looked around wondering what had happened to suddenly make her brother so happy. She saw Elise scowling and her brother Tom looked confused. What was going on with her family?

The next day was a busy one in the Carter household. Between the extra family members and the ball that evening, the house was alive with activity. Lily tried, on several occasions, to speak with her brother Tom. Between visiting his fiancé and wedding preparations, she was unsuccessful. Elise and James had spent much of the day in James' office and when Elise wasn't there, she was entertaining Amelia and Aunt Clarisse. Finally, late in the afternoon, Lily was able to speak with her brother James.

As she entered his office he was busy looking over papers. She silently prayed that everything with the business would work out soon. Her brother was working himself ragged. "You seemed happy yesterday, what's the occasion?"

James looked up and flushed slightly, an uncommon occurrence for him. "It is good to have Tom here and the wedding so close." He looked back down at his papers and Lily's eyes narrowed suspiciously.

"You are not fooling me." Lily closed in on her brother. "Elise has looked ready to skin a cat, Tom did not seem himself yesterday and now you are being evasive. What is going on?" She stood with her face only inches from his. There were very few secrets in her family and she did not like that there was one now.

James looked back at his sister and stared for a few moments. "Alright, there is more to it than that but I have to get these papers out today to reach home by next week. Why don't we sit down tomorrow and talk?"

Lily slowly backed away and nodded her ascent. She turned to leave then turned back again, "First thing in the morning." Then she left the office without another word. She would have liked more information than that but tomorrow would be soon enough and she had a party to get ready for.

Two hours later, two carriages pulled up to take the Carter's to the Winchester Ball. Mark had arrived a half-hour before to travel to the ball with the family. As they stepped outside he turned to Lily.

"You look stunning." He helped Lily into the second carriage and climbed in himself.

Lily, in an attempt to employ one of Elise's strategies, placed her hand on his arm and looked at him through her lashes as she softly thanked him. "It is wonderful to have you back with us."

Mark gave her a soft smile in return and kissed her hand. There was an intimacy in his gesture that momentarily stunned Lillian and she forgot her lessons as she pulled away from him. Mark stiffened momentarily but then turned towards the door as Amelia climbed in.

Mark helped her into the seat across from them. She too smiled at Mark and thanked him for helping her but did not pull away. The two stood together for some seconds before breaking apart as Tom climbed in to complete the group. Lily decided to watch Amelia more closely for pointers.

She looked over at Mark and thought that he looked extremely handsome this evening. Despite his good looks, however, he did not seem to make her feel the way Eric Sampson did. She doubted she would have pulled away if it had been Eric smiling at her. Despite Elise's advice to have fun, she decided that she should not encourage Mark any further, she did not feel that way about him.

Twenty minutes later they pulled up the impressive drive of the Winchester home. Lily could feel the anticipation growing as she smoothed down her blue silk dress. The dressmaker had been right, it matched her eyes perfectly and it was by far her favorite dress.

As the Carter's approached the entrance, Danielle's family met up with them. Danielle took Tom's arm and they lead the group through the double doors. Danielle's parent's, Douglas and Lucille Handler, followed. Mark offered Lily his arm and the two walked in silence behind them. Lily wondered if she had hurt Mark's feelings, he was far quieter than normal.

"Mark, is everything alright?" Lily turned towards him, her concern showing clearly on her face.

"Fine." He paused as he looked at her upturned face. "Are you worried about me?"

"Of course. You've been quiet and I…" she did not know quite what to say.

"It has been a long time since a lady, as pretty as you, has worried about me. I have to admit, I like it." He gave her a devilish smile and for a moment he looked like he had just a few days ago.

"Well, I am happy to oblige but everyone seems so tense, I cannot figure it out." Lily gave a small shrug but she noticed that Mark tensed up immediately.

She looked at him but he said nothing. She wanted to ask him further but they were about to be announced.

As she entered the ballroom she noticed the stares of many men. She smiled shyly at a few of them and they immediately smiled back.

The group progressed towards the dance floor but the ball was extremely crowded and progress was slow. Finally, they reached some available chairs and sat as they watched the dancers. James met a few of his business associates and was deep in conversation while Lily and Elise watched the dancing.

"Where did Amelia take off to?" Aunt Clarisse asked as she sat next to Elise.

"I am not sure perhaps Mark knows." But Mark was gone as well. Elise raised her eyebrows but before she had a chance to speak James approached with two gentlemen.

Carl Fisk and Michael Conway, this is my lovely wife Elise and my sister Lillian."

"How do you do?" Elise smiled at Carl while Lily held out her hand to Michael.

"Pleased to meet you." Lily gave him a small smile and looked up through her lashes.

"The pleasure is all mine." Michael kissed her hand and still holding it turned to her brother. "Where have you been hiding this beautiful creature? I must ask you to dance."

"Of course." She said with a smile and the two were off to the dance floor. As she began the first steps of the waltz she noticed Eric Sampson dancing with a pretty brunette. She felt a quick stab of jealousy and wondered if he was escorting the woman. She pushed him out of her mind and concentrated on her partner.

Two hours later, Lily had danced with a number of men and was enjoying herself thoroughly. Her ribs began paining her and she realized she had not sat and rested since she arrived. The doctor had told her to take it easy but she had felt so well she hadn't been paying attention. It was time for a break. She sat near Aunt Clarisse and watched the dancers as a man approached from her right.

"I was hoping for another dance." Michael smiled as he again kissed her hand.

"Oh thank you, I would love to but I am in need of a rest. I fear I am a little worn out." Lily smiled from where she sat but felt slightly light headed and did not want to rise.

"Perhaps I could sit with you then?" He again kissed her hand.

"That would be lovely." The two sat and chatted while the dancers passed by. As they were talking an older man, dressed in uniform approached.

"Michael, you must introduce me to this enchanting creature." He was a tall man, although not as tall as her brother and Eric, and he had steel grey hair and eyes. He was in good shape and would seem attractive to many women but there was a hardness about him that made Lily immediately ill at ease.

"Of course, Colonel Kingsley this is Miss Lillian Carter." Lily stood as Michael made the necessary introductions, although he did not seem particularly pleased.

"How do you do?" Lily held out her hand and the Colonel took it in a very firm hold. She felt a shiver run up her spine but it was not a pleasurable sensation.

"Very well thank you, pleased to meet you. I know your brother of course. We are negotiating a contract for ships. I was hoping to ask you to dance." The Colonel smiled at her but it did not look natural like smiling was not something that he did often.

"Oh, I am sorry, Mr. Conway just asked and I was explaining to him that I was hoping to rest a bit." Lily was glad for the excuse. She couldn't explain it but she did not want to be alone with this man.

"Well then, why don't we all sit and chat." As the Colonel moved towards the chair a third man approached the group. Lily turned to see Eric smiling down at her.

"Miss Carter, how wonderful to see you. I was hoping we would run into each other before now. How are you feeling?" Eric took her hand and gently pulled her towards him and away from the other two men.

"Much better thank you, although all of this dancing has worn me out a bit." She smiled as he kissed her hand glad for his sudden presence.

"Colonel Kingsley, how are you, it has been a long time." Eric turned towards the other man as he tucked her hand into the crook of his arm and pulled her closer to him. Lily gladly moved as he wished, feeling much more comfortable by his side than she had a moment before. He continued to keep his other hand on top of her own.

"Mr. Sampson, it has been quite a while. I was sorry to

hear about Caitlin." The Colonel paused. "She was such a… vibrant woman."

Lily could see Eric's jaw harden but his voice was calm as ever. "Thank you for your condolences. Now if you will excuse us…"

"You are not going to take the beautiful Miss Carter away are you? We were just getting to know one another." Kingsley stepped forward and unconsciously Lily moved closer to Eric.

"Actually, I am. Her brother has asked me to escort her into the card room. You will have to excuse us."

"Perhaps another time then Miss Carter, it was a pleasure." He reached for her hand and she held it out although she did not move away from Eric and he did not let go of the hand tucked in his arm. The Colonel turned and left.

Michael shuffled uncomfortably for a moment then turned to Lily "I am sorry we were interrupted, I enjoyed our conversation immensely."

"As did I, thank you for keeping me company. I am sure I will see you soon." She turned to Aunt Clarisse just to let her know where she was going.

"Alright dear, I will be there as soon as I can track down Amelia, she is off somewhere once again."

Eric maneuvered her through the crowd but their progress was slow. Lily could feel her head beginning to ache and she began to feel slightly dizzy.

"Do you think we could sit for just a moment?" She asked Eric "I am afraid I may have overdone it this evening."

"Of course, I know just the place." He steered her to their right and soon they were out on the veranda that lead into the gardens. As the cool air hit her face she took a deep breath already feeling better.

Eric led her into one of the gardens with a small stone bench to one side. The two sat down and Lily looked up at the stars drinking in the beautiful view.

"It is a beautiful view isn't it?" She asked as she gazed up.

"Yes it is." Eric did not look at the sky but at the

woman sitting next to him although Lily did not notice. Her hair danced in the breeze and many of her curls were lit with moonlight.

Lily closed her eyes and took a deep breath completely unaware of how desirable she looked or how intensely the man next to her was looking at her.

She turned her focus from the sky back to Eric. "Where do you know the Colonel from?"

Eric's jaw once again hardened. "He was a friend of Caitlin's before we were married."

His answer took Lily by surprise. "For some reason I cannot picture the Colonel with many female friends although I do not know him very well."

"Why do you say that?" Eric looked at her intently.

She laughed nervously then answered. "You will probably think I am silly but he made me feel uneasy."

"I don't think you're silly at all. In fact, you would do well to trust your instincts." Eric relaxed after her answer. "And I think you're right. The Colonel does not have many women that he calls strictly friends."

"Oh." Realizing he meant the Colonel's lovers she felt herself blushing all the way to the roots of her hair and despite the dark, she looked down at her feet to hide her blush.

Eric gently put his finger under her chin and lifted her face back up. "Don't be embarrassed." As he said these words, the tips of his fingers, which had been on her chin, slid down her neck and over her collarbone.

Lily's entire body tingled as his lips touched her skin. She had never felt anything like this before and it was utterly amazing. Without thinking, her head tilted back as his lips moved up her neck and along her jaw. His hands slid down her arms and then wrapped them around his neck as his lips touched hers. He pulled away and then kissed her more deeply. His lips felt so wonderful and she could feel herself growing warmer, heat curling in her body. She pressed herself closer to him and his hand ran up her abdomen and gently cupped her breast. She gasped at the sensation but her gasp was quickly lost as he opened her lips with his own and deepened the kiss further. Lily could not think a reasonable thought, she could only feel and she knew that she did not want this to end. As he pulled her into his lap and continued to kiss her a moan escaped her and her hands traveled up into his hair.

Suddenly Eric broke away. "Did you hear something?"

"Hmm?" Was all she could muster. She was still in his lap with their bodies pressed together and all she could think was that she wanted him to kiss her again.

He stood up holding her around the waist and moved them into the shadows of the garden.

The clear voice of the Colonel floated towards them as he walked by the entrance of the garden. "I met a very interesting girl this evening. I've been curious about her for a while and I would like some more information. I would like you to find out what you can about her."

"Girl? That does not sound like your usual tastes" A second man remarked.

"Well, my usual tastes do not make suitable wives." Both men laughed and continued walking, the rest of their conversation lost in the breeze.

Lily felt herself shiver, she wondered who the poor girl was. Eric's arms tightened around her, his lips formed a hard line. Did he know who the Colonel was talking about?

He leaned down and gently kissed her lips. He removed her arms from around his neck and again tucked one of her hands into the bend of his arm. "We should get you to your brother before he begins to worry."

Lily nodded feeling slightly embarrassed by how strongly she had reacted to his kiss. As they walked backed towards the doors to the ballroom she did not know what to say to him.

"Promise me one thing." Eric stopped walking and turned towards Lily. "Promise me you'll stay away from Colonel Kingsley."

She nodded her head, unsure of what to say. He quickly dropped one more kiss on her lips before turning towards the doors.

As they walked inside, it was apparent that the party ball had thinned out since they left and they quickly made their way to where some of the guests were playing cards.

She easily spotted her brother and Elise as she and Eric moved towards them. Aunt Clarisse had obviously found Amelia and the two were sitting on a nearby settee. Mark, Tom, and Danielle conversing to one side and all looked up at their approach, Amelia winked at her as she passed but James looked far less amused.

"Where have you been?" James stood the hand of cards forgotten. " I sent Mr. Sampson for you ages ago."

"My apologies James." Eric addressed her brother. "I found her shortly after you sent me but it seems she overdid it on the dance floor and was not feeling well. I sat with her for a time until she the crowd thinned out and we could make our way here."

James seemed satisfied with the explanation but at the blush on Lily's face Elise grinned from ear to ear.

"Perhaps we should take you home, if you feel you have overdone it. Eric, thank you for escorting her back. I didn't realize it would be such an involved task." James shook hands with Eric.

"Not at all, it was my pleasure." Eric turned towards Lily and kissed her hand. "It was wonderful to see you again." He nodded at the rest of the party and then turned and left. Lily had hoped he would mention when they would see each other again and was mildly disappointed but after their kiss, she was sure he would call next week.

Chapter 9

Lily woke the next morning feeling extremely happy and memories from the night before flooded into her mind. She stretched and then jumped out of bed eager to start the day. She dressed and then headed down to breakfast. She was the first to arrive and poured herself some tea and grabbed a biscuit as she sat to wait.

James and Elise joined her shortly after followed by Tom. The four sat and chatted about the goings on in Kennebunk and Tom's wedding, now only a few weeks away. Lily found herself drifting from the conversation and thinking of Eric and the ball last night.

Amelia and Aunt Clarisse entered the breakfast room and sat down. James and Tom soon excused themselves. They had several meetings scheduled.

"Isn't it Saturday? Those two are always working." Amelia exclaimed. "Although it does gives us an opportunity to discuss last night. Be honest Lily, did you really need to sit down or was something else going on with the handsome Mr. Sampson?"

Lily looked down at her plate then up at Amelia who laughed and squeezed her cousin's hand. "I really did need to sit down but…"

"Then romance took over." Amelia finished her sentence. "Trust me I understand. When are you expecting to see him again?"

Lily hesitated her doubts resurfacing. "I am not sure, he didn't say."

Amelia's brow furrowed. "This is not good. We must find a way to get the two of you together soon!"

"I agree." Elise chimed in. "Let's invite him for dinner tomorrow night with the Handlers." She stood from her chair. "I'll go make out the invitation."

Lily sat in the kitchen peeling potatoes for the cook as she hummed a dance tune she had heard last night. Unable to sit idly and wait for Eric's response to Elise's invitation, she had decided to make herself useful. Her niece and nephew played at her feet and danced around to the music she hummed.

May entered the kitchen and headed towards her mistress. "There is a gentleman here to see you miss."

Lily jumped up from her stool then sat back down. She was not expecting anyone and was not dressed for entertaining. In fact she was covered with potato peels and wearing her oldest clothes.

"Tell him I couldn't possibly, tell him I need some time, tell Mr. Sampson…" Lily was going a mile a minute.

"Oh no, not Mr. Sampson, Mr. Summers miss. What should I tell him?" May asked

Before Lily could answer Emma and Jamie went running out to see their new favorite uncle. Two minutes later he returned with them to the kitchen.

At the sight of her dress covered in potato peels and the sheen that had broken out on her skin from the heat of the kitchen Mark broke out into a large grin. "I'm assuming a carriage ride is out of the question?"

Lily laughed and stood doing a small twirl that sent potato peels everywhere. "Why Mark Summers, what are you saying about my attire. Do I not look like a lady?"

He grabbed her hand and kissed it peels and all. "You still look beautiful, I must admit."

"Miss," May popped her head into the kitchen. "I've got a quick bath drawn if the gentleman doesn't mind waiting."

"Not at all. I will be out in the garden when you're ready."

Forty-five minutes later, Lily emerged looking as fresh as if she had spent hours primping. As she approached Mark, she again pirouetted. "Do I look more like a lady now?"

"You do." Mark smiled faintly as Amelia stepped around him from behind an arbor.

"Cousin, you look lovely." Amelia kissed her cousin on the cheek. "It was wonderful chatting with you Mr. Summers. Have fun you two." And with that she was gone.

"Well, did you still want to take a carriage ride? I should probably see if Elise can chaperone." Lily asked wondering why Mark was, once again, so far away.

"That's all right. Let's just take a stroll around the garden. He placed her hand in the crook of his arm and the two began walking.

"Lily when I first saw you at the picnic, I couldn't get over how beautiful you have become. But I always thought you were a pretty girl. You have your mother's eyes. They are the color of the sea on a sunny day, warm and familiar. I missed being around you and your family so much. In many ways, you were more of a family to me than my own." Marks's parents had never taken much interest in their only offspring and left him to his own devises. Lillian's family had taken him under their wing and her parents had treated him like one of their own.

"Thank you Mark, we consider you family too." Lily patted his arm. She was curious to know where he was going with this but she was content to wait and comfort him.

"There isn't anything I wouldn't do to insure your happiness or the happiness of your brother's." He paused and then turned to her.

Mark held both of her hands as he looked into her eyes. "I guess what I am trying to say, what I am trying to make official is… Well, will you marry me?"

Lily looked at him with her jaw hanging open, unsure of what to say. She was not sure how much time passed before she finally put a thought together. "Why are you asking me this?

Why would we need to get married to ensure my brother's and my happiness?"

"You mean James didn't tell you? He asked me to marry you so the business doesn't go bankrupt."

Lily stared at him with her mouth open. "My brother asked you to marry me?" Anger welled up inside of her.

"Yes well, arranged marriages are not that uncommon and it isn't as though we don't like each other."

"Mark would you excuse me, I need to speak to my brother." And with that Lily let go of his hands and began walking then running towards James' office.

The door was closed but she barely slowed her pace as she pushed open the door and charged into the office. Both of her brothers were leaning over the desk and both looked startled by her entrance.

"James Carter have you gone completely insane?" Lily stood stick straight and stared fixedly at her brother. "I understand that I need to marry to save our families future but I thought we agreed that I would have the season to try and find a husband of my own. Someone of my choosing! How dare you arrange a marriage for me without even consulting me."

James straightened up and spoke slowly. "I am sorry. I received a letter from Tom last week. The situation was worse than I thought and there isn't time for you to spend the season looking for a husband. Mark is a good and honorable man and would make a fine husband."

"Of course he is but that isn't the point. I deserve one season in Boston. I deserve one chance to learn how to be fun and carefree before I marry. Does my life have to be completely dedicated to my family? Am I to sacrifice everything for the sake of the business?" Lily could feel her anger turning to tears but she fought it not wanting to cry now. She wanted to hold her anger and unleash it on James.

James moved around the desk towards his sister. He reached out and hugged her. She tried to push him away but he wouldn't budge. After struggling for a few minutes she gave up and stood stiffly in his arms. "You're right. It isn't fair to you and I didn't tell you because I wanted you to enjoy this time for as long as you could. I'm sorry you have had to give up so much for us but I can't think of another way. If I could, I would give you all the time in the world to find the perfect husband." James paused and pulled away from his sister.

With each word Lily felt a little of her anger melt away. Tears were running down Lily's face and she felt her spine loosen as she sank into her brother's hug. She knew he was telling her the truth but she did not want an arranged marriage.

"Please just think about it." James said as he hugged his sister for a second time.

Lily turned to leave the room unable to speak and saw Mark standing behind her looking completely miserable. She let out a small gasp. "Oh Mark, I am so sorry."

"Don't be." He took her hand in his. "Do you want to talk about this?"

"Do you think we can wait just a little while. I need some time to think and…"

"Of course, I'll stop by tomorrow. Try not to be covered in potato peels this time." Mark smiled at her and kissed her on the forehead then exited the room.

She walked slowly down the hall and Tom easily caught up to her. "Lil' wait." He stood there staring at her. "I am sure we can find another way, I'll talk to James again." He hugged Lily. "We've always had each other. I don't want the business to get in the way of that. I can't lose you for Seacoast Shipping."

She looked at her brother, wishing that he could be right and that there was another way. If James said that he could not find an alternative then there wasn't one. She had told Eric that losing her parents was the hardest thing that had ever happened to her and it was. But she was worried that she was about to lose herself.

She did not say a word of this to Tom. She had already said enough harmful things. Lily gave his hands a gentle squeeze and then turned and continued walking. Tomorrow she would tell her brothers that it would be alright and that she was fine but today she needed for herself.

Chapter 10

      Lily sat in the morning room in one of her finest day gowns waiting for her fiancé to arrive. After talking with James, they agreed to wait until after Tom and Danielle's wedding to make the engagement public.

      She wondered vaguely what she would do if Eric came to court her. It didn't seem right to lead him on but the family had decided to keep the information private. She thought of the feel of his lips on hers and heat welled up in her body again. It was hard to believe that she would never feel that again. Anger replaced her desire but she quelled it. This marriage was a necessity. Anger wouldn't change that.

      At promptly eleven, Mark arrived and was escorted to the morning room. No one was there to chaperone and Lily wondered if her family was giving the couple a chance to talk or if this was part of her new status as an engaged woman.

      "Hello." Mark reached for her hand and kissed it.

      "Good morning." Lily responded, unsure of what else to say.

      The two stood awkwardly for some seconds then sat down. The silence built until finally Mark spoke.

      "I owe you an apology. My proposal yesterday, besides shocking, was seriously lacking in romance. I would like to try again." He took her hand. "Lily, you are one of the most beautiful women I have ever met. You are kind and giving and would make a wonderful wife and mother. I would be honored if you would agree to become my wife." Mark paused for a moment then smiled a devilish grin. "How am I doing so far?"

Lily smiled back. As she did, she heard the ruffle of skirts and wondered if Elise had arrived to chaperone. No one entered so she returned her attention to the man in front of her. "Oh, you are doing very well indeed. All we need is a romantic kiss to complete the picture." She said with a laugh.

At those words Mark leaned over and placed his lips over hers. He withdrew slightly and then kissed her again, deepening the kiss.

Lily found the kiss to be very…pleasant. Mark lips felt nice and warm and his cologne had a wonderful scent. As he moved her closer to him, it felt good to be close to him. She had felt very alone the past day and his strength was comforting. If not for her kiss a few nights before, she might have thought it wonderful. But, there was no changing history. Mark's kiss did not make her body ache for more.

Mark withdrew and the two looked at each other for a moment.

"You haven't answered."

"What? Oh yes, of course I will marry you." Lily answered slightly embarrassed by her gaff. "You'll have to forgive me. I had barely gotten used to the idea of joining society to be courted. I hadn't really considered engagement. I mean I knew it would happen I just thought…" Lily paused for a second.

"That it would happen more naturally?" Mark asked with a grin.

"I suppose so." Lily blushed slightly. "But I think you will make a wonderful husband as well. You're so caring and kind, not to mention handsome. I'm lucky to have you." She said and meant it. She had spent the night thinking and while Mark didn't make her weak in the knees, he would make a fine husband. He would also remain close to her family, which would be a blessing.

"Well, now that we have all of that worked out. I have to go discuss some details with your brother but perhaps I will see you later." He kissed her cheek and left the room. As soon as he was gone, an emptiness filled Lily once again. While he was kind and handsome, it was clear he did not love her any more than she him. Maybe in time they could grow to care for one another. Lily sighed. She would have to hold on to that hope for the sake of her family.

The next few weeks passed without any further incident. Lily and Elise were now making daily trips to the Handler's to help with all of the last minute wedding preparations. Mark visited everyday as well but they seemed to be growing more distant rather than closer together. Lily tried not to think about it too much but every time her thoughts lingered on her upcoming marriage, she filled with dread.

Equally distressing was the fact that Eric had not come to call on her since their kiss. She knew she was engaged but he did not know that and she thought for sure he would want to see her again. Her fears that she was just not exciting enough welled to the surface but she pushed them back down. Their kiss had been exciting, at least for her.

She sat polishing silver, unaware that she was frowning as these thoughts flitted through her mind. Elise walked in and sighed when she viewed her sister-in-law again looking so distressed. Lily was so engrossed however, that she did not see or hear Elise.

"Lil' are you alright?" Elise asked softly.

Startled, Lily jumped slightly in her seat. "Fine, why do you ask." She did not look at Elise, it was easier to lie that way.

"You know you can talk to me about it." Elise sat down next to Lillian and put her arms around her.

"Really, I'm fine. Mark is a good man and I'm sure he will make a good husband." Lily repeated for the hundredth time.

"But you don't love him. You are going to be married to him for the rest of your life and you don't love him nor will you be able to love anyone else." Elise stated, wanting to get the truth out in the open.

Lily looked at Elise and the tears began to flow. She put her head on Elise's shoulder and cried for the life she was never going to have. Soon sobs wracked her body, letting out all of the emotions she had been holding in. Finally, after several minutes, her cries slowed and then ceased.

Elise continued to hold her and Lily did not try to pick up her head. She felt comforted being close to someone she loved and for now that was enough. Finally she spoke.

"I am very lucky in one respect." Lily spoke into Elise's shoulder. "I will be able to stay close to all of you."

Elise gave her one final squeeze and then Lillian pulled herself up.

"I wish it could be different for you." Elise bit her lip.

"Thank you, so do I." Lily shrugged her shoulders. "But, I have got to learn to play the hand I have been dealt. It is just hard."

"Well, we're going to the theater tomorrow night, that should be fun. Maybe it will cheer you up."

Lily's head snapped up. She had forgotten that she would have to continue participating in the social scene until the wedding.

"What is it?" Elise looked intently at Lillian.

"Nothing, nothing. The theater should be fun." Lily bent her head down and resumed polishing the silver platter she had been working on.

Chapter 11

Lily dressed for the theater carefully. She wore an organza silk pale blue gown. Her hair cascaded down her back, loosely pulled up. She had one beautiful diamond necklace given to her by her mother that she wore with the dress. The stone sparkled against her bare skin and drew attention to the cleavage just below it. She felt reckless this evening and it showed in the way she stood in front of the mirror. She had done as her family had asked her all of her life because she loved them and it was her duty. She would do as was required of her but a little rebellion never hurt anyone. Tonight, she did not feel like following the rules.

As she came down the stairs the eyes of her entire family and her fiancé turned towards her. She held her back stiff and straight but her usual smile was not on her lips.

"Lillian, you look stunning." James stepped forward. "Mother's necklace is perfect with that dress. You look...just like her." James stared in disbelief.

"I will be right back." Elise hurried back up the stairs.

"Lily leaned in and whispered into James' ear. "What do you think mother would think of this marriage you have arranged for me?" The question was meant to sting and it had it's desired effect. Their mother had been engaged to another man when she ran away to marry her father. They had loved each other passionately and her mother had been daring enough to go out and get what she wanted.

Amelia stepped up and took her arm walking her towards the door. "I don't know why you are moping so much. Mark will make a good husband."

"You marry him then." Lily bit back. She knew she was being mean to her family but she couldn't help it. She was angry at them and she just couldn't hold it in. Wearing her mother's necklace brought her mother closer to her.

Elise came back down the stairs. "Lily wait." Elise hurried across the foyer. "Wear these too, in fact, keep them. The set should never have been broken up." Elise held out her hand and dropped onto Lily's palm the earrings that made a set with the necklace. They were gorgeous stones and even in her hand sparkled and shined.

"I couldn't." Lily began.

"They should be yours. Take them." Elise picked one up and clipped it onto Lily's ear then the other. She leaned over and said. "You have a great deal of power, you just have to find it."

Lily sat in the carriage and pondered Elise's words. Perhaps if she asserted herself more, she would not be in this mess. She thought of Eric. She just assumed he wouldn't be interested in her, she hadn't done a thing to actively pursue him. And Mark. She hadn't encouraged him one way or the other. She had sat next to him like stone waiting for him to love or reject her. She didn't remember always being this way. She used to go chasing after her brothers constantly. What had happened to her?

The carriage pulled up to the theater and Lily stepped out. She felt the eyes of several men turn towards her, all filled with admiration and desire.

Mark offered her his arm and she accepted. She was unaware that her conviction added an extra sway to her hips and a confident tilt to her chin. As they entered the lobby, Mark took her coat. As she stood admiring the art on the walls, Elise walked up beside her.

"I don't know what has changed but men are looking at you like they are bees and you're the honey. If you keep this up, you may have another marriage proposal by the end of the night." Lily started to laugh then looked at Elise. Now there was an idea. She smiled at a passing gentleman. He smiled back and paying no attention to where he was going, ran into a potted plant.

The group made their way to box of seats reserved for them. Danielle's parents had been kind enough to invite them along and as Lily sat down she began to feel excited about the show ahead. She loved the theater, especially opera. The party in the next box entered and she looked up to smile at its occupants. The smile froze on her face when she saw Eric accompanied by a tall red haired woman. For a moment, she could almost swear that it was Caitlin. Her spine stiffened. Of course it wasn't her, but the resemblance was remarkable and Lily felt a stab of jealousy similar to the first time she met Eric. Her lips set in a harder line. She couldn't control the fact that she felt jealousy but she could control her reaction. She was not going to run and hide nor was she going to simply smile at Eric and pretend she didn't feel anything. He had kissed her, to her that meant something.

James had stood from his seat to shake hands with Eric and the family had followed suit. Lily rose and moved towards the couple.

"Miss Carter, it is wonderful to see you again." Eric kissed her hand. "This is Mrs. Kathryn DeMarco, Caitlin's sister."

No wonder she bore such a resemblance to Caitlin. Lily smiled at the other woman. She had to admit, she felt slightly relieved but it did not change the fact that Eric had never come to call. "How do you do Mrs. DeMarco."

"Very well, thank you Miss Carter. I must say those are exquisite diamonds." Lily touched the stone around her neck.

"Thank you." She smiled about to turn away and Kathryn caught her arm.

"You must tell me how you know Eric. My brother–in-law is so tight lipped."

"Actually, I met Caitlin and Eric several years ago when my family traveled to Boston. My brother James and Mr.

Sampson are business associates." Lily drew herself up.

"Please, there has to be more to it than that. Toby speaks of you reverently and has mentioned something about a great rescue. I am sure the two of you are more acquainted than you are letting on."

Lily looked at the woman standing before her. At one time she might have been intimidated by her but today she was not. "Mrs. DeMarco, are you saying that you don't believe me?"

"Of course not, but Toby..." Kathryn began.

"I am sure Toby would be happy to tell you the story." Lily returned to her seat. She saw Eric look down, a satisfied smile on his face.

Elise nudged Lily in the shoulder. Lily turned to her beloved sister-in-law, annoyed by the interruption.

"What is it? Lily asked.

Elise only laughed. "It's you. You look absolutely stunning sitting there and Mr. Sampson has not been able to take his eyes off of you!" Elise exclaimed.

Lily glanced over to see Eric staring at her with desire clearly evident on his face. She simultaneously blushed and felt the hairs on the back of her neck stand up. Something in her responded to him.

"What do you know about Kathryn" Lily asked Elise.

"Kathryn is married to Mr. Henri DeMarco, a wealthy French aristocrat now in his late sixties, I believe. Rumor has it that his health is failing, but Mrs. DeMarco seems to spend a great deal of time abroad. It is also mentioned that she is unfaithful to her husband, frequently." Elise, who didn't enjoy the theater nearly as much as Lily, was happy to gossip.

"Why do you think she and Eric are together?" Lily couldn't help asking, even though it revealed her jealousy.

"Toby is her nephew." Elise shrugged. Lily nodded, of course it made sense.

The first act ended and everyone headed back out to the lobby to stretch their legs. Lily felt alive as she walked next to Tom and Danielle, the music had filled her heart. It helped a little that she had relieved some of her jealousy towards Kathryn DeMarco. As they reached the bottom of the stairs Lily, found Kathryn directly next to her.

"I am sorry to jump out at you but I was hoping for a word." Kathryn pulled her out of the crowd. "I didn't mean to pry earlier. I hope I didn't offend you."

Lily muttered a noncommittal answer as she waited for the woman to get to the point.

Kathryn continued undaunted. "It is just that it is clear that you and Eric have some sort of relationship...

Lily interrupted her. "What makes you say that?"

"Dear, he barely looked away from you through the entire first act." Lily felt herself blush at Kathryn's words. "Anyway, I wouldn't feel right if I did not explain to you what happened between Eric and my sister."

Lily shifted uncomfortably, she was not sure she wanted to hear what Kathryn had to say. "You needn't explain anything, Eric and I are simply acquaintances. Thank you though, for your concern." Lily turned to leave.

"Wait, I know you say that but I can see the way he looks at you, it is the same way he looked at Caitlin."

Lily paused, turning back to the woman.

Kathryn took this as her opportunity to share the information she had wanted to give. "They were happy at first but when the baby came...Caitlin tried to make it work." Kathryn sighed dramatically. "But once she became pregnant, the infidelity started. It broke her heart. Finally, she confronted him and they had a huge fight. We think they had an altercation, there were a number of unexplained bruises on her body. She fled the house and that was when she had the accident." Kathryn paused staring at Lily.

"It may almost be better this way. I don't know how she would have continued in the relationship. Please, don't make the same mistake my sister did."

Lily stared at Kathryn unable to process what she had just heard. She felt like she had stepped into the plot of an opera herself. Unable to hear anymore she muttered, "I have to go..." And hurried blindly from the lobby down a long hall. She did not look back and, once Lily reached the corridor, she began trying doors. She just needed a few minutes to compose herself. Lily could hardly believe what Kathryn had told her. Could there be any truth to it? She did not know a reason that Kathryn would lie.

Relief flooded her as a door finally pushed open. She rushed into the room and closed the door behind her grateful for the respite. It took a few moments for her to register a man and a woman locked in an embrace in the center of the room.

"Oh, I am so sorry, excuse me." She stuttered as she tried to find the doorknob again to leave.

The man turned slightly towards her and in an instant she recognized Mark.

Unable to speak, she turned to grab the doorknob, yanking it open. Clearly she heard Amelia's voice say, "Lily, wait!"

Another wave of shock ran through her as she turned back to see her fiancé and her cousin standing together.

She stood speechless, or perhaps her words just crowded her mouth and couldn't get out. She knew she should feel betrayed by Mark, they were to be married. But somehow, all she could feel was relief.

"Lily, I am sorry." Amelia rushed forward, seizing her hands. "I would never do anything to hurt you. It's just that, well, we fell in love. I know it is crazy and sudden but as soon as I met him, I knew and he had just told your brother that he would marry you and I tried to stay away but..." Amelia's words trailed off.

Mark stepped forward. He started to speak, then stopped, unsure of what to say.

She reached up and once again this evening touched her mother's necklace. She felt as though her mother was there watching over her. She reached out her hands to the two of them. With a sigh and a small smile she spoke. "James is going to be so disappointed."

Amelia paused for a moment and then an enormous smile broke over her face. She hugged her cousin as hard as she could and then stepped back to Mark. Relief clearly showed on his face as well but he hesitated.

"Lily, I'm sorry..." He started but she waved her hand. "What am I going to tell James?"

"We'll talk to him together tomorrow." Lily replied. "But now we should be getting back or James will be worried."

The three of them left the room, hurrying back towards their seats. In the hallway a man stepped from the shadows with a look of satisfaction on his face.

As they entered the box, Lily was immediately reminded of why she had been seeking refuge in the first place.

Kathryn looked over at her as she entered but quickly looked away. Lily sat down, no longer paying attention to the opera unfolding in front of her, she was caught in her own drama. Kathryn had made some serious accusations about Eric. That his womanizing had drove Caitlin to her death seemed farfetched for the man who was such a dedicated father. But she had to admit, there was an inkling of doubt as well. Why would he kiss her and not so much as write her a note or come calling? Perhaps she was just like those other woman in his life, a mere diversion. Well, she told herself, she was not going to be played the fool anymore! She knew she had to find a husband, but he was clearly not the man!

She snuck a peak at him. He was sitting watching the opera looking more handsome than ever in his evening attire. Even sitting down, he looked muscular and virile. A lock of hair had fallen across his forehead and she wanted to reach out and push it back. She would not, she told herself, think these thoughts. She turned back towards the opera, determined to pay attention.

As the show ended, the small group began shuffling out of the box. Lily said good night to the Handler's, promising to meet at their home first thing Monday morning to continue wedding preparations. This weekend, she and Elise were finishing some embroidery on Danielle's dress.

As she filed down the crowded corridor, she could see the heads of Eric and Kathryn making their way through the crowd. It was time to get over Eric Sampson. She wished that she could take some time to think about what had gone wrong but her family was planning on attending Senator Winthrop's ball the next night and she must begin the business of finding a husband.

Chapter 12

Lily sat in the morning room working on the embroidery at the cuff of Danielle's wedding gown. Elise was working around the collar since her skills were clearly better. Elise's finger moved quickly and she smiled to herself as she worked.

"When is Mark supposed to be here?" Elise asked. Lily had told her of last night's events.

"Soon." Was all that Lily said. A knot of apprehension was building inside of her. James was going to be very upset and though she didn't want to marry Mark, she was did not know who might fill his shoes.

"I think you should stop working while you wait." Elise smiled more broadly. "You have dropped four stitches in that row so far and it is going to take me forever to fix it if you keep going."

Lilly looked down at her work and realized that it looked horrid. She began pulling it out cursing her lousy skills. Just then, Mark entered the room. He smiled broadly at her. "Hello ladies. Lovely morning isn't it?" Mark seemed full of his usual vigor and Lily realized their prospective marriage had been weighing heavily on him as well.

She grimaced and stood. "That is easy for you to say. You don't have to live with James."

"Don't worry. For better or worse, I intend to take full responsibility. Hopefully, he can forgive me in time." The smile slipped from Mark's face but returned quickly as Amelia entered the room.

She smiled shyly and Mark kissed her hand. The two looked lost in each for a moment then Amelia pulled away and sat down. "I'll fix these stitched Lily, while you two are with James."

Lilies eyebrows shot up. Amelia must really be grateful. While she was quite good at embroidery, she usually avoided it all costs saying it was old woman's work.

Lily and Mark walked towards James' office and Lily knocked on the door. Tom answered and held the door open for the two of them as they entered to find James behind the desk.

Tom greeted the two of them with a friendly hello and James smiled as he looked up from his papers. "What can we help you with?" James asked cordially.

Lily looked into her lap and Tom straightened as he looked her way. "Perhaps you would like to talk to James alone?"

"No Tom, stay." Lily looked from one brother to the other. She may need Tom here when James heard the news.

Mark took a deep breath. "Something has happened." He paused, seemingly trying to figure out what to say next.

James eyebrows furrowed as he looked from one to the other. "Lily's not...you haven't taken advantage of her have you?" James started to stand looking very menacing.

"Of course not. Don't be ridiculous." Lily soothed her brother.

"I've met someone else." Mark stated directly. "After talking to Lily, we have decided not to get married. I'm sorry James."

"You've decided what?" James stood this time his face contorting into rigid, angry lines.

Mark stood as well and the two stared each other down from across the desk. Lily became aware of just how tall and broad her brother was. He equally matched Mark in height and he looked quite menacing.

"It's not fair to her James. She deserves someone to love her." Mark leaned into the desk.

James leaned closer as well his eyes narrowing. "And I am sure it's her best interest that you were thinking of when you called off the wedding. How selfless of you."

"Now that's rich. You accusing me of being selfish. You can't seriously tell me you were thinking only of her when you signed her up to marry a man she hasn't seen in years and doesn't love." Both of their voices were rising and she was sure Elise and Amelia had caught that last statement.

"She is my sister and I will decide what is appropriate for her future. Who is this woman you've met? Will you be staying in Boston? Why don't you just turn your back on all of us." James yelled now inches from Mark's face.

"I'm not turning my back on you, I'm being honest with you and Lily and myself. Do you want us to spend the rest of our lives miserable for your precious business? What has happened to you? The man I knew would never have been this selfish."

James turned purple and opened his mouth to speak when Amelia came rushing in with Elise hot on her heals trying to pull her back.

"This is all my fault. If you are going to mad at someone it should be me." Amelia stood next to Mark and the two clasped hands.

James mouth dropped open and his hands clenched the desk. "Get out, both of you."

"I will not." Amelia snapped. "This was my father's house and…"

Lily stood, "Enough." She did not say it loudly but she said it decisively and with an air of authority. She had never spoken to James that way before or Amelia for that matter but it was time she stepped in. "My brothers and I need some time alone to speak. Please leave us."

"I will decide when this conversation is over not you. I am not finished…" James was winding up again when Lily cut him off.

"You have said enough hurtful things for one day. Someone has got to save you from yourself." James stared at her speechless for the moment and Lily took this as her cue to continue. "If you will all excuse us." Mark and Amelia shuffled out of the room but Elise gave the three Carter's an enormous smile as she walked out.

Lily turned back to her brother James. "I appreciate all you've done for me. You've raised me and ran a business to support the family at a time when you should have been out exploring the world and having fun. It can't have been easy to leave Harvard to come back to Maine and take on the family. I know you have sacrificed."

The tension slowly left her brother's shoulders and he sat back down in his chair. "I did what was necessary. There wasn't any other choice."

"I know that and we are all proud of you. But you have to understand something. I am almost the age when you left school. I'm not a child anymore."

"I don't think you're a child or I wouldn't be trying to find a husband for you."

"That's just it.' Lily took a deep breath. "Mother and Father left us equal shares of the business because they trusted all of us to make decisions for ourselves when we came of age. You need to give me that same trust. I am old enough to find my own husband, I don't need you to find one for me. I think our parents knew when we were ready to marry, we would be ready to take on our part of the business."

"She's right you know." Tom chimed in for the first time. "We need to give her the opportunity to find her own way in the world."

"But I wanted to keep you safe. I wanted…" James paused.

"I know you did." She reached for her brother's hand. "Thank you for trying. But you can't keep out the world and I would have been miserable married to Mark. The polite distance would have killed me."

James nodded his head and looked down at his papers. "What do we do now?"

"Same as before. I'm going to find a husband." Lily said this matter-of-factly. It was just a few weeks ago that she could barely think of marriage but being engaged, even for a short time, had caused her to face the reality and, in retrospect, to do some growing up.

"Are you sure?" Tom looked at his sister. "It is a big commitment and shouldn't be entered into lightly."

"I think I'll be ok. Now if you will excuse me, I have a ball to get ready for." She smiled at her brothers and walked out of the room closing the door behind her.

Both of her brothers stared at the door she had just exited. "What have you done with my sister? She suddenly is so much like our mother it's like looking in the past." Tom shook his head.

James took a few moments to answer. "She is like mom but truthfully, I think she has become herself again. She became so quiet and withdrawn when mother and father passed I was worried for a long time. Then I think I just adjusted to her meekness. I forgot what a spit fire she used to be."

Tom gave his brother a side-ways grin. "I hope you're ready for this. Grandpa still cringes when he talks about mom's time in society."

Chapter 13

Lily had dressed for the Senator's ball with a great deal of care. She almost wore her diamonds again but decided against it since she had just worn them the night before. She chose a more understated sapphire, again from her mother. She was running out of dresses she realized, as she descended the staircase to be announced. At every other event she had been announced with her family or with Mark. Tonight she was being announced alone. She was making a statement.

The night passed quickly. Lily found herself dancing with a myriad of men, many proclaiming their love. She smiled and batted her eyes but she did not give any of them too much encouragement. None of them really made her heart beat quicken and she did not want to mislead anyone. Besides, Elise had told her to play hard to get.

As the party began to wind down, a few men started to push their favor and Lily began to feel pressed in. Alexander Preston, a handsome socialite had been particularly attentive. Lily had heard he had a reputation for falling madly in love and then quickly falling out again. This was not what she was looking for and to escape his advances she ducked out while he was in conversation and headed towards the powder room.

As she headed down a corridor she passed a few ladies who smiled and waved. Some of them she had seen before and she returned their greetings. She was about to enter the powder room when a hand reached out for her arm. She jumped slightly but did not avoid the vice like grip that encircled her upper arm.

"You are a very difficult woman to catch alone." Colonel Kingsley stepped out from the shadows. "In fact you are a difficult woman to catch at all. You have been surrounded all night. There has been a change in you my dear. You look devastating but I rather enjoyed the quiet you. It is an appealing quality in a wife."

Lily tried to casually step away but his grip was firm. "Well, thank you for the advice Colonel Kingsley. If you will excuse me, I think I should be getting back or my family…"

"Oh but my dear, you just got here and I was hoping to get to know you better. Tell me, about your home. Maine isn't it?" As the Colonel spoke, he was propelling her further down the hallway and Lily did not see any other guests about. She began to worry.

"Yes Maine, really I should be getting back." The Colonel stopped and Lily felt a glimmer of hope that he was going to do as she asked. Instead, however, he began to lower his head towards hers.

She pushed against him with her free hand as hard as she could but he did not move an inch and instead grabbed the back of her neck, trapping both of her hands between their bodies. She opened her mouth to scream but he brought his lips down over hers in a hard kiss that seemed almost cruel. She tried to pull away but he turned her and trapped her against a wall.

Her heart was pounding in her chest and as she struggled she barely moved against him. He opened her lips with his and thrust his tongue into her mouth. She began to feel sick and struggled more desperately and more uselessly but his grip was like a vice and his body a wall. Fear was rising in her to the point she was unable to think.

"Sorry to interrupt, but Miss Carter's family is leaving and would like her to join them."

The Colonel raised his head and though her eyes were swimming with tears, she recognized Eric Sampson standing ten feet away. Her body went limp with relief.

"Of course." Colonel Kingsley replied. "I will escort her myself momentarily. Thank you." His hand was traveling quickly up her body and she was sure he was about to cover her mouth so that she could not protest.

Eric stood stone still for a few moments and then turned to leave. Lily felt panic rising in her. "No wait." She cried out before the Colonel could gage her.

Eric turned slightly again and the Colonel grip on her arm tightened. "I'm sure Mr. Sampson wouldn't mind escorting me." Her voice was shrill but she attempted to remain calm.

Eric moved stiffly forward and held out his arm for her. Slowly, the Colonel released his hold on her. Her hand was numb from his grip but she forced her fingers to grasp Eric's arm.

Eric turned to leave and she allowed herself to be steered by him leaving the Colonel standing with clenched fists.

"You forgot to say goodnight." Eric's voice was hard but Lily hardly noticed. She was shaking so badly she could hardly walk.

"I told you to stay away from that man. No good will come from a relationship with him." Eric paced quickened. "Then again, what the hell do I care?"

Lily barely heard him. The pace caused her to stumble and she began to fall. His hand automatically wrapped around her upper arm to catch her, which caused her to cry out in pain.

"What's the matter with you?" Eric turned towards her and for the first time noticed that she was shaking like a leaf. Her face was pale and her large blue eyes looked like saucers on her face. Her dress came off her of her shoulders. Quickly he reached behind her and undid her first few buttons on the back of her dress then pulled the sleeve a few inches down her arm. It was highly inappropriate, but Lily hardly noticed. Black and blue marks were already forming where the Colonel had held her arm.

"Jesus, I'm sorry." Eric pulled her into his arms and she laid her cheek against his chest. She wanted to cry but didn't, more because she always seemed to be crying or fainting, in front of this man.

Eric tucked her into the crook of one of his arms and

tried a doorknob that blessedly opened. They appeared to be in a study. Eric steered her towards a settee and pulled her into his lap as he sat down. He folded his arms around her and only then did she start to cry.

"I'm sorry I'm always crying around you. I don't normally, I…"

"It's alright honey. Just sit still for a minute and recover yourself." He pulled out handkerchief and she began to dab at her eyes. She rested her head into the crook of his neck and closed her eyes. He smelled so good. His hand was running up and down her back and every nerve began to tingle. She lifted her head up and looked into his eyes.

"Thank you." She breathed as she stared at his face. He was so handsome and his lips were so beautiful and so close.

He smiled at her. "You're welcome." He brushed his thumb over her parted lips and she felt her lips tingle and her body getting hot all over.

"I should be getting back. My brother is looking…" Even as she said this her eyes drifted to his lips again.

He kissed her slowly and fully. "He isn't. I was being selfish, I didn't want you kissing another man." His lips took hers again, this time with more pressure and passion. She felt lost in the desire rising up inside of her. She was unaware of being laid down on the settee or of being shifted underneath Eric but as his weight settled on her she pushed her body against his, longing to be closer.

She felt his hand undoing more of the buttons on the back of her dress as it loosened and he pulled it slowly down rubbing her breast under her shift. She moaned with desire and his lips kissed a trail down her neck and over her collarbone. His lips moved lower and began to kiss her clothed breast as he cupped it. She gasped as her body grew hotter.

She rubbed against him wanting to be closer to him and her hands were tangled in his hair.

His lips came back up and met hers again, the kiss becoming more intense. His hand had grasped her ankle and started sliding up her leg, only her stockings and pantaloons between them. As his hand reached her thigh she moaned again, lost in the sensation and longing for more. She wanted his hand to keep going but she was unsure to what end.

Eric's hand, however, stopped and she felt him pull them both up to sitting.

"I think I should get you back to your family." Eric kissed her neck a few more times and then her lips intending to break contact.

"Hmm." Was all that Lily said as his lips met hers one more time. She was sure he had intended the kiss to be a farewell one but she wasn't thinking, she was feeling, and she met him with all the passion she had. As the kiss deepened and lengthened Lily felt her body begin to hum and vibrate. She began to feel frustrated by all the clothing between them.

Eric suddenly broke away. "Lily, if I don't stop soon, I'm not going to be able to and you're going to find yourself no longer a virgin and a wife."

Lily blinked a few times as reason slowly returned. She looked down to find the top of her dress around her waist and she began to blush furiously. Even in the candle light, it was noticeable.

Eric laughed as he pulled up her dress and began to do up her buttons, kissing her still exposed collarbone and neck.

Lily began to forget about her embarrassment as Eric kissed her lips one last time quickly, then he stood them both up.

He tucked a few tendrils of hair back into place, then turned her around. "Good as new." He smiled as he placed his hand under her chin and brushed his thumb across her lips with a sigh.

She was at a loss for words as he stood looking at her.

"Should, should we go." She tried to sound calm but her voice shook slightly. She felt dizzy from the range of emotions she had felt in the past few minutes.

"In a minute, I need a few moments to compose myself as well." He gave her a devilish smile and she looked at him confused for a moment until she looked down and saw the evidence of his desire. A blush even worse than the one moments before spread across her cheeks.

He rubbed his hand across her cheek and kissed her forehead. "You are so beautiful."

"I… well, I…" He laughed again and then lead her towards the door. "We'd better go."

As the pair approached her family no one spoke. They clearly had been worried about her extended absence and, as this was the second time, James was not going to be easily pacified.

He stood as they approached, not saying a word although Eric did not look the least bit intimidated. Lily however, felt guilt rising in her for making her family worry.

"Where have you been?" James said in a low voice. His eyes rested on her face and then her lips and Lily's hand unconsciously rose to cover them.

"Something very serious has happened." Eric said in a calm voice.

"Who the hell do you think you are?" James voice held a low fury. "This is outrageous, I should…"

Eric held up his hand. "Lily was accosted by Colonel Kingsley. I know you have questions and I would be happy to answer them but first I think you should take Lily home. She has had a very trying evening. I will be by first thing in the morning to answer all of your questions." With that he turned and left giving Lily's hand a quick kiss before he turned away.

James stared after him with a look of suspicion on his face. He turned to Tom. "I find that man in compromising situations with Lily all the time and he always has some fabulous explanation but I am beginning to wonder."

"Really." Tom said trying not to smile. "I seem to remember when a certain someone first met his wife…"

"That was hardly the same thing!" James said turning towards Lily. "I want an account of your evening. You may consider yourself an equal but I am still your older brother and your guardian. We're leaving."

He turned and headed toward the front doors where the carriages waited outside. Lily sighed and followed the rest of the family falling in behind her. Amelia slid up next to her and whispered into her ear. "He is one fine figure of a man."

Lily smiled but said nothing. Despite his kisses, she would be surprised if Eric came calling and she was not going to sit around waiting.

Chapter 14

The next morning dawned bright and early and Lily groaned as May entered to wake her. She had been up late into the evening telling her brother's about the events of the night before. She focused on Colonel Kingsley and on Eric's rescue but left out any details of her and Eric's kiss. James seemed satisfied but said little. Tom had a great deal of questions.

"You were lucky that Eric came along when he did. How did he happen to be down that corridor?

"I didn't think to ask." Lily began to wonder herself.

"Why did he interrupt, it would have seemed that you were perhaps in a lover's embrace and not in trouble?" Tom continued.

"Perhaps he thought her behavior indecent." James answered absent-mindedly

"Maybe." Tom looked at Lily who was looking at her lap.

"I should get to bed. I don't want to be too tired for church." It was a silly excuse but the conversation was making her uncomfortable.

Lily was dressed and ready before anyone else in the family and sat eating breakfast alone. She prepared herself for the morning events by trying recall all the men she had danced with and what they had mentioned about themselves. Last night's kiss with Eric changed nothing. He didn't seem interested in actually courting her and she was not going to sit around pining after him.

James entered the breakfast room. "Mr. Sampson is here to see you." He sat down across from her.

"Don't you need to talk to him?" Lily asked, butterflies rising in her stomach.

"I already have. Your stories match." James said with a grunt. "As for Colonel Kingsley, you are not to leave my sight. I don't know what this man is after but it is not good. I don't think you should take even trips to the powder room alone. Understood?"

She nodded and rose to meet Eric. What could he want to see her about? As she entered the room, he was sitting near the fireplace. He rose as she entered.

"Good morning Mr. Sampson." Lily sounded stiff to her own ears.

"I think, at this point, you can call me Eric. Good morning." He leaned over and kissed her hand. "How are you feeling this morning?"

"Much better, thank you… Eric, for everything. I am not sure what might have happened last night…" She sounded awkward to her own ears.

"No need to thank me, I feel like a fool for not coming to your aid sooner." Eric answered and then hesitated.

Silence fell between them and Lily sat wondering how conversation could be so uncomfortable while touching each other was so natural.

"Lily, I want to apologize to you." Eric leaned forward. "That night on the veranda, I never should have kissed you."

Lily sat there feeling stunned. He was apologizing for kissing her? He made a mistake? "I see." Was all she could manage.

"I let the situation get out of control and, as I am sure you do not do this kind of thing very often, it is my fault."

"No, I don't." She felt anger welling up inside of her but she tried to keep her cool.

"Anyway, I know you are engaged and…" Eric did not have a chance to finish.

"You kissed me when you thought I was engaged?" Lily voice stayed quiet but fury was slowly building behind it.

"Don't look at me like that, you returned my advances and you are actually the engaged one."

"Neither time that I," She paused her voice growing steadily louder. "returned your advances was I engaged."

"What are you talking about? Of course you were...are engaged."

"I am not. Mark is marrying my cousin Amelia, which is beside the point. I don't know what kind of woman you think I am but I do not go around kissing arbitrary men and certainly not while I am engaged to another." Lily stood her voice rising even higher. "When I kiss someone I mean it. I am sorry you do not share my convictions Mr. Sampson." She put a great deal of emphasis on his name. "Now if you will excuse me, I have to get ready for church."

"Lily wait, I can see that I have offended you." Eric reached for her hand which she yanked away.

"Offended me? You have used me, you have trifled with my emotions, you have treated me like a, like a... I don't want to say and now you wish to apologize. I have had all from you that I can take. I wish you luck in life now please stay out of mine!" With that she stormed out of the room and up the stairs passing several of her family members along the way.

Elise turned to Tom. "I told her to play hard to get but telling him to stay out of her life seems a bit harsh." She turned with a smile on her face. "Still, he'll be back."

Amelia's face held a look of concern. "I hope you're right."

As her initial anger cooled a lump of dread filled her stomach. She had said horrible things to him and, worse, had told him to stay out of her life. While she had told herself that he wasn't going to court her, a hope had always flickered deep down and she had extinguished it herself. She sat with her head down in the church pew, praying to God to show her a clear path to help both her family and herself because right now she couldn't see it.

She was so engrossed in her prayers that she did not notice the many furtive looks that came her way or the whispers that surrounded her as she walked out of the church. Alexander Preston met her at the doors and kissed her hand.

"You escaped from me last night." He said with a gleam in his eye.

"Oh yes, I am sorry. Something came up, I had to leave." She said clearly distracted and not fully paying attention to the conversation.

"Well, I will forgive you if you promise that I can be the one you leave with." He gave her a knowing smile as she stood stunned. Recovering herself, she pulled her hand from his and rushed after her family.

Amelia stood talking to a group of women and did not make it back to the carriage with the rest of the family. When she entered she looked troubled.

Elise sat next to Lily. "I am surprised you didn't take this opportunity to mingle more. Or speak to some of the men you met last night. Actually, I'm surprised they didn't seek you out."

"Many of them were scared away I'm afraid." Amelia said in a low voice. "There is a rumor that you have been... compromised." Amelia took a deep breath and reached for Lily's hand. "Last night at the ball."

James' face turned a few shades of purple. "What are you talking about? She wasn't compromised. You can't tell me that kissing the Colonel..."

"It isn't kissing in the hall that she is being accused of. It has something to do with being alone in the study with a yet unidentified man."

Lily felt cold fear wash over her. If the rumors hadn't been true she could have dismissed them and held her head high but they were true or at least partially so.

"Sampson." James gritted out from between his teeth.

Lily turned to tell her brother that she had not been compromised but his face was black. "Not one word!" And they rode home in silence.

Amelia continued to hold her hand but Lily stared out the window miserable. She would never be able to find anyone to marry her now and she had told the one man she had any feelings for to stay out of her life. She would die alone and miserable, she knew it.

When they pulled up the drive to the house, a carriage was parked outside. They entered the house to find Colonel Kingsley standing in the parlor.

James already in a foul mood did not even pretend politeness. "If you value your life, you will get out!"

James advanced, making a formidable looking opponent. Kingsley stepped back a half a step before drawing himself up. "Please, I wish to make my apologies and explain my actions. I have been in the army too long and have forgotten how to treat such a gentle creature, I am sorry Miss Carter for any scare I may have caused you. I have heard the rumors surrounding you, most untrue, but I wish to help." The Colonel held out his hands in a sign of peace and James stopped advancing.

"Step into my office." Was all James said.

Lily stood rooted to the spot. "How could he possibly help?" Her heart was hammering in her throat.

"By offering to marry you." Elise said with a grim note to her voice.

"You don't think…" Lily knew her brother was furious with her but to engage her to a man who had tried to attack her?

"He wouldn't." Elise grabbed one of Lily's hands. Lily reached for Amelia's with her other but Amelia was nowhere to be found.

Across town Eric was sitting in his study contemplating having a drink despite the early hour. He was angry with himself for allowing his emotions to become so entangled with Lillian Carter. She had accused him of some damn fowl things and it would do well to take her advice and stay out of her life. Unfortunately, he couldn't shake the feeling that she may have had a point. It didn't matter, however, he would stay away from her.

A knock at his study interrupted his thoughts and his

butler entered. "Sir, there is a woman her to see you and she claims that it is an emergency. Her name is Amelia Clark."

A frown marked Eric's face but he signaled for Amelia to be let in.

She entered and Eric was struck but the similarity between the two women's eyes. The same shape and color, he was haunted by those eyes but his were surrounded by honey colored hair and a shy smile. "What can I do for you?" He asked, shaking his thoughts.

"Let me get right to the point. Lily is in trouble. There is a rumor that she was compromised last night at the Senator's ball."

"Kissing in the hallway is a forgivable offense. It will just take a little time." Eric dismissed her words.

"Not kissing in the hallway. Isabelle Gardner mentioned something about the study actually." Amelia stared pointedly at Eric as she said this.

He straightened in his chair. "Nothing happened." He said in a flat voice.

"I am sure that you are right. Lily is a good girl but society will not forgive her for what they think she has done and worse Colonel Kingsley is at our home right now trying to 'help' Lily out of her predicament."

"James would never..." Eric began then stopped.

Amelia knelt down in front of him and grabbed his hand. "Please, you can't let her marry him, you have to do something."

"There is little I can do. It's James who..." Eric began.

"You know perfectly well that if you proposed, James would accept. If you do not, Lily will become a spinster or the wife of Colonel Kingsley. I have heard stories and I'm afraid for her." Amelia did not get up. "I don't know why you do not want to court my cousin but I can tell you that you will not find a more loving and caring woman to help you raise your son. She would lay down her life in a second for him, she already has. She would stand by you no matter what."

Eric looked into her eyes and he could see Lily in them pleading for his help. Dammit! She was right. Lily would make an excellent wife but he could already feel his emotional connection with her growing and he just didn't want to make himself vulnerable like that again. But could he live with himself if she married Kingsley? Amelia had an inkling of what kind of man Kingsley was but Eric had intimate knowledge and it wasn't pretty. At the very least he had to give James additional information to make sure that he did not betroth Lily to Kingsley.

He stood up and pulled Amelia with him. "I need some time to think. I will be over later this afternoon. Try not to worry, it will all work out."

Lily sat in the courtyard, staring off into space. How had things spiraled so out of control so quickly? Yesterday she had been ready to find a husband and save her family and today she was the ruin of them. She heard someone come up behind her but she didn't turn. She was too ashamed to face her family.

"I want to talk to you." James voice was cold.

She turned slightly then. "I'm sorry. I've let you down. I've let the entire family down. I don't know how... I don't know how I let things go so astray." She took a deep breath. "If I have to marry Colonel Kingsley, I will." She felt a sick dread in her stomach at the words but she didn't flinch or show any outward sigh of emotion.

James shoulders slumped slightly then he sat himself down next to her. "You are not marrying that man if I have to throw myself in front of a train. He is a snake. But, I don't know how we are going to get out of this."

The butler stepped out onto the courtyard. "Eric Sampson is here to see you sir."

Lily jumped and James stiffened. Then he stood quickly and headed for the doors. He turned back to his sister. "Don't move."

Eric was waiting for James in the office. James entered and sat himself behind the desk. "Unless you are here to propose marriage I'm not sure we have much to talk about." James' voice was hard.

"I'm sure Lily has told you that nothing has happened between us." Eric replied casually.

"Something has happened. You took my sister into a room unchaperoned where you stayed for a lengthy amount of time. It is an unforgivable offense."

"I came here to warn you that you can't marry Lily to Kingsley. He is a cruel man particularly towards women. Her life will be as good as over."

James stared at Eric before answering. "We may not have a choice. Lily needs to get married this season as you well know. It will be impossible to find another husband with her reputation as it stands."

"You would do that to your own sister?" Eric sneered.

James leaned forward. "My sister is very important to me but so are my children and my wife. I can't sacrifice the future of my family and that of my brother's for Lily. She chose to walk into that room with you now she must suffer the consequence."

Eric sat staring fixedly at James. He had seen James play poker and knew he was an excellent bluffer. He wondered if he was bluffing now. If he was, he was damned good.

James sat back in his chair. "You could help my sister, you know, help all of us. It is you who put her into this predicament."

Eric's face hardened and he started to get up.

"Don't leave yet. I know you are well aware of Lily's personal attributes. I wanted Lily to find a husband on her merits not on her dowry but I can assure you that the marriage would be beneficial for you."

"James, I don't need money..." Eric stopped as James shook his head.

"Not money, land. Land on the harbor that was bequeathed to my father when he married my mother. It was preserved for Lily's husband. Land on the Boston Harbor."

Everything suddenly made sense to Eric. He wondered how far Kingsley would go to get his hands on that land. His instincts told him far.

"You said that you haven't told a great deal of people about this land, who might know?"

James stared at him momentarily. "I suppose anyone who took the time to check public records."

Eric took a deep breath. "He's after the land."

"What?" James stared at him.

"Colonel Kingsley does not live off an army salary. He does some trade with the East. I know he imports porcelain and silks from China but I have heard that he has some illegal operations as well."

"How would you know that?" James looked skeptical.

"My wife was very close to the Colonel. Too close." Eric pursed his lips.

James nodded his head.

"Port land and warehouses would help with any business but if needed to stash some illegal goods for a time it would be crucial."

"If you are trying to convince me not to betroth them…"

Eric waved his hand. "I think the Colonel started the rumor to force your hand and I don't think he is done trying to persuade you to marry him to Lily."

"If I refuse what else can he do?" James stated simply.

"He can finish what he started last night."

James stared at him then nodded his head. "I hate to admit it but that would explain his actions. Still, if Lily leaves society and returns to Maine he has no opportunity."

"True, but you have the wedding coming up and if he knows Lily is the owner of that property he may have some knowledge of your financial situation. He may know you need to marry Lily. It is not a secret in Boston Society." Eric sat back and ran his fingers through his hair.

James stared hard at a spot on the wall. "He knows Lily needs to marry. I mentioned her engagement to Mark when he was here about a contract. He asked me why the rush and I made a vague reference to finances. He must have thought last night she was still engaged."

"The only way Lily would be completely safe is to be

married." Eric stated.

James frowned looking skeptical. "You think he's that much of a threat?" James paused.

"Regardless, we are back to what you want. Lily married. I assume you would like the wedding to happen quickly?" Eric voice remained even.

"Well, before the end of the year. It's a bit short but…" James was cut off by Eric's reply.

"How about by the end of the summer?" Eric smiled coolly.

James began to protest "What will people say?"

"Well, once we are married all will be forgiven and they already think it. Actually, it is the perfect guise for a quick marriage."

"This is not acceptable." James laid his hands on the desk.

"I know you don't know Kingsley but I do and I am telling you he is a threat to Lily. I am not going to let her get hurt. These are my terms. We are to be married by the end of the summer and she is not to attend any social engagements without my presence. James, you are getting what you want remember?"

"Then why do I have the feeling I just lost?" James and Eric shook hands.

"Do you want to tell Lily or shall I?" Eric asked with a half-smile.

"I think you had better. The last time I engaged her she nearly chopped my head off." James grimaced at the memory.

"A bit of a spit fire when she's angry isn't she?" Eric grinned.

"You'll find out soon enough." James said with a small laugh.

"Just one more thing, I don't think we should share any information about Kingsley with Lily until it is necessary."

"Agreed. Lily is waiting for you out on the courtyard." The two shook hands once again and Eric headed for the double doors.

As Eric stepped outside he could clearly see Lily sitting on a bench with her back to him.

"What did he want?" Lily asked without turning.

"Not too much." Eric answered approaching her on the bench.

"Oh, I am sorry, I didn't know, I mean I thought you were James." Lily stumbled over her words.

"Obviously." Eric kissed her hand briefly. "Do you mind if I sit?" He asked.

"Please do." Lily moved over slightly and he took the seat next to her. "I said some awful things to you this morning."

"Most of which I deserved." Eric smiled as she stared at him unsure of what to say. "Let's neither of us apologize since we've both made errors."

Lily nodded her head.

"Lily, I am an honorable man despite my actions. I have inadvertently gotten you into a great deal of trouble and I intend to get you out of it."

"What are you talking about?" Lily felt her pulse rising.

"James and I have discussed it and provided you are amenable to it we are to be married at the end of the summer."

Lily's heart slammed in her chest. A flurry of emotions passed through her body at once. Excitement, fear, disappointment battled in her mind. While no man made her feel the way he did, this proposal held even less romance then Mark's had. Still, she had little choice in the matter. She needed to marry and the man she felt more connected to than any other was proposing. She had little prospects besides this but a small voice in her cried out 'but he didn't say he loved you or even wanted you.'

Lily swallowed her doubts and smiled. "Of course."

"Excellent." He kissed her cheek. "Toby is going to be absolutely thrilled when I tell him. Why don't we have a picnic sometime this week to celebrate?"

"That would be lovely." She nodded. He seemed far more distant today while proposing marriage to her then he had the night before. It filled her with apprehension.

"If you will excuse me, I have some arrangements to

begin making. I have something for you that I will send over later this afternoon." He stood and she followed suit.

She looked at him and the reality of what was happening sunk in. They were going to be married. She would live with him, see him every day. What kind of husband would he be? The kind she imagined or the one that Kathryn accused him of?

"Have a good afternoon." Was all she could think to say as he departed. She sat back down. She had been ruined and saved all in a day.

"Damn it!" Colonel Kingsley sat in a wingback chair in his study. While his body looked relaxed, his face clearly showed the fury he was feeling.

"You didn't really think her brother would agree to the marriage?" Kathryn sat nearby a smirk on her face.

The Colonel grabbed her forearm and pulled her close. "That is enough." He held her arm for a second more and a slight fear flared in her eyes. He smiled and let her go. "He wouldn't have had a choice if Sampson hadn't interrupted. That man has been a thorn in my side for far too long. I thought you had convinced her not to marry him."

"You might have appeared the more attractive candidate if you hadn't tried to force yourself on her." Kathryn snapped.

"I thought she was engaged. It seemed the quickest way to solve my problem." The Colonel shrugged. "I've made a few miscalculations."

"Just a few. You are not engaged to Lily Carter and Eric has not suffered at all! Right now he is engaged to a beautiful heiress." Kathryn took a deep breath about to continue.

A second man, also in uniform, sat in the shadows. "We will make sure the two don't get married, but we will have to do it soon. Our leave is almost over and we need to have our business secure before we go. We can't keep bringing goods into port that we can't store."

"Quite right." Colonel Kingsley nodded. "It shouldn't be difficult provided Kathryn can complete her part."

"I don't think I'm the one you need to worry about." She bit back.

In response, Kingsley raised his hand and smacked her hard across the face. "I told you, that's enough."

"We will wait till after the wedding. If she isn't there, her family will not be able to hide her absence. You, of course, want your bride to be able to enter back into society?"

"Of course." Kingsley smiled. He was going to enjoy this.

Lily smiled as Toby ran through the field singing at the top of his lungs. Exuberance was not something he lacked. She wished, at the moment, she could say the same for his father. Conversation had seemed stilted and, other than kissing her hand, he had not touched her once since they had departed for the picnic.

"The ring looks beautiful on you." Eric glanced at her left hand.

"Thank you." Eric had sent her a beautiful diamond ring cut similarly to that of her mother's necklace. It was a lovely gift.

Toby ran over to Lily and sat down next to her. "Miss Carter what do I call you now?"

She put her arm around him and hugged him close. "What would you like to call me?"

"Well, I could call you Lily or Flower but I never had a mom before so I was thinking that when you and my dad got married I could call you mom, if that's ok?" He looked at her uncertainly.

"I think that would be wonderful." She smiled at him and gave him another squeeze.

He stood and then whispered in her ear. "Do you think I could start practicing a little, you know, when no one was around?"

"I think that would be fine." She whispered back.

He gave her a grin and then ran off into the field to play once again.

"He is quite taken with you already." Eric sat up straighter.

"And I with him. He's a wonderful boy." Lily replied.

"Thank you." Eric's tone was stiff and Lily sensed that something was wrong.

"Is it difficult for you?" She asked. When he gave her a quizzical look she clarified hesitantly. "To hear him call someone besides Caitlin mom."

"Oh." Eric paused. "No, I guess I just wish there wasn't such a large void in his life. He has missed having a mother."

"I understand." Lily nodded and dropped the subject. She made a mental note to try and have more patience. While Eric seemed cold and distant at times, she had to remember how difficult it must be to have lost his wife. It must be even harder to see another woman taking her place.

They sat for a few more minutes in silence and then Eric turned to her. "After the wedding I will have to stay in Boston for a few weeks but then I thought we could travel up to Maine and begin looking for a house."

"Really? Oh that is wonderful!" She felt joy bubbling up inside of her.

"We wouldn't be able to live there year round but we could be there part of the year and I am sure James and Elise will be in Boston part of the year as well." He returned her smile enjoying her happiness.

"Of course, but that will be just perfect. Thank you so much. I would miss them if I could only see them a few weeks a year." Without thinking she leaned over and kissed him on the cheek. "Thank you." She repeated.

"You're welcome." He looked at her lips and she felt that pull towards him that was beginning to feel familiar. As she leaned towards him, however, he sat straighter and pulled away.

She felt disappointed and a bit angry but pulled herself together. She didn't understand him. He was so affectionate at times and then so cold at others.

Toby came back from his trip around the field with a fistful of flowers for her. She smiled and Eric began unpacking food for them.

The rest of the picnic was cordial and polite. Lily enjoyed both of their company but she wished that she could feel the closeness now, she had shared with Eric before. As they drove home Toby curled up next to his father and the two sat together. Lily wondered if she would ever become part of their circle, if they would feel like a family.

Chapter 15

The morning of Tom's wedding was a perfect New England summer day. The sun was shining bright but the temperature was mercifully mild, a rarity for late June. The house rose early and there was a buzz of excitement that filled the air as people bustled about.

Lily began dressing in a beautiful sapphire gown, one of many that Eric had sent over the week before. The thought of him made her sigh in frustration and she paused in her dressing. They had seen each other several times over the past few weeks, but with each visit Eric seemed further away from her. She couldn't explain the distance and she didn't have the slightest idea of how to bridge it. If she had thought things were strained with Mark, it was doubly so with Eric. At least she and Mark had history connecting them, some common ground. How could she be so terrible at being engaged? Her nerves fluttered at the thought of actually being married. At least, she thought with a smile, she wasn't marrying Colonel Kingsley.

She finished dressing and May came in to begin arranging her hair. She put on her diamond necklace and earrings and then her ring, a gift from Eric. Stepping back, she looked in the mirror and smiled. At least she looked calm and well put together. She was to arrive at the Handlers in an hour to help attend to Danielle. She looked down at her ring one more time and her thoughts again drifted back to Eric. Why would he agree to marry her if he didn't want to even get to know her? She sighed and pushed these thoughts aside. Today was about Tom and Danielle.

The ceremony was beautiful and Lily blinked back tears as she watched Tom and Danielle stare blissfully at each other. She sat with her family, Eric and Toby just on the other side of her. She had been the object of many stares but she tried to ignore them and focus on her brother and new sister-in-law. As the ceremony ended, people began to file out and meander to the drive where their carriages would take the guests back to the Handlers' for a reception for the new couple. In the rush Lily was separated from her family, only Toby remained by her side holding her hand. In front of her was Mrs. Johnson and her daughter, Isabelle. Lily prayed that they would not see her. She did not want to face their snide comments today. Blissfully they did not notice her but as words from their conversation drifted back to her, she realized that the two women were discussing her.

"He is so handsome and frankly, well off, how could he be engaged to her? Can you believe she was found in room with a man, really! Is the family forcing him? Do you think it was him? It couldn't have been?" Isabelle rambled on.

"She is quite beautiful, unfortunately. But it couldn't have been him, rumor has it that it was Colonel Kingsley." Her mother replied.

"Then why would he be marrying her? Everyone knows the Carter's don't have any money." Isabelle sulked.

"I've heard that she has a dowry, the family can't access it until she is married. Besides, she has something far more valuable; land on the harbor." Mrs. Johnson shrugged her shoulders. "Mr. Sampson hasn't stayed single because he wanted to be married. He just can't refuse such a good piece of land."

Lillian felt her insides churning and fought down the nausea that was building. Normally, Lily ignored gossip but she couldn't deny this. Mrs. Johnson had a great deal of personal information about her and her explanation about Eric's reasons for marrying her made so much sense. It explained his coldness, she was a business transaction. She fought down the rising tears as she pictured the life before her. Eric remaining distant and impassive towards her, possibly taking other lovers to fill the time. All the while her own feelings growing for him! How would she bare it? Lily willed herself towards her carriage. She was lost in her own world of despair when a group of men caught her attention. Standing across the street from the church entrance, they stood out from the rest of the passerby. Their clothes were travel worn and dusty from time spent in the woods. Their faces were hard and their eyes were all staring directly at her. She felt a shiver run down her spine as she stepped into the carriage helping Toby in behind her. Eric snapped the door closed behind them both and Lily exhaled, realizing that she had been holding her breath.

"Where are James and Elise?" Lily asked surprised but relieved to see Eric sitting next to her niece, nephew and the new governess.

"Riding with Tom and Danielle." Eric said as he looked out the window, directly at the spot where the men had stood.

"They are very disconcerting." Lily commented as she felt another shiver run up her spine. Without realizing it, she outwardly shivered.

"Why." Eric's attention snapped back to her.

"It is silly, I'm sure but I felt that they were staring at me." Lily sighed, sure Eric would laugh it off but he didn't.

"Lily, don't go anywhere alone today. Stay close to me" Eric's eyes bore into hers and she nodded her ascent. She wrapped her arm around Toby, who snuggled into her side. She was unaware of how fetching they looked snuggled up together but Emma and Jamie quickly jumped off their seat and into the remaining space on their aunt's lap. She kissed each child's head and snuggled them closer, drawing strength from their presence. She looked up to see Eric still looking at her but his eyes had softened.

"We are going to have to start working on providing you with more children as soon as we are married." Eric's face broke out into a full smile, the first Lily had seen in a long time. She felt herself blushing but she too smiled. The thought of children surrounding them suddenly seemed to fill the void she had seen in her future but it also brought the conversation she had heard crashing to the fore front of her mind.

"That would be wonderful." She murmured softly and hugged the children once again. Her mind was full of all that she had heard surrounding Eric and his last marriage. This time she didn't notice that another man was staring intently at her; her soon to be husband.

As they entered the Handler's home Eric tucked her hand into his arm as the children milled around them. "Remember what I said, stay close." He whispered. One of his finger's brushed a hair away that trailed across her cheek. It was an unconscious gesture that left little doubt in the minds of the people around the nature of their relationship. Whatever people had thought Eric's motives for choosing Lily as his bride, it seemed obvious now. Obvious to everyone, that is, but Lily. It was strikingly apparent to Kathryn DeMarco , who stood by the entrance watching the couple begin to mingle.

For the next two hours, many well-wishers congratulated Tom and Danielle on their marriage and Eric and Lily on their engagement. Eric had been right. While people may have been talking behind their backs, to their faces there were nothing but enthusiastic. Apparently Eric held enough influence in town to silence any dissent on his choice of bride or the accelerated time line for their marriage.

Lily found herself enjoying the reception immensely. The Handler's home looked beautiful for the event and many friends and family she had not seen for a long time were there. She felt herself relaxing for the first time since her engagement. She also found herself looking forward to her marriage. For whatever reason, it hadn't occurred to her that she could soon have children of her own. Just the thought made her smile.

"What are you smiling about?" Eric asked next to her. Lily blushed, not realizing that she had been outwardly expressing her joy.

"I was thinking about what you said earlier about children, actually. I hadn't thought beyond Toby but now that you mentioned it..." she trailed off, unsure of what to say.

"It hadn't occurred to me either until I saw you surrounded by children but frankly, it's a beautiful picture." He smiled at her again and it nearly took her breath away. "After Toby, Caitlin was sure that she did not want any more children. I had resigned myself to that fact but, I must admit, I always did." He paused again and Lily unconsciously held her breath. She had never heard him talk about Caitlin and this information fascinated her. "It is obvious you'll make a wonderful mother to Toby and to any other children we have."

"Thank you." Lily replied trying not to sound disappointed. She had hoped to hear more about his first marriage. She had so many questions, she didn't dare ask. Usually, he was so distant and their relationship so new that she did not want to pry. Lillian also had to admit that while being a good mother was a better motive than land to get married, it was not what she really wanted to hear from him. She knew it was impossible, but she wanted him to tell her how passionately in love with her he was. She did not have time to articulate any of this, however, as another couple approached to engage them in conversation.

Eric stepped away to get them refreshments while Lily continued talking to some old family friends. Eric had meant what he had said about keeping Lily close and had not strayed from her side for more than a few minutes all evening. But as the conversation lengthened, Lily realized that some time had passed since she had seen Eric and she began to wonder if she should try to find him. On the one hand she felt relatively safe in the middle of a crowded room with close friends and family but on the other, she had promised Eric she would remain close to him at all times. Another five minutes passed and she finally excused herself to go find him. After checking several rooms, she finally stepped out onto the patio. She knew Eric would probably not want her to but she told herself she would just look for a moment and then return to the ballroom. As her eyes scanned the property, she saw a man standing in the shadows that looked strikingly like Eric, talking to a tall red haired woman.

She hesitated, they appeared to be arguing and she did

not know if she should interrupt or go back inside. Suddenly, a hand reached out and clamped over arm and then quickly over her mouth. She began to struggle and looked to the two people she had seen for aid. She struggled, twisting and turning trying to break free while her feet kicked wildly. Her foot finally struck a footed pot which crashed to the brick patio, making both people turn towards her. She could clearly see Eric's face and wanted to cry with relief. A man stepped from the shadows and hit Eric with a blunt object in the head, sending him crashing to the ground. She, thought for a moment to try to call out to Kathryn but the other woman simply stepped into the shadows and disappeared.

Two more men stepped out and she recognized the travelers from the church earlier. A sick dread began to fill her stomach as she realized the seriousness of the situation. Lillian began to fight with every ounce of strength she had. More men grabbed hold of her and she continued to fight. She heard what sounded like a moan come from the direction where Eric had been standing. It sent her into a frenzy, trying to delay her attackers. As she struggled she heard one of them say.

"Ain't know use. Just knock her out." and with that she felt a sharp pain at her temple and then nothing.

Chapter 16

She woke slowly and became aware of her situation in small increments. First she felt a rolling motion that added to the nausea she was experiencing. She smelled the distinct odor of horse beneath her and the rough voices of men all around her. She kept her eyes shut as she tried to piece together where she was and what was going on. After a minute or more she realized she was no longer in a dress but in some sort of rough pants and shirt and her breasts were clearly bound. Her hands, tied in front of her, automatically gripped the horn of the saddle while her back slumped against an unknown attacker. She tried not to stiffen away from him. She did not want him to know she was awake but clearly he was already aware because he whispered softly in her ear.

"Keep your eyes closed and lean against me. I do not want the others to know that you're conscience and I have a great deal to tell you." She did as he commanded but he said nothing more for at least two minutes.

"It is my job to keep you safe but in order to do that you must do as I say." He paused for a minute and then continued. "These are not good men you are among and they will take any opportunity to do unspeakable things to you so you must listen to me at all times."

"I have put you in men's clothing to keep you as inconspicuous as possible, do not worry, I have not violated you in any way." She shifted slightly in the saddle testing her parts.

Her nether regions were the one part of her body that was not soar, so she assumed what he said was the truth. He stopped again and it must have been five minutes until he continued. "I know that it is difficult to do but you must trust me that I will not harm you and that my intentions are to help you if I can. Beyond that I cannot say much more."

Lily frowned as she pondered his words. A man, who had kidnapped her, tied her up and now carried her from her family and home asked for her trust? He couldn't be serious? Still, she had to credit him in a few places. He had clearly taken measures to keep the other men at bay, for now, and had not touched her himself. For the moment, she would do as he asked.

Another man called for the group to halt and Lily felt fear rise up inside her. When the group was riding, no one was paying any attention to her but she doubted that would be the case when they stopped.

"Hey Tracker, she awake yet?" A voice called from her left. She still had her eyes closed and had no intention of opening them.

"Not yet." The man behind her replied.

"Funny, I thought I saw you whispering in her ear. Sure you're not trying to sweet talk her for yourself?" Lily immediately recognized the voice of the man who had suggested she be knocked out and she felt her skin crawl at the sound of his voice again. Yes, she would stick close to Tracker.

"I was trying to wake her, and no, I am not trying to keep her for myself. We have strict orders, and you would do well to follow them." Tracker said evenly but his words did nothing to calm Lily. Orders? From who? Was this Tracker saving her from these men only to deliver her to someone far worse? Perhaps his offer of help was just a way to keep her quiet and obedient for the trip. She would have to pay careful attention.

Another man piped in "Owh, a little fun never hurt nobody, why you gotta be so rigid?" Lily kept her eyes closed and her body still but it was difficult. She kept telling herself to breath evenly.

"Enough, let's eat a little grub then we hit the trail again. We gotta put as many miles between us and her men as possible." They began to make a quick camp and Tracker lifted her off the horse and set her down in his lap while the other men worked.

"Ain't you gonna set that girl down and help?" The voice that Lily now recognized asked, a hint of his plans, if Tracker did as he suggested, tinted his words and Lily found herself praying that Tracker would say no.

"Not on your life Slim." Tracker responded, quietly but the other man did not respond and it seemed to Lily that Tracker had some authority in the group. He was clearly better spoken and she wondered briefly how he ended up with these men. How many were there? Tracker had told her to keep her eyes closed. Should she listen or try to find out more information about the men around her? She did not want one of them to see her awake so she decided to begin gathering information when they resumed the journey to wherever they were going.

As they mounted back up on horses, Tracker again whispered in her ear. "You're doing fine. Watch out for Slim, he's the most dangerous. I am going to loosen your wrists once we get started. Try to flex them so that they don't get to tired."

Lily was puzzled by his words. She was still groggy and her head ached terribly. Why would he be showing so much concern for her? She had no idea how much time had passed or what direction they were heading. It was dark out and until the sun came up she would have no way of getting answers.

The ride continued and, with every passing mile, Lily felt her head pound harder and her nausea grow. When she felt she could take no more and was about to scream from the strain, the sun began to lighten the sky ever so slightly. It made its way over to the horizon and Lily could see that it was to the south and east of them which would mean that they were heading towards Maine. She almost smiled before she began to wonder if they had just made a direction change to confuse her. She would have to watch the landscape because if it was Maine, there was a chance that she could escape and make her way to her family. It was a landscape that was familiar to her.

This time Tracker called for a halt and the men pulled to a stop. No one spoke and she assumed they must be as tired as she felt.

"Eat this." Tracker handed her some food that she ate without tasting but she felt her headache and nausea lessen immediately.

Tracker unrolled his sleeping roll and then picked her up and carried her towards the woods.

"Where are you taking me?" Even she could hear the fear strangling her voice.

Tracker smiled, not in a malicious way but one that was clearly amused. "I, ah, thought you might need to relieve yourself."

"Oh...I...thank you." She felt a blush creep up her face as he set her down next to some bushes.

"Go in there. I'll wait right here for you." He turned his back on her and she quickly headed for the center of the bushes. Lily contemplated using this opportunity to try and escape but she was bone tired and could barely hold her body up to relieve herself. She couldn't imagine actually escaping from a man who had not suffered a head blow and who was far more used to long periods on horseback. She saw little choice, Lily returned to Tracker and allowed him to lead her back to camp.

"Lie down." Tracker told her as he motioned towards his roll. She gladly accepted with a nod of her head and immediately closed her eyes ready to collapse. They bolted open seconds later when she felt a body press against hers.

"What?" Lily cried in a half strangled voice trying to sit up. She heard several men snicker from close by and she clamped her jaw shut.

"Slim, you're on first watch. Kyle, you're second." he directed the men. Then, he said to her, in a quieter voice. "Get some sleep, you'll need it." Again, she did as she was told and Tracker wrapped her in his arms. This time she did not protest, and considering the men that surrounded her, it actually did make her feel safer. She closed her eyes and fell immediately to sleep.

Lily woke from an exhausted sleep, completely disoriented. She had no idea where she was or how long she had been asleep. Lillian wondered why she had woken at all. She was at least warm, and relatively comfortable although she realized that she was asleep on the ground and wrapped in someone's arms.

"I am sorry to wake you but most of the men are asleep and I thought you might like a few minutes to wash up and get yourself...ah...ready." A voice from behind her whispered softly and the reality of her situation came crashing back to her.

"Can I turn around?" She whispered back hoping to ask a few questions.

"Of course." He said.

She shuffled quietly around but stopped when she looked down to see a revolver in his right hand, resting on her stomach.

"It is only for your protection." He calmly assured her and she continued to turn. She looked into his face and had to admit, it was not unpleasant. He had dark brown hair and his eyes were like liquid pools. He did not look like he smiled very often but his face held no cruelty either. He seemed slim and wiry but memories of the hours he held her on horseback were coming back to her and told her that he must be strong.

"Where am I? Why am I here?" Lily asked the man she knew only as Tracker.

"I don't have time to go into any detail. Stay close to me and don't speak to any of the men, it will only provoke them. Keep your head down and pull your hat as low as you can. These men are dangerous." Tracker's face hardened with every word and Lily felt herself tensing.

"I believe you." Lily didn't doubt his words but she doubted his motives in sharing this with her. "Why am I with these men?"

His face relaxed and a small smile touched his lips. "Right. I believe that your hand is wanted in marriage."

She stared at him stunned for several moments, unable to fathom what he had just said to her. "What?" Was all she could mutter.

"Someone found your engagement unsatisfactory, to say the least, and has decided to make you his wife instead." Tracker added quietly, no longer smiling.

Lily's eyebrows furrowed. Who would kidnap her for marriage? But even as she thought the words, she knew who it was. "Colonel Kingsley." She whispered softly as a slow dread began to fill her stomach. She suddenly realized what his kisses the night of the ball meant. He had intended to force her to marry him. Since that attempt had failed, he would try another.

Her fear must have trickled into her voice because Tracker grimaced. "I had to go through with the kidnapping, it was necessary. But I will do everything I can to see you safely back home." He spoke softly but firmly and Lily wanted to trust him although she thought it was foolish to do so. Men began stirring nearby them and Tracker rose, pulling her up so that she could get ready for the ride ahead.

The day was endless. The sun rose in the east and to the south of them and continued to travel overhead, telling Lily that they were heading Northeast. She had missed the first part of the journey and did not know their original direction but to her estimation, they were travelling to Maine. They rode, stopping only briefly to water the horses and eat a few bites of pack food and then continue on. They saw no one and passed through no towns and Lily began to wonder how she was going to get out of this mess. The men around her spoke very little. It meant she could learn nothing about them or where they were heading. It also meant that they also already knew the path that they were taking and would likely continue to avoid civilization. As the hours past she grew more apprehensive. Tracker's promise of help seemed unlikely at best and as he rode behind her, saying nothing, she thought that she should try to come up with another plan. But as she wracked her brain, she could think of little that would help her out of this situation. She was never left alone, she had no weapons and little idea where she was. Lily sighed to herself, but she felt Tracker behind her chuckle.

She wanted to turn and vent her frustration on the man

she considered her jailer but couldn't. "Relax." He whispered in her ear.

"You talkin' to that girl again?" Slim's voice cut through her like a knife and she shrank back into Tracker.

"Hey Slim, she sure does look like a boy in that git up, don't she?" Another voice called. "I saw her in that dress though and she didn't look like no boy. No way. She looked damn good."

"Shut up Curly." A third voice called. "You heard the boss."

"Yeah Curly. He don't want her touched. That is why he sent his lap dog to watch her." Lily heard Slim's voice coming from her right, and glanced briefly to catch a glimpse of the man. He was staring directly at her, leering in a way that made her blood run cold. He was a thin and wiry man with gray hair pulled into a ponytail. His eyes were hard and when he smiled, Lily could see that he was missing several teeth.

Tracker said nothing, but pushed his horse slightly ahead of the group and ground in her ear "Don't look at them. Keep your head down."

Lillian did as she was told, fear filling her insides till she could feel every nerve tingling. With sick dread, she saw the full extent of her situation. There were maybe five or six other men besides Tracker. Although one seemed willing to follow orders, at least two were not all that interested in delivering her to the Colonel. Could Tracker hold them off? Even if he did, what was to be said about the man who awaited her at the end of this journey? What could be said about Kingsley who had first attacked her, then had her kidnapped and kept company with men like these? Reaching her mystery destination seemed no more safe than traveling with these men. Her musings were interrupted as the group came to a halt. Lily could see Slim, and who she thought was Curly, talking at the back of the group.

"Rings, take her." Tracker turned to a man on her left and Lily felt wild panic growing inside her. At least with Tracker, she was safe from immediate attack.

"Rings will keep you safe, I need to talk to the other men." Tracker stopped and lifted her easily from the horse, standing her on her feet. Rings reached down and just as effortlessly picked her up, settling her on the horse in front of him.

"Slim and Curly" Tracker words came out in clipped tones. "Double back and see if we are being followed."

"Are you kidding me, how far we gotta go?" Curly shot back indignantly. "I'm sick of this saddle, I want a rest."

"You'll go until you can't go any more or until you find sign of someone." Tracker returned evenly.

"Isn't this supposed to be your job?" Slim spoke more deliberately and although she didn't lift her head, she could feel his eyes burning into her.

"I have been ordered to stay with the girl at all times. You know that. You have to keep look out this time." Tracker shrugged.

"Just trying to keep me away from that Girly aren't you? Come on Curly, lets git goin' so that we can git back." From beneath the brim of her hat, She saw Slim turn and ride his horse back the way they had come. Curly followed.

Tracker turned back to rest of the men. "Anyone else who doesn't want to follow orders?" They grumbled but said little else.

Tracker turned his horse and headed in the opposite direction of Slim and Curly, tossing his bed role on the ground. "Make camp here, I'll be back in a little while." He rode off without another word.

Rings dismounted from the horse, then pulled her down, handing her some hardtack. "Eat this then go to bed. And don't try nothin funny."

"I, ah, need a minute alone." She did as Tracker had instructed her and didn't make eye contact.

"Go behind that bush, you got one minute and I'm comin' after ya."

Lily did as she was instructed, wondering if there was any chance she could escape. She hadn't been behind the bush thirty seconds debating whether or not to run when she heard Rings moving towards her. "You're too quiet girl, whatcha doin'?"

"I'm almost done." Lily called back. Rings was clearly keeping a close watch on her and she doubted she would get very far. She would have to wait for a better opportunity.

Lillian came back around the bush and sat down to eat her hardtack and lay down. Her stomach grumbled, she had barely eaten anything, but she ignored it. These men weren't going to give her anymore food and she didn't want to draw any more attention to herself. Besides, she was exhausted and she lay down on the bed roll. Without Tracker there, however, to give her information or to make her feel safer, she found that she could not sleep. The men lay down and seemed to fall asleep around her except for Rings, who sat up leaned against a nearby tree.

Finally he spoke. "Go to sleep, girl. You're gonna need it."

"Somehow, it's hard to relax." She replied, the sarcasm evident in her voice.

She heard him chuckle. "You'll have to learn to curb that tongue when you're married."

Lily didn't reply and as the minutes ticked by she felt herself relaxing and until she finally fell into an uneasy sleep. She woke often, clearly unable to relax into a deeper sleep and her dreams were vivid and frightening. She knew she was asleep but it felt so real. She was in a field seemingly alone but somehow she knew that people were lurking out of sight. She started in one direction, only to see the grass moving in an odd way. Frightened, she turned in another direction and saw a shadow approaching her. Lily felt her body tensing. She spun around again when suddenly Eric was next to her. He put his arms around her and whispered in her ear. "Don't worry, I'm here. I'll keep you safe." She felt the tension from her body melt.

"Eric." The name sighed from her lips and she fell more deeply asleep.

Lily woke early, the sun was not yet over the horizon and she wondered for a few moments where she was. Reality came quicker everyday as did her dream of the night before. She turned quickly, had she been rescued? Tracker lay behind, roused by her movements. "Sorry, it's only me." He gave her a small half smile. "Who's Eric?"

Lily scowled, she couldn't help it. She was angry with herself for seeming to give everything away and disappointed that her dream was not a reality. "My fiance." She answered simply.

"Ah yes, Eric Sampson. I guess it hadn't occurred to me because I assumed your marriage had been arranged." Tracker smiled again, which made him look far more handsome.

"It was. Although the circumstances are a bit... complicated." She smiled back unable to help herself.

"Really? I wish I had time to hear the story." He responded but the smile had slipped from his face.

Lily hesitated, wanting to ask him some questions but unsure of how to proceed. He beat her to it.

"I'm sorry to leave you last night. It was necessary." He whispered in her ear.

"Why?" She whispered back.

"It is dangerous for both of us if you know too much. I will tell you that we are not that far from Portsmouth and that we are headed into Maine. I will try to slow our progress to allow your brother and fiance time to catch up to us."

"They're following us?" She felt hope rising in her chest. She wanted more than anything to be back with her family and back with Eric.

"Yes, I believe they are. You may have to faint today, to slow us down. Can you do it?" Lily nodded and tried to keep from smiling. "Just fall into me when we take a midday break."

Tracker let her have a few minutes to herself then gave her some more hardtack and some berries he had picked on the trail. She thought to herself that it wouldn't be hard to faint. She had hardly eaten anything and she had a nagging headache that hunger and a lack of water fed, in addition to a lump on the side of her head. As she approached Tracker's horse she groaned to herself. Two days in the saddle had made her more sore than she could have imagined and the thought of climbing back onto a horse made her insides tighten. She would give anything to be back home. One thing was for sure, if she made it back, it didn't matter to her if Eric felt the way she did. Lily was going to put everything she had into her marriage and hope for the best. She couldn't imagine marrying anyone else and the thought of never seeing Eric again made her realize how much she cared. She would put any trepidations she had aside. It didn't matter if he still had feelings for Caitlin and the infidelity that Kathryn had accused him of was only an accusation. Even if it were the truth, she would do what she could although her heart twisted painfully at the thought. Kathryn seemed less than trustworthy at best. It suddenly occurred to Lillian that Kathryn must have been in on the kidnapping. The men would never have let her go otherwise and Eric, as well as herself, would not have gone out onto the patio without being bated. That woman had been the bate. No wonder Kathryn had been so eager to talk to her while they were at the theater. Filling Lily's head with poison. Kathryn was trying to keep them apart.

As they mounted up, Slim rode up beside them. "Mornin, Girly. How did ya sleep?" He leered at her.

Lily pulled down the brim of her hat and tried to ignore him. "Sweet thing like you needs her beauty rest." He leered at her. "You gotta wedding to git ready for." He cackled at his joke started to move on and then stopped. "The boss wants you pure and you better hope to hell you are or there'll be hell to pay. Don't think Tracker's gonna save you. Spreadin' for him don't change nothin'. I got my eye on you."

"I'm not the one the boss is worried about." Tracker returned quietly, one eyebrow raised.

"Well, the boss ain't been seein' the way you're always talkin' her ear off." Slim gave her one last leer then rode on.

"I don't like him." Lily spoke quietly.

"You shouldn't. He is dangerous, even in this crowd." Tracker kicked his horse into a trot and the day's ride began.

Chapter 17

Every muscle in her body screamed as the men picked up the pace. She began to worry that she wouldn't have to fake fainting and she may do it before she was supposed to. The summer heat was beating down on them and the trees only seemed to hold in the humidity. She had had very little to drink and she felt herself growing more and more dizzy. The only thing that kept her going was that her family might be somewhere behind her.

Tracker said little and she was sure that Slim's comments had affected him. Tracker didn't want Slim to become suspicious.

At noon, they stopped near a small river and Lily looked at it longingly. She would give anything to do as she had done as a child and wade into the water. Perhaps, however, she could get a drink.

Tracker set her down and she began to sway on her feet. It was half acting and half real. She was exhausted. As Tracker stepped down off the horse behind her, she let her knees buckle from under her and she began to fall backwards. It suddenly reminded her of the incident with Toby and made her more homesick than ever.

Tracker caught her easily and she lay motionless in his arms enjoying being laid down on the ground. It might be nice to take a break.

"That girl faint?" She heard someone ask.

She could feel the men coming to stand over her and the need to run began taking over her mind. It took every ounce of energy to lay still while they stared down at her. A hand grabbed at the collar of her shirt and traveled down the fabric to the first button. "You bound em'." she heard Slim say and then someone knocked his hand away. Curly's voice was next.

"Who's gonna know if we just have a little fun?" A hand grabbed at the top of her pants. She could feel her heart beating faster and faster and tried to keep her breathing even. She had to trust Tracker.

"The boss will." She heard Tracker speak quietly.

"He doesn't have to know it was us. She looks loose enough to me. She probably done it with a bunch of guys." Curly was sounding more excited by the second and at that instant she felt someone pick her up. Lily almost screamed but held motionless.

"I'm getting her a drink of water." She heard Tracker say over his shoulder as he carried her to the water. She could have cried with relief but another voice spoke close to her ear.

"You awfully friendly with that girl. I think you should give her to me. What do ya say boys? Tracker gettin' to friendly?" Slim turned to the other men.

"Leave it Slim," another voice called "bosses orders."

"Don't leave that girl alone Tracker, I ain't seen one as pretty as her in a long time and what the boss don't know won't hurt him." Slim touched her hair and Lillian's skin crawled.

"You don't think he would know?" Tracker never raised his voice but it always made it's point.

"Not if you're not there to tell him. I could even tell him that you run off with her. The men would probably back me up, the way you been chatterin' in her ear." Slim had lowered his voice so that only Tracker could hear. Lily's insides clenched at the implication of his words. If she were not with Tracker and not delivered to the Colonel then Slim would not be returning her to her family; she would be dead.

"I think you can only get away with taking the boss's female companion once don't you?" Tracker returned without breaking stride or changing his tone. His words, however, seemed to have had their intended effect. Slim stopped talking and Lily could only assume that he had left. Tracker again lowered her to the ground and began to pour small amount of water from his hands onto her lips. She choked a little then opened her eyes. He nodded that she could revive and she began to try and lean over to drink a little water on her own. But she didn't have to fake the shaking.

"Bags, she needs some more food, can you try to catch us something?" Tracker called over his shoulder.

"Yeah, but it takes time." Bags called.

"Just a little something for her if you can't bring something for all of us. I'll build a small fire while you hunt so that we can do this as quick as possible."

Lily heard his words and her insides clenched. Tracker had been right, when they were moving, the men left her alone. But now that they had stopped, she worried that they would get unruly.

"Have you done this before?" She whispered.

"No, I haven't. But they have." The tension that hadn't been in Tracker's voice when he had been talking to Slim was there when he answered her and the fury behind it was evident.

"I'm sorry. I didn't mean to... I've upset you." She stumbled to find the words to comfort him. She didn't know why but his anger upset her so much.

"Don't be. I'm sorry. I have learned to control my feelings around them at all times but it is harder with you. You actually have feelings that reflect my own. You care and you ask questions. I..." He stopped. "I can't do this right now. I have to keep my guard up, especially with the men resting."

She nodded her head and he carried her to the shade of a tree. She sat and looked at the water while the men milled around. Two built a fire, which seemed crazy in the heat but then Bags came back with a rabbit and two pheasants, Lily was surprised at his speed.

"He has skills." Tracker smiled, "They all do." He added.

Curly helped skin the rabbit while Bags plucked the

118

pheasants, then they set them to roast. She could smell the meat and her mouth began to water. She hadn't realized how hungry she was. She put her hand to her stomach to try to quell the grumblings and then Tracker got up to bring her some meat.
Rings had found some blueberries in the woods that were almost out of season but she was thankful that he had found some. Tracker brought her what seemed like half of the meat. He himself had a small leg of rabbit and she looked at her helping with guilt.

"I shouldn't have all of this." She started to push it away.

He smiled, a genuine smile "You are the one who fainted. You need your energy."

She tucked her head down so that the others couldn't see her smirk and dug into her food. The strength she would get from this could only help her.

They soon packed up but she had to hope that the time they had spent allowed her family to get closer to her.

Four days passed in the same exhausting pattern. They rose early, ate little and rode all day. They could only push the horses so fast and Lily hoped that her family was getting closer but she was losing hope on that front. At least Tracker stayed with her and strangely, she felt relatively safe.

She again had only hardtack to eat and while she had spent some time on a ship, she found this diet increasingly difficult. Tracker said less and less and she wondered at his silence. He usually spoke at least a few words of encouragement to her.

They finally made camp in the evening and even Lily could sense that something was not right. Curly and Slim were talking to themselves and Curly kept throwing glances her way. Finally, Slim sauntered over and winked at her as he turned to Tracker. Lily felt her skin crawl.

"I think that we're gonna backtrack and have a look. See if her men are following us." Slim turned back and headed to his horse. Tracker's eye's narrowed.

Tracker unrolled his bed roll then called to Rings.

"Watch over her." He turned and Lillian felt fear rising up inside her.

"Ain't you supposed to be stayin' with her." Rings asked as he moved toward them. "I ain't the lady sitter you are."

"I need to do some scouting but I will get her settled to make your job easier." Tracker said curtly and began to lead her into the bushes.

Once they were out of sight Lily turned to him to protest. Tracker pressed something into her hand and as she felt the cold metal touch her fingers, she felt a chill run down her spine. "Don't leave." Was all she could choke out. Fear was building inside her.

"I have to. I want to protect you but I have to complete my mission." He looked away and Lily felt herself choking.

"Delivering me?" Was all she could get her throat to say.

"No, of course not. If that were the case, I wouldn't be giving you a gun. I have to find enough evidence to put the Colonel in jail for the rest of his life. Slim and Curly are up to something and it could be the break I have been waiting for."

So many questions rose in Lily's mind but she didn't have time to ask any of them. He stuffed the gun in her waist band and led her back to camp. "Don't fall asleep." He said as he tucked her into the bed roll.

She couldn't imagine falling asleep but she wondered how long she would have to lie awake. She tried to move as little as possible and keep her breathing even so that Ring would think she was asleep. Her skin began to itch and crawl with the exertion of holding still and she wanted to vent her frustration. It felt like the darkest loneliest night of her life, except for maybe the night her parents died. But as she lay there listening, a plan began to form in her mind.

This might be her opportunity to escape. She just had to get away from the camp and then in the morning, she could head east toward the ocean. From there, she could get home. She occasionally smelled an ocean breeze and thought that they were loosely following the coast, only skirting settlements. Her only concern was that James and Eric might be close and she would be giving them the slip as well. But after considering it, she decided it was worth the risk.

Slowly, she sat up to test the sleeping men around her. Rings was snoring softly as he leaned against a nearby tree. She slowly stood and contemplated which way to go. Lily wanted to avoid any beaten paths without getting completely lost or injured. She thought back to the direction she had seen the sun set and headed the opposite way. With any luck, she would have a jump on her plan to head east.

She crept through the woods, trying not to make any noise while still making progress. After an hour had passed she began to breathe easier. It didn't seem anyone was following her and Lillian hadn't heard any alarms being raised. She felt the gun that Tracker had left her with in her waist band. It gave her some measure of comfort. She continued on for another half an hour when she heard a small noise in the distance. She froze and crouched down. Lily heard nothing for a few minutes and she was about to stand when she heard a noise a few feet away.

Lily froze in place, she didn't even breathe. Slowly her hand moved to where the gun was and she placed her fingers around the butt of it. She didn't dare pull it out. She was afraid she would make a noise. She stood completely still for what seemed like several minutes and heard nothing. She realized that she had been holding her breath and slowly exhaled. Suddenly, she heard a sound that made her blood freeze.

"Hello Girlie. Thought you'd be headin' this way." She heard Slim's voice from close by. She wanted to run but knew it would do no good. She would probably fall and hurt herself making it even easier to find her. She stood completely still and said nothing.

"Don't think I don't know it's you. You're pretty quiet but not as quiet as us. We've been traveling through the woods for a long time. Bet you're wonderin' how we found you." She could almost hear the smile in his voice.

"You shoulda known better Girlie. You woulda been safe in the camp. But we knew that if we left, Tracker would follow and you would try to escape. Fell right into our trap." he cackled and she heard a second laugh further away that could only be Curly.

But where was Tracker? "If you're wonderin' if Tracker is gonna save you, he ain't. We threw him off the trail a few hours ago though it ain't easy to do. Looks like it's just the three of us." She could hear that his voice was moving closer but she couldn't identify the direction. He knew where she was though. Slowly, Lily pulled the gun from her waist band. Maybe Slim wouldn't have counted on this.

"You ain't sayin' too much Girlie. Not that I mind. I like a woman that keeps quiet. But don't think you're gonna slip away, you ain't. It's too perfect. You escape and no one will ever know that it was us who caught up to you. Tracker might wonder but he can't prove it." Slim was close by and she thought she saw a movement to her right. She prayed she had six bullets and shot.

The blast that close was deafening. She gripped the gun tighter as she heard a scream pierce through the night. Shock and relief flooded her body just as a hand gripped her upper arm. Slim's leering face came suddenly into sharp focus in front of her and she raised the gun but he was too quick and snatched it out of her hand. He grabbed her wrists even as she struggled until he had both wrists in one hand and then clamped his other hand over her mouth. She struggled as hard as she could but he was so much stronger than her that he quickly wrestled her to the ground.

"Poor Curly." He didn't sound sorry at all and his hand left her mouth to begin pulling off her clothes. Lily didn't have time to think, she just acted. She reached up and bit him hard on the cheek. Her hat had come off in the struggle and he grabbed her hair, pulling hard, snapping her head back. It freed her hands and she began to scratch and claw at him. He smacked her hard across the cheek bone with the back of his hand and she felt, for a moment, like her head would explode. He ripped at her shirt and several buttons came undone. Thankfully, her breasts were still bound and giving up, he began to pull at her pants. She fought, but her hands were again trapped and her head pinned under his. She felt a sickening cry rip from her chest but it only seemed to excite him more. She closed her eyes and felt the hot tears run down her cheeks as he worked her pants down.

"You're a fighter Girlie, knew you would be." Lily heard Slim grunt out. She wanted to continue to fight but she didn't know what to do. He freed one leg from her pants and began unbuttoning his own. Feverishly she began to fight again but slowly he was working his legs in between hers.

What could she do? He was poised on top of her ready to enter. Lily knew once he was done, he would kill her. No one knew she was here and he certainly didn't want her sharing her story. She pictured her family, Eric and Toby and said goodbye in her mind. Lillian braced herself for the pain when she suddenly felt Slim go still.

His weight slumped down on top her and then suddenly he rolled off of her. Tracker stood above her. She could have cried with relief but she couldn't force out any words. He picked her up and Lily could feel herself begin to shake. "He almost..." She couldn't finish the sentence.

"I know." Was all he said as he carried her swiftly through the woods.   It was still dark but she didn't have the mental ability to wonder how he was doing it. She just held on as he righted her clothes and carried her to his horse.

"You're alright now." He soothed her, stroking her hair as he mounted his horse.

"Is he dead?" She asked softly.

No, I just knocked him out. He'll know it was me but..." Tracker chuckled softly "He won't be able to say a word. He wasn't supposed to be here with you so he won't be able to accuse me of anything. I wonder what he's going to tell them?"

"What about Curly?" Her voice trembled as she asked.

"I only saw a blood trail" he stated softly "he's probably still alive but Slim will kill him."

"What, why?" She sat up for the first time feeling a little clearer in the head.

"They are not nice men. Slim won't want to carry him or tend him. Nor will he want a second accounting of what happened from Curly. Curly's the worst at keeping lies straight. If the others suspect that Slim is lying or working against them, they'll kill him." Tracker's voice was hard.

"I have never hurt anyone, I can't believe I..." He stopped Lily.

"He would have done far worse things to you than just shoot you. You shooting him may have been what saved you. Slim would have been much quicker if he hadn't been trying to..." Lily stopped him.

"I get the picture. Where are we going?" She asked inadvertently holding her breath. What would he do with her?

"We are heading for a small town called Bucksport." He shrugged.

"Why?" Lily felt both relief and fear course through her body.

"I think you should be able to get home from there but we have to hurry. I need to be back by sunrise to cover my tracks." He kicked his exhausted horse into a canter.

"Shouldn't covering your tracks be easy for a man named Tracker." She said with a small smile.

He laughed. "You noticed all the nicknames, huh? We are men with a great deal to hide and our identities are the first and largest of our secrets."

"I see." Lily said and she did. Having only a nickname made it far more difficult to implicate them in any crime.

"But my name is Michael." He chuckled. "It's been awhile since I have used my first name with anyone and it feels kind of nice."

"You don't have any family?" She asked.

"I had a sister but she passed away a few years ago." The grief was still evident in his voice and she patted his hand. "You remind me of her. You both have a very warm heart."

Lily was slightly embarrassed by his comment and changed the subject. "What does the Colonel do that you are trying to prosecute him for?"

"I don't know that there are very many laws that he hasn't broken but smuggling is the bread and butter of his career outside of the army. I am still tracking down illegal goods that he is bringing into the country but he also brings a great deal of goods in from overseas that he sells without paying tariffs or taxes." Tracker hesitated and Lily assumed that he was unsure of how much to tell her.

"But why are we in Maine currently?" She asked having been curious for some time why he would kidnap her and bring her to her own state.

"Well, the Colonel is stationed here. The American government has a large army presence in Maine. I believe they are concerned about an attack from the English through Canada. There, as you know, have been several border disputes as well." Lily nodded. Maine had gone so far as to declare war over one such dispute. Luckily it had been resolved before any bloodshed.

"Also, as you can imagine, Maine is a new and still largely uninhabited state. It is easy to bring illegal goods through it. But I think Colonel Kingsley is getting lazy because now he is trying to get the goods through the Boston Harbor."

"Ah, yes, where I come in." She shook her head. "Seems like a horrible reason to get married to me."

"People get married for far less. Besides, I think he has some notions of legitimate children and a more settled life, at least in appearance." Tracker added.

"Somehow, I don't see him as the fatherly type. She said as she let out a loud yawn. It had to be nearing sunrise and she hadn't gotten a moment of sleep.

He said nothing and Lily quickly nodded off with the rocking of the horse.

She woke suddenly when the horse stopped, completely disoriented. "We're here." Tracker said softly in her ear.

"Where?" Was all she could mutter.

"Bucksport." He dismounted and pulled her down. "Find some bushes to hide and get some more sleep. In a few hours, try to find a public place to look for your brother and fiancé. Try the tavern and inn, Jed Prouty Tavern, I think it is. Here is money for a meal. Keep watch for any of the men. The town is one of the first places they will think of but I will try to stall and divide them. Good luck." He mounted back up and disappeared into the trees.

Lily stared at where his back had disappeared. She

wished he could stay with her but she understood why he hadn't. He clearly had been working for a long time to implicate the Colonel and he couldn't risk it all now for her. Still, Lillian felt completely alone. She wondered if James and Eric would really be in Bucksport and a small flutter of hope rose in her chest. She was exhausted but she didn't know how she was ever going to get any sleep. It was easier with Tracker but now she was alone and this time she had no gun.

A nearby bush looked promising for cover and she crawled underneath. Roots were sticking in her back and branches were in her face but she did feel protected. Amazingly she fell instantly asleep.

She woke two hours later with the early morning sun peeking through the branches, the day already heating up. She tried to collect her thoughts. Tracker had told her to go into town but Lily wondered what time her family would be up and possibly setting out. Had she missed them? She scrambled out from under the bush and then stopped. Which way to town? She could have laughed at the absurdity of it if it wasn't so serious. A breeze picked up and she turned her face into it. Well, Lily thought, I will head towards the ocean.

Chapter 18

She followed a trail that grew sandier as she progressed and soon she found herself glimpsing the rocky shore. She looked to her right and saw little but open ocean and woods. To her left, however, sprawled several buildings on the inlet of what must be Bucksport. She was clearly on a point and could see all of the town nestled into the harbor. She smiled, it was a short walk. Lillian headed back up the trail she had been on and when the woods thickened, she turned towards the town. She decided to stay off beaten paths and instead, stayed in the woods. It made her progress slower and she was growing increasingly worried that she would miss James and Eric but she swallowed her fear. She would take an even bigger risk by being exposed on the road by herself and would surely risk recapture. If she and Tracker had gotten here as quickly as they did, it would not take her other captors long to arrive.

Finally, she came to a building that was clearly on the outskirts of town and headed for the town center. Her stomach grumbled and she reached into her pocket to touch the coins that jingled there. She could already taste the food in her mouth. It didn't matter how good or poor the cooking at the Tavern was, it was going to taste like a feast to her.

She had a few other problems to worry about as well. Lily didn't know how long she would have to wait and she needed to remain inconspicuous. She would try to find a table in a corner and watch people as she ate. In addition, she would try to order, drink and eat as slowly as possible, although, it was going to be extremely difficult considering how hungry she was.

As she turned down Main Street, the town was beginning to busy, with many people out and about. A few gave her curious looks. At first, she thought that she might look odd as a young boy but as Lily looked down at herself, she realized that she was filthy. She bit her lip, unsure of what to do. Time was of the essence but she didn't know if the Tavern would even let her dine looking like a total vagabond.

Lily took out the money from her pocket and counted what she had. She had enough to at least buy a cheap shirt but then she would have to go without food. She could have broken down and cried at that very second. Lily, however, pulled herself together and walked into the general store.

The clerk finished with a customer and then turned to her. His look hardened somewhat but he asked. "What can I help you with Son?"

Lily was taken aback by the reference but stepped up. She tried to deepen her voice as much as possible then asked. "I'm looking for a shirt. Every day wear is fine, I am not looking for anything of quality or dress."

He stared at her and she began to feel uncomfortable, worried that she had given herself away as a woman.

"My goodness, son, what happened to your clothing?" He asked smiling. "I can tell by your speech that you are from a family of quality but by your clothes, I thought you were a street urchin."

Lily stared, unsure of how to answer. What excuse could she possibly give him? She hadn't thought of this and she stumbled over what to say.

"Oh...uh... I was dragged by my horse. The beast got away and I am left rather dirty. I'm just trying to get home without my mother worrying too much." Lily glanced at him to see if he accepted the excuse.

He smiled at her in an affectionate way. "Does your family have an account? We could just charge a new outfit..."

"No!" Lily said too suddenly and then tried to calm herself. "I'm sure my horse will head home, I have a little money... I just need something simple."

He nodded and Lily sighed in relief. He brought her a simple shirt and she paid him, then looked woefully at what was left.

"Thank you." She smiled at him. "Could you tell me where the Jed Prouty Tavern is?" Lily asked.

"You don't know?" He asked and Lily again felt her heart beating faster. She had never been good at lying, anticipating what to say. She stared at him for what seemed like forever then finally an idea struck her.

"We just moved here. It's my first time in the town." He seemed to accept her answer and Lily felt relief wash over her.

"How wonderful. We are growing rapidly. People are realizing what a wonderful town Bucksport is." He looked at her then held up his finger for her to wait for a minute. He came back holding up a pair of pants and a hat. "Take them. They were my sons before he out grew them, they should fit you. I meant to resell them but you seem like you're in need. There is a pump just a block down you can use to clean up. The Tavern is just down the street from there." He turned to a woman who had just walked in and Lily hastily left.

She headed down the street in until she found the pump. She pushed her hat back, not wanting to take it off and reveal her hair wrapped in a handkerchief. Lily washed her face then rolled up her sleeves and rinsed her hands and arms. She would have given anything for a bath but since she couldn't, Lily splashed some water under her arms, soaking her filthy shirt.

Lily stood up and realized she was making a spectacle of herself. She also realized she should start watching for the men who had captured her. She quickly stepped down from the platform and headed for an alley between a barn and home. Lillian quickly took off the dirty shirt and replaced it with the clean one. The fresh fabric felt wonderful on her skin. Glancing to make sure no one could see her, she slipped off her shoes then took off her pants and replaced them, tucking in her shirt. Feeling slightly cleaner and a little more presentable, she headed for the Tavern.

She walked up to the door and butterflies filled her stomach. Would they throw her out? Would her brother be there? Would Eric? She pushed open the door.

The Tavern was actually a Tavern and Inn and it was clearly an upscale facility. It smelled of rich mahogany and leather. Lily relaxed immediately; she couldn't see Slim in a place like this. She headed for an empty table in the corner and sat in a chair that gave her a view of the dining area.

"What can I get for you?" an older woman, looking slightly harassed, asked her.

Lily lowered her voice. "Coffee."

"Nothing else?" She looked surprised when Lily shook her head. She left and then quickly returned with the coffee. Lily sipped it enjoying the hot liquid but she could smell something delicious from the kitchen and tried not to think of her grumbling stomach.

She tried to drink slowly, she had no idea how long she would have to wait or how long they would let her stay. She did not, however, have to wait long. Two groups of men walked in at exactly the same time. The first group of three was her brothers James and Tom with Eric directly behind them. Eric's dark eyes pierced the room sending her heart into palpitations of joy. She almost jumped up from her chair and ran to them but the hat behind Eric caught her eye. It was clearly that of Rings. Next to him was Bags and another man she did not recognize. Her family sat across the room from her while her captors sat just a few tables away. They began to talk immediately.

"How could you lose one lone girl?" The man she didn't know asked.

"Shut it Jack. I done told you, somethin happened last night. Curly's gone, Slim's hurt, Tracker was out all night and nobody don't seem to know nothin. Somethin's fishy but I can't sniff it out. It ain't no coincidence that we was so close to deliverin her and she slipped away but I don't know if it's Tracker or Slim that's to blame but it sure ain't both of 'em. Those two never work together." Ring's looked ready to spit and Lily ducked her head, thanking the Lord for the new hat.

She didn't dare get up, she was too afraid that Rings would recognize her. He was sitting directly between her and her family. She wanted to scream with frustration, she was so close and yet couldn't go to her family. Lillian couldn't hear anything that her brothers and Eric were saying but she could recognize the cadence of their voices and she ached to be with them. Lily thought about getting up and making a mad dash for them but it didn't make sense. Even if her brothers could take these men, as they were evenly matched, she would expose their whereabouts and more of the Colonel's men could come. Obviously he had more men in his employ then were transporting her, she just didn't know how many. She would have to bide her time a little longer.

"How come we're here?" Jack asked. Rings said nothing but nodded his head ever so slightly towards her family. Lily held her breath. They were watching Eric, James and Tom! How would she ever get to them unnoticed?

She quietly put the money on the table for her coffee so no more conversation would be necessary. She left as generous a tip as she could to buy more time. She watched Eric and her brothers get up, they too looked worn and beaten from the trail. Eric called to the matronly woman that Lily assumed was the mistress of the house.

"Could I have bath water brought to my room?" He smiled kindly and the woman returned his smile.

"I'll have someone bring it up as soon as I can." She replied. Eric nodded his assent and they left the room.

Lily wanted to cry as she watched them leave. She tried to console herself that she knew that they were here and they seemed to be staying but she hated to watch them walk away. She didn't know what rooms they were in and she didn't know how to send them a message.

Rings turned to the matron as she asked if there would be anything else. "Yes ma'm, who do we see to book a room?"

Lily watched the three men follow the inn keeper's wife out to purchase their rooms. While she was glad to not be in the same room with them, she had no idea how she was going to contact her family. Should she wait outside to see if they left? It didn't seem like they were planning on it anytime soon. Besides, she could risk being seen by Rings and his men first. At least Slim wasn't here, Lily thought. Tracker must have sent him in another direction. She said a prayer for small miracles. The matron of the house returned and called for a boy to fetch bath water. Suddenly, Lily smiled, she was a boy.

Lily got up from the table and, as casually as she could, watched a boy head for a back door. She held her breath as she followed him out. He began to pump water into three buckets. When he filled the third, Lily stepped out, lowering her voice. "Want help carryin' those?" She asked.

"I don't know if I'm supposed to have help," the boy returned.

"Aw, no one'll even notice. I been thinkin' about gittin a job and this'll give me a chance to try it out and help you out too." Lily had grown up around the Maine accent and imitated it easily.

"How come I never seen you before?" The boy asked.

"Just moved here, I'm Billy. Billy Sampson." She stuck out her hand and the boy shook it. She hoped it didn't seem as awkward as it felt.

"Jake Cutter. I guess you can help if you don't talk to nobody or git me in no trouble. I gotta have this job. The tavern girl didn't come in today so everyone is extra busy. I could use the help." Lily sighed with relief as Jake handed her a bucket and she grudgingly carried it to the kitchen, where they dumped it into a pot to heat.

"Let's bring up the tub." Jake turned and Lily followed as her heart hammered in her chest. Would she finally be rescued? The two grabbed the tub and began to lug it up the narrow back staircase. He stopped in front of room 208. This must be Eric's room. Lily held her breath as Jake knocked on the door but no one answered. Jake pulled out a keyring and opened the door. They carried in the tub and set it down by the fireplace. Lily looked around, there were very few belongings in the room and nothing that she distinctly recognized as Eric's. She hoped she was helping with the right bath.

"Let's go git the water. Just be careful not to spill it over the stairs. You got to mop it up then and start all over." Jake was warming up to her. She was helping him and apparently not causing any trouble. She nodded and they refilled the buckets to bring the now warm water upstairs.

Lily held her bucket as still as she could. She was beginning to feel faint as the day warmed up and she hadn't had any food. She gritted her teeth and stayed behind Jake. At least he was carrying two of the buckets. He headed back for 208 and again knocked.

"Who is it?" Lily heard Eric's voice call, her heart started beating wildly.

"Here's your water sir." Jake called.

"Come in." Eric replied and Jake opened the door.

Lily saw him sitting at the small desk in the corner of the room. She tipped her hat way back to expose as much of her face as she could. She wanted to cry with frustration. Lily couldn't expose herself in front of Jake but she didn't want to leave the room now that she had arrived.

They filled the tub with the water, then turned to leave. Lily hesitated. Should she say something, anything and hope he recognized her voice.

"Just a second." Eric's voice halted their progress. "Could one of you deliver a message for me?" Eric looked up and their eyes met. Hers pleaded with him to recognize her. Surprise momentarily crossed his face but he quickly masked it. He turned to Jake. "Perhaps you could deliver this message to the front desk, it is urgent. If you," Eric turned to her "wouldn't mind staying for a few moments, I have another that needs to be delivered to the store."

Jake looked relieved and nodded. With all the work he had to do, Lily was sure that he found the arrangement satisfying. Lily herself could have cried with relief. Jake took the message and hastily left the room.

As soon as the door clicked closed, Eric stood from his desk and crossed the room. Lily was momentarily disappointed that he did not come to her but she realized that he was locking the door. She heard the bolt give a distinct click then he turned back to her and, in what seemed like two steps, crossed the room and gathered her up in his arms. Their lips met and Lily lost herself in the kiss. It felt so wonderful to be held in his arms, to feel safe. She didn't even realize that she was crying until he pulled away to wipe the tears from her eyes.

"Don't stop." She murmured as she sought his lips again.

"Sweetheart, I would love nothing more to lay you on the bed and keep you there for several days but..." he paused. "I think I should tell your brothers that I found you and..." he started to continue but she interrupted.

"Just a few minutes, please. It has been so difficult to get to you and I have been so alone." A sob escaped her lips and he wrapped her in his arms sitting them both down on the bed.

Lily sat there in the warmth of his embrace and wanted nothing more than to cry out all her frustration, anger, and loneliness but she had to be strong. They were still in danger and she had to warn her brothers.

"OK, I'm ready." She lifted her head up and he kissed her again long and deep. She felt herself growing dizzy and when he stood up, she swayed back into him.

"Are you alright?" He asked.

"Fine, I just haven't eaten very much today." Lily shrugged but Eric had placed his hands around her waist.

"My God Lily, have you eaten anything at all?" He felt her arms, then her shoulder.

"A little. We didn't stop very often." Lily rested her head on his chest.

"I am going to go get your brothers. I will get you some food as well. Why don't you take a quick bath. Lock the door behind me." Eric started to turn away.

"We're being watched." Lily told him as he turned to go.

Eric nodded then smiled. "I'll be back soon." He kissed her one more time then left.

Lily wasn't aware that she had fallen asleep until she heard the key turn in the lock. She bolted up then just as quickly sunk under the soapy water to try to cover herself somewhat. She sagged with relief as she saw James and Eric walk in.

One look at her in the tub and James scowled at her.

"Lily, why are you naked in a tub, for Christ sakes?"

Lily frowned slightly. She thought her brother would be happier to see her.

"James, I didn't sleep. I'm just tired. Please, I..." She didn't know what to say. Please understand that I have been through hell.

"We'll come back." He started to turn when Eric interrupted.

"James, I don't want to leave her alone again. I don't think it's safe." James' glare turned to a look of murder.

"I don't care what you think, it's not appropriate for you to see my sister without her clothes..."

"Keep your voice down James, they could be in the hallway." Lily nervously looked at the door, straining to hear any sounds.

James glared at her but Eric didn't allow him an opportunity to say more.

"We are going to be married in less than two months. It doesn't matter whether or not I see her without her clothes. The important thing is that she is alive, James." Eric stood without moving and James stormed out of the room, closing the door behind him.

"What just happened?" Lily felt tears welling up in her eyes. Her brother had always loved her and the brother she knew would have been overjoyed to see her, not angry.

Eric sighed. "Lean back, we may as well wash your hair while we have a few minutes." He poured water over head, then began to lather her hair. "He is angry at me for starters. James thinks I am to blame for getting you in this mess. He's most likely right. I think he's angry at you as well, for choosing me..."

"Technically, I didn't choose you." She smiled at him although she was amazingly aware of his gentle hands in her hair and the fact that she was naked. At the same time, she was surprised by how natural it felt.

He smiled back, a chuckle breaking through his lips.

"Too true." He rinsed out her hair and Lily turned slightly in the bath to be able to better see him. "I'm sure he thinks that if your reputation had been intact, you would have had more options."

She looked at him and burst out laughing. "What is so funny?" Eric looked at her incredulously.

"I wouldn't want to marry anyone but you anyway." Lily smiled at him softly and he leaned forward and kissed her lightly on the lips. When he started to pull away, she reached up a wet hand and wrapped it around his neck, deepening the kiss. She had never done this before but she wanted to kiss him so much.

"Lily, we have to stop." He said as he pulled away for a moment before the kiss resumed.

"I don't want to." She said when he tried to pull away a second time.

He cupped her face. "There is nothing I would like to do more than pull you out of that tub and carry you to the bed but I can't. James would..."

"Eric," her voice was full of her desperation. "Please." Was all she could get out. She took a breath. "I barely made it back here alive and with my..." she paused, blushing slightly "I don't want to wait. What if..."

He pulled her up out of the tub and handed her a towel to rub herself dry. "You are going to be fine. We'll get you out of here." He smiled at her then kissed her forehead. "Get dressed. We'll talk about this later and I promise, we will keep you safe." He smiled reassuringly but Lily remained unconvinced.

She turned away from Eric and began to wrap her breasts. Now that they were not being intimate she was feeling more awkward about her nudity. She turned briefly to see him staring at her from across the room and she blushed.

He smiled a little but said. "You look too thin." Concern colored his face.

She nodded. "I haven't had very much to eat." She pulled on her pants, then socks but groaned at the thought of the boots.

Eric smiled more broadly, "Leave them off for now,

Tom should be up with some food any minute."

Lily's face could have split with a smile. She didn't know if she was more happy about seeing her brother Tom or eating a real meal.

She ate voraciously as the three men sat in silence. She knew that they must have a hundred questions for her but she couldn't wait another second to eat. She felt her energy returning and her head clearing from the fog it had been in. When every ounce of food had been consumed, James cleared his throat.

"Lily, we need to ask you some questions." James shifted in his chair as she nodded.

He didn't say anything, perhaps he was unsure of where to start. Tom began. "Lily, you said you were followed here. How do you know?"

Lily nodded, Tom was right. The story of the kidnap could wait, what was important was who was here at the Inn and what they knew. "I was in the tavern while you were having breakfast." All three men looked startled by this information and Lily smiled and shrugged. "I was trying to blend in." Tom and Eric both smiled but James' face continued to look black. "I was in the corner when Bags, Rings, and a man I believe is named Jack came in. He wasn't traveling with us though. I could hear their conversation and they said that they had come to watch you because they thought I would come here to try and find you. They were hoping to intercept me I guess."

James' face grew even blacker. Eric looked thoughtfully. "They know who we are, what we look like and what direction we might be heading. We will have to find a way to disguise ourselves. At least until we can get to Portland."

Tom nodded. "We will have to find new clothes and horses, perhaps we could find another traveler to accompany us. Look like a completely different group.

"I agree." Eric thought for a minute. "Maybe even a wagon makes us look like settlers."

James had said little but finally spoke. "For now we will have to keep Lily out of sight. She will eat here and sleep here but not with Eric. Eric can stay with Tom and I will stay with

Lily."

Of course Lily knew that James would not allow her to stay with Eric even though he was to be her husband but she couldn't help but to feel disappointed. She wasn't at all sure that she wouldn't be kidnapped again and she wanted Eric to take her virginity before someone else had the chance.

Suddenly an idea occurred to her. "What if Eric and I got married?" Lily blurted out.

"What!" James spluttered.

"Hear me out James. The reason I was kidnapped was because the Colonel wants to marry me. What if I am already married? Doesn't that make all of this unnecessary?"

"Your reputation is already in tatters. There is no possible way I am going to return you to Boston already married. It is suspicious enough that you disappeared in the middle of Tom's wedding. Absolutely not." James' face had turned murderous again.

"But James..." Lily began.

"He's right, Lily." Eric shook his head. "If the Colonel finds out you are married, he may stop trying to kidnap you but will most likely try to kill both of us. It is far easier to keep you safe when everyone wants you alive."

Lily wanted to cry in frustration but said nothing. She could feel a fire building inside of her, a fire of anger and resentment. She felt like her mother again, always so bold and brash. She had the urge to slip out in the night with Eric and leave her family behind. Be married and slip away from all the pain. It scared her because her family had always been the most important thing to her, her safe harbor.

"Hey, are you in there." Tom smiled at her. She smiled back and nodded, unsure of how long the conversation had been going on without her. Eric was looking at her with a great deal of concern. He said nothing, but continued to study her.

"How did you get away?" James asked. His question was cold but he seemed less angry.

"To tell you how I got away, I have to tell you who I was with and" she paused it was painful to say it out loud but she mustered up her courage. She couldn't meet any of them in the eye. "what I have done."

She felt the tension rise in the room and James looked ready to commit murder again. She couldn't help that though, she had to be honest. Lily tried not to share the fear, the constant fear. Instead, she focused on the facts. She told them what she knew about Tracker, the Colonel, Slim. When she got the part by the river, she couldn't express the danger she knew Slim posed.

Tom interrupted for the first time. "How did you know he wanted to hurt you?"

Lily paused, collecting her thoughts. "He thought I had fainted, he made a reference to another woman, like me, that he had killed or maybe Tracker brought it up. Something he said told me that he would do the same to me if he had the chance."

Tom nodded and this time, when she looked up the dark expression that had colored James' face had spread to Eric. Taking a deep breath she continued.

Lily glossed over the endless riding and skipped to the night Tracker left her with the gun. Eric was gripping the side of his chair, his knuckles growing whiter by the second. She told them how Rings fell asleep and she slipped into the woods. She got to part with Slim and she stopped. She didn't know how to share this part.

"What happened, Lily?" Eric's voice was soft but there was an edge.

"I don't think I can, it was too..." She stopped.

He moved from his chair, and sat next to her on the bed. James started to stand but stopped when Tom put his hand out. Eric held her hand. "It's alright, you can tell us."

James cleared his throat. "It's alright, let her finish another time. We know enough to form a plan and we should start putting some pieces in place. Besides, Lillian looks like she could use some sleep." She nodded, relieved that she did not have to share. Eric was glaring at her brother but she couldn't concentrate on what was happening. Once she stopped talking, she could feel the exhaustion creep in and she was already falling off the edge of consciousness into sleep.

Chapter 19

Lillian woke unsure of where she was or what time it was. She sat up and looked around but could find no clues. Her mouth was dry and pasty and she was relieved to see water on the night stand.

"Feeling better?" James' voice carried out of the corner and she started to smile, relieved to hear her brother. As his face emerged from the shadows, the tension in it was palpable.

"James, what is wrong?" Lily ignored his question, in favor of her own.

He shook his head. "Just trying to keep you safe and get you home and married." The last word came out of his mouth as a sneer.

"I thought that was the point. I was to be married." Lily felt her anger rising.

James' face twisted. "Not to him, look at this mess."

"This is not his fault. It's the Colonel's. You should know that." Lily's voice was rising.

He stood, a retort on his lips, when three firm knocks came at the door. He stomped over to the door and yanked it open to let Tom and Eric in.

Tom smiled his good morning but no one smiled back. Eric came over to kiss Lily on the forehead and James jerked towards them. "Until you are married, you are to keep your lips off of my sister."

Eric turned, he had remained silent with James but Lily

could see he was drawing himself up, ready to challenge James.

Tom stepped in between them. "Why don't I stay with Lily while you go down to breakfast?"

Lily started. "Breakfast? How long did I sleep?"

Eric smiled "About fifteen hours. Feeling better?"

"Much." She wanted to wrap herself around him to get lost in his embrace.

James cut in. "I don't want to go to breakfast with him."

"Oh good, then Eric can stay with Lily and we'll go down. Then I can tell Mrs. Embry that Eric is still asleep. It will stall her coming to make up the room and give me an excuse to bring up breakfast."

James' mouth opened but he closed it and started out of the room. Before he stepped out, however, James turned to Eric. "You know what you promised." Then James left.

Once the door closed, Lily looked at Eric. She wanted to ask him what was going on but, more than that, she wanted the comfort of his arms. She launched off the bed and skipped the two steps to him. He caught her up in his embrace and buried his head into her tousled hair. She had fallen asleep before she had had time to braid it.

"I must look terrible." She giggled self-consciously but not letting go.

He chuckled back. "You look amazing but we have got to start feeding you more." He touched the hollow in her cheek.

She turned her head so that his thumb was against her lips then placed a small kiss on it. She looked at him and then leaned in to kiss him but he put his hand up to stop her. "I promised James that I would not."

Lily snorted, "I don't care what James wants. What is the matter with him?"

"I told you, he thinks I am to blame and that you have not chosen well. If he could, he would find you another suitor."

"But our engagement had already been announced, how could he?" Lily felt herself beginning to panic.

"It is his right. I don't know how you would be received in society. I am trying to appease him as best I can." Eric's lips narrowed into a line. Lily knew that it was not a role he was used to. He was usually a man in charge. She had seen it in his interactions with other men.

"Thank you. I know it must be difficult to deal with him. I love him and I am trying not to strangle him!" Eric laughed and she smiled too. "Eric, are you sure you want to marry me? I seem to be bringing you an awful lot of trouble."

"Lily, this is not your fault and neither James nor Kingsley is going to stand in the way of our marriage." Lillian felt his tension as his arms tightened around her. She knew she had been hoping for a declaration of his feelings but his commitment was something. It would have to be enough.

"Do you think we should run away?" She asked quietly.

Eric looked at her surprised. "I didn't think it would be an option. It would alienate your brother permanently and you might lose all of your family."

Lily looked at him and all the fear she had been trying to suppress rose into her eyes. "I need to feel safe. I don't think I can feel that until we are married." He rubbed the back of his hand along her jaw line and their lips moved towards each other. A knock at the door pierced the room. It was not the three knocks from before and it was too soon for Tom and James to be back. Fear rippled through Lily, as Eric motioned for her to hide under the bed. She climbed under, holding her breath.

The knock came again and Eric went to the door. "Who is it?" He asked sounding perfectly calm.

"It's Mrs. Embry, I know the Mr. Carter said he would bring up breakfast but I thought you might like it now."

Eric slowly opened the door, he appeared to be checking to see if Mrs. Embry was, in fact, alone. "Thank you Mrs. Embry. So kind of you."

She giggled, not unlike a school girl, and Lily had to suppress her own laugh. Mrs. Embry, the inn keeper's wife, was blushing and talking a mile a minute as she set down Eric's food. She was asking him how he liked the room, how he liked the inn, the town. Eric told her how wonderful it was and thanked her for her the hand delivered breakfast. She left smiling and blushing and Lily was reminded how charming Eric was on top of being incredibly handsome. No wonder she was contemplating running away with him.

Just as she was about to crawl out, she heard a voice that stopped her cold.

"Is Mr. Sampson alone?" She heard Rings' voice clearly through the door.

"Do you know Mr. Sampson?" Mrs. Embry asked, clearly a little protective.

"We have a mutual friend. I hoped that our friend had arrived." Rings was clearly on his best behavior. Even his accent was diminished.

"Well sorry to disappoint you but he is alone." Mrs. Embry didn't sound like she had warmed up at all.

"He hasn't been takin extra meals?" Rings was getting insistent.

"No, he hasn't." Mrs. Embry was sounding more miffed.

"Not the brothers neither?" Rings asked.

"No. They usually come down together but this morning Mr. Sampson slept in. Now if you will excuse me, gentlemen," she paused on the word "I have work to do."

Lily could hear Mrs. Embry's retreating steps then she heard Jack. "Where in tarnation is that girl?"

Bags chimed in "Do you think Tracker hid her? He's got a soft spot for that little filly."

"I don't know where he coulda hid her. He's off with Slim, lookin' south. Who'd be taking care of her?" Rings seemed genuinely confused.

"Maybe Slim killed her." Jack suggested.

"Could be. Slim's like that and, Curly bein' dead, somethin' went down. What Slim says about it don't seem right." Rings seemed to be thinking hard.

"How long do we gotta wait?" Bags asked.

"Till they leave or we get orders otherwise." Rings voice was faded out, clearly they were headed down the hall.

Lily breathed a sigh and started to climb out from under

the bed. Eric met her as she got half way out and picked her up. She didn't realize she was shaking until she met his still body with her own. Lily tried to speak but her teeth were shaking so hard she couldn't get out the words. Eric tucked her head under his chin and held her tighter.

Three hard knocks came at the door. Eric set her down on the bed. He had to pry her arms from around his neck. "I have to get the door, they will worry." He soothed her then went to the door.

Lily lay on the bed unable to control the shaking. She told her muscles to stop but she seemed unable to control them. James and Tom entered the room and James' face went from the angry black look he now wore to chalk white. "What happened?" He whispered. He reached out his hand and stroked her temple as Eric relayed the conversation they had overheard.

"Why did she react like this?" Tom asked. "Is she that afraid of them what did they do to you?" She could see the panic in Tom's face rising. While James had always been more of a father figure, being the oldest, Lily and Tom had grown up as siblings and friends. She hated to see him so upset.

"No, nuh nuh no." Lily finally stuttered out shaking her head. She sat up, still shaking her breathing ragged. She took three deep breaths and the shaking lessened. "It isn't what they did to me it's what I did."

"What are you talking about?" James' words were a little harsh but there was a gentleness to his voice.

"When Tracker left, he gave me a gun. At first I thought it was to protect myself but then I realized I could escape. When I had been traveling for about an hour, Slim and Curly found me. They said it was part of the plan. They would leave, Tracker would follow, and I would escape. Slim said he was going to kill me. I couldn't see. I raised the gun and fired. I heard this cry...I..." Lily couldn't speak anymore the shaking took over her body.

"You killed Slim." James sounded appalled.

"No, Curly." Eric came over to the bed to wrap his arms around her.

James turned around and in an instant jumped at Eric. Eric, looked momentarily surprised but quickly recovered and knocked James off his course. The two were evenly matched in size, both being over six feet and broad shouldered. James slammed into the desk, then turned to make a second attack. Tom jumped in front of his brother in an instant and Lily sprang off the bed to launch herself in front of Eric.

"This is your fault!" James hurled his words across the room.

Eric's face twisted in pain, he clearly thought James was correct.

Lily head shook back in forth without realizing she was doing it. "No." She said softly, then louder. "No James, this is not his fault. It is my kidnappers'. It is fate. Eric has no control over this."

These words seemed to only infuriate her brother. "Why are you standing up for him? What is it about him? Because he is handsome? Rich? His first wife came to an abrupt end and you are about to do the same! You don't think this has something to do with him! Well I know it does!" James turned towards the door and stormed out, slamming the door behind him.

Lily stood there stunned. She knew little about Caitlin's death but James seemed to think he knew more and that Eric was responsible. It was one thing to hear Kathryn say it but her own brother was entirely different. She turned her face to Eric's and it was again tortured. She put her hand on his cheek. "What happened?" She asked softly.

He looked at her in surprise. "You're not going to blame me?" He asked.

She smiled. "Everything I have seen with your son and with me tells me that you are good. I think you at least have a right to explain your side."

Eric smiled back and rubbed her cheek. When he smiled like that, the hairs on the back of her neck stood up. Lily had a sinking feeling that it didn't matter what he said. She was hopelessly in love with him.

Tom cleared his throat. "I know you want to clear this all up but Eric needs to do some last minute preparations so that we can leave tonight. The sooner we get out of here, the better we all will be."

Tom turned away and busied himself at the desk while Eric said goodbye. He wrapped his arms around her and whispered in her ear. "I promise I will tell you everything that happened with my first marriage soon. You have a right to know before we get married. Then you can decide if you still want to go through with it."

Lily pressed her body closer to his. "I'm sure I will..."

He leaned down and kissed her. "Just wait until you hear it all." He let her go and walked out the door. She was left feeling empty and alone.

Tom cleared his throat again and Lily turned and smiled weakly at him. She drifted up next to him and laid her forehead on his shoulder.

"It's going to be alright Lil'. I don't think Eric's transgressions are that awful. James is just being protective. And now that we have you back, we are not going to lose you again." Tom stroked her hair as he talked.

"Where is Eric going?" She asked.

"To purchase clothes for you, I think." Tom continued to soothe her.

"Won't that look suspicious?" She asked.

"Frequently your friends don't notice when only one of us leaves. When they do, we have gotten pretty good at shaking them long enough to complete our business. Much of what we have been doing doesn't give them much of a clue as to our plan and since they still don't know you are here, I think they are only half-heartedly following us. Truthfully, I think that they think you are dead and that it doesn't matter what we do. They'll know tomorrow that you are not."

"Shouldn't we stay here then? Won't they give up after a while?" Lily asked.

"We risk you being exposed and then being trapped here. It is better to leave while we have the advantage." Tom put one arm around his little sister. "Try not to be too mad at James. I think deep down he feels guilty for pushing marriage on you. He's blaming Eric outwardly but inside blaming himself."

Lily snorted. "What do you know about Eric and Caitlin?"

Tom hesitated but seemed to make up his mind to continue. "I know Caitlin had other lovers."

Lily gasped. This is not at all what she had expected to hear.

Tom sighed. "It is also rumored that she and Eric quarreled the night of her death. She died in a carriage accident, I believe but the carriage had seemed to have been tampered with."

Lily was stunned. She had always assumed that it was Eric's love of Caitlin that had held him back but could he be suffering from more than a lost love? Was he responsible? Kathryn had made it sound like he was but Lily didn't trust Kathryn to tell any truth that wasn't to her advantage. Clearly, Kathryn was on the Colonel's side.

"Do you really think Eric was responsible for her death?" Lily asked, biting her lip.

"Lily, I like Eric a great deal but don't block out important information because of your feelings. This is your life we are talking about and it's important you have all of the facts." Tom gave her a squeeze to emphasize his point.

Lily knew that he was right but it was hard to separate her feelings from her judgment.

At just after midnight the four of them struck out. They didn't even check out of the hotel. They left a note with payment for the Inn Keeper. Lily was disappointed that she was still traveling in men's clothing but she had let it go. Judging by the tension when she had asked, James and Eric had disagreed over that as well. When they reached the outskirts of town, she saw a wagon waiting on the side of the road. Fear bubbled inside her but James approached easily.

"Mrs. Madison, thank you for meeting us at this late hour. I trust you had no trouble getting here?" James smiled cordially.

"No, I didn't. Thank you for asking. I would ask why we are leaving at this hour but I am sure that you will not tell me." Mrs. Madison stated matter of factly.

"Ann Madison, these are my brothers Tom and Billy. Our friend, Eric." Lily almost jumped out of her skin. She was to pose as a boy all the way to Portland? It was one thing to do it for a few minutes but for several days? White hot furry swept through her as she realized why. She would not be able to so much as touch Eric, nor he her, if she were posing as a male. She could have chewed nails and spit them and the look she shot James said as much but he only smiled angelically.

Tom took over driving the wagon and Ann rode next to him. She wanted to ask why a lone woman would agree to travel with a group of unknown men but she couldn't find an opportunity to ask. She had her own horse, obviously a boy of her age would not ride with another man. She felt herself growing angry again and she was afraid Ann would hear her voice and know that they were lying. She supposed that James might just be trying to protect her but she was fairly certain that he was just trying to keep her and Eric apart.

She felt herself growing more and more tired and Ann eventually went to lay down in the back of the wagon, though she couldn't have slept much. Lily knew that Ann was perfectly safe but it must be very strange to be traveling with a group of unknown men. She knew the feeling well. She wished she could lay down, or at least snuggle against Eric. She cursed James again but continued to ride.

At about sunrise she started to fall asleep in the saddle. She woke herself up the first few times but then she felt herself slumping over. She closed her eyes for just a second and fell soundly asleep.

"Billy, Billy, wake up." She heard Eric's voice through a fog. She was still on her horse, her head resting against his neck.

"Sorry." She croaked, rousing herself. Eric rode over to James and she could hear the two of them whispering to each other in short bursts but she could not understand what they were saying.

James rode over to the wagon, Ann having poked her head out because of the stop. "I am sorry Mrs. Madison but my youngest brother is suffering from exhaustion. Would you mind riding next to Tom while Billy lies down for a bit?"

Ann looked relieved and nodded her head. Lily climbed into the back and fell asleep before she even realized the wagon had resumed moving.

She woke a few hours later, hungry and still tired. They stopped and made a brief meal, although more elaborate than hardtack, and then packed up. Ann, looking exhausted, climbed into the back of the wagon again.

Lily thought back to their previous discussion and realized that they must be posing as settlers. The sun was rising behind her and she realized that they were heading west instead of south. Perhaps they were trying to throw her kidnappers off their tracks? She had to admit, it seemed like a pretty good plan. Wouldn't it look better though, if she were also a woman?

"James," Lily rode up next to her brother "why am I dressed as a male?" Lily's indignation showed clearly in her voice.

"To protect you, of course. Keep your voice down, you wouldn't want wake Mrs. Madison." James smiled clearly pleased with himself.

Lillian gave him a withering look. "But all of my kidnap, ers recognized me as a male. They would be less likely to recognize me as a female."

"Lily, no man that sees you as a woman is going to forget you. But as a male, change your hat and apparently they can sit next to you in a tavern and not know who you are." James was enjoying himself.

"You realize that you are endangering Mrs. Madison. They could mistake her for me." Lily shot back, exasperated.

He nodded. "An unfortunate possibility, but I don't think it will happen."

"How could you be so callous?" She fell back in her spot between James and Eric, not waiting for a response. Eric kicked his horse up slightly and leaned over to whisper in her ear.

"He's right about one thing." He grinned. "No man is ever going to forget once they have seen you."

Lily stared hard at her brother's back. This was not over.

They continued most of the day, their trail finally arcing south near sunset. They stopped and had dinner, a nice meal, and Lily was thankful they had a wagon that could carry provisions. The horses were tended and then James lay out the bed rolls. She was between her brothers, while Eric kept watch. Ann was, of course, in the wagon. Lily was exhausted after a long day and night of riding but she couldn't seem to fall asleep. She ached to be in Eric's arms. Now that she was back with him, polite rules of decorum interested her little. After what she had been through, it seemed more important that she be near him. They would be married soon and she didn't see why that precluded her from all physical contact. She just wanted to feel safe.

Lily finally fell asleep late into the night but her dreams were restless and all night she dreamed of being kidnapped, or that she was separated from Eric and she couldn't find him no matter how hard she looked. Towards dawn, she began to have a dream that she was alone in the woods. She could hear Slim's voice calling to her. She tried to run but the more she ran the closer he seemed to get. His voice was right in her ear "I'ma comin' for ya girlie." He cackled.

Lillian woke in a cold sweat and sat up. She felt so alone and afraid. She couldn't even talk about how she was feeling for fear of being discovered. After a night of rest, Ann would not be retiring to the wagon today. She was forced into silence.

The day seemed to drag on, even more so because she was exhausted. She craved sleep but when the time came to actually fall asleep she again had difficulty and was plagued by nightmares. By the next day, Lily could feel her shoulders slumped with exhaustion but she was too tired to do anything

about it. She also noticed Tom, Eric, and James whispering and looking at her with concern but she didn't know what they were saying and couldn't bring herself to muster the strength to ask.
When they broke for camp, Ann and Tom went to gather fire wood.

Eric immediately wrapped his arms around her and she slumped against him. Her eyes closed of their own accord.

James started to protest but Eric gave him a sharp look and growled. "Not now James."

James was silent and Lily was thankful for the warmth of his embrace even for a few minutes.

Finally, James spoke. His voice was the gentlest it had been in days. "Lily what is wrong?"

"Can't sleep," she mumbled "nightmares."

"James, we can't let this continue. She looks like the walking dead." Eric gave her a small squeeze.

"What choice do we have? We have to continue, we have to get her to safety."

Eric thought for another minute. "We could say that she is sick and let her sleep in the wagon."

James thought for a second. "Then what would we do with Ann? Where would she sleep at night? She might also try to tend Lily and that could get... complicated."

Eric nodded and Lily thought it was nice to hear them speaking cordially.

"James, could Eric sleep next to me?" Lily asked.

"Lily" He started to protest.

"Please James, you'll be right on the other side of me and then, if I need to, I can hold his hand in the night when Slim comes to get me." She paused "I mean in my dream. He comes to get me in my dream." She was already falling asleep in the warmth of Eric's arms.

James nodded his head, concern seeming to override his desire to keep them apart.

"Sweetheart, you've got to wake up and have dinner. Then you can go to sleep." Lily roused herself as the meal was prepared. She shoved down what she could then lay down on the bed role. She was already falling asleep and knowing that

Eric would be next to her helped her start to drift off. She heard Ann, however, ask a few questions about her.

"Is Billy alright? That boy looked tired all day. He isn't getting sick is he?"

"I hope not." Eric replied but Lily could hear the concern in his voice.

The next morning, Lily woke feeling better and realized that she was holding Eric's hand in her sleep. No wonder she had slept well. She heard someone stir and saw Ann coming back from the woods. Hopefully the woman had not noticed that Lily was grasping Eric's hand.

She quickly placed her hat over her bandana that held back her hair. It was braided and tucked into the wrap that bound her breasts. It was extremely uncomfortable but she could do little about it other than cut her hair and that was not going to happen.

"Good morning." Lily nodded to Ann, using her best male voice. Ann looked surprised and Lily realized that she had not spoken to Ann the entire trip.

Ann smiled and returned the greeting then began building up the fire. Everyone in the camp began to stir and shortly after, they hit the trail again. James insisted that Lily ride on the seat of the wagon with Tom and Ann for a few hours. While it was a welcome change to not not have to sit in the saddle, Lily was nervous because it meant a lot of potential conversation with Ann. She didn't know how long she could fake being male.

As the group set out, Ann remained silent. It was early and most everyone was still tired. But as the morning heated up, so did the conversation.

Ann looked over at Lily, "How are you feeling this morning?"

"Better, thank you." Lily didn't want to say too much.

Ann looked disappointed so Lily decided it would be alright to ask the other woman some questions. If she herself kept quiet, she wouldn't give too much away. "What brings you on this trip?"

152

Ann frowned slightly. "My husband and I were planning on settling down near Bucksport but he..." Ann hesitated then spoke again "he passed away."

"Oh, I am so sorry." Lily's brow furrowed. "You poor thing!"

Ann looked at her surprised. "Thank you. It has been very difficult." Ann put down her head and Tom gave her the eye over Ann's bonnet. Lily realized that she had reacted far more like a woman than a man. She bit her lip. This was not going well.

By noon, everyone was hot and exhausted. The wagon bumped over several rocks and made a sickening crack. Lily felt the wagon bumping along despite the fact that there were no more rocks. Tom pulled the wagon over next to a river and got down to take a look. James and Eric dismounted to join him.

Ann looked over at her. "I may as well make us some lunch. Who knows how long this will take to fix."

Lily nodded then realized that she should have joined the men. It would seem awkward now and she couldn't help Ann. She considered wading in the water but knew that James would not approve. She suddenly smiled to think how like her father, James had become. She climbed down out of the seat and sat silently on the river bank when she heard a noise coming down the trail. It started as a low rumble, and grew steadily louder. She felt her insides clench. Lily looked over at the three men checking the wagon wheel but they had stopped. They too were watching the trail. Quickly, Lily got up and crouched down next to Eric, wanting to be near him as the hooves of approaching horses echoed the pounding of her heart.

A group of about ten uniformed men stopped just in front of the wagon where Ann was partitioning out a small meal. Not knowing that they might be in danger of uniformed men, she smiled easily and asked if she could help them, as Tom stepped up next to her.

A blond haired man, clearly high ranking, answered her question. "We looking for some travelers, perhaps you have seen them?" He smiled, clearly inspecting Ann.

It was Tom who responded. "If we can be of any service. I'm Tom Mitchell, and this is my wife Ann."

"Lieutenant Colonel Andrews. May I ask who you are traveling with?"

Lily was surprised that Ann did not even blink when Tom announced that she was his wife. This must have been part of the original plan. Lily wondered what circumstances had caused Ann to go along with this charade.

Tom smiled at the Lieutenant Colonel. "Of course, my brother Jim is gathering some firewood. My brother Billy and Sam are fixing the wagon wheel."

Eric whispered, "Keep your hat low and tip it slightly, say nothing." Lily nodded; he did not have to tell her twice.

They both stepped out from behind the wagon and tipped their hats. Eric also seemed to be keeping his hat low and Lily wondered if he knew Lieutenant Colonel Andrews.

"I am sorry for the interrogation. We have been traveling a long way looking for a lost girl. Perhaps we could join you for a bit?" Andrews asked.

Tom nodded his accent and Ann began to lay out more food. The men with the Lieutenant Colonel began to dismount and Lily felt fear curling inside her. She wanted to run away but she knew it was a mistake. She told herself to breathe. She was unconsciously inching closer to Eric, also a mistake.

Ann turned back towards the wagon and looked at her. "Billy" she called "would you help Jim fetch some firewood?"

Lily nodded, relief making her feel limp. She left in the direction that James had headed, glancing back at Eric, who was still working at the wheel. A soldier had stepped around to assist him and Lily was relieved she had an excuse to not be there. She sent a silent thank you to Ann. She wondered, however, how much of the situation Ann understood. Was it coincidence that the other woman had sent her off? Lily found it hard to believe, Ann had never asked her to do anything before.

James was not far off and he seemed to be standing in a field waiting for her. He smiled when he saw her, clearly relieved, and then began gathering more firewood. "Get as much as you can. We'll stall for as long as possible." He didn't ask her any questions so she could only assume he had overheard the exchange.

"James, how much does Ann know?" Lily asked, her eyes narrowing. Did Ann know that she was a girl? Had she been hiding for nothing?

"She knows that you are under our protection and that you are to be around as little as possible when we have visitors. She knows that we are trying to keep our identities secret." James shrugged.

"Why would she agree to this?" Lily asked, again surprised that a lone woman would agree to travel with a group of men who were hiding their identities.

"We gave her some basic information and agreed to pay her a handsome sum to help us. She and her husband had very little and when he died, she lost what little they had. She is trying to get back to her family, but she needs money."

Lily felt a swell of pity for Ann. She could only imagine the desperation that Ann must have been feeling to make her join an unknown and potentially dangerous group to try to get to family. While her own situation was dire, at least she had her family working for her.

After a while, James motioned her to return to the camp and Lily felt dread fill her again. It was more controlled this time, with time to prepare herself she decided she needed to throw herself into the role of adolescent boy.

They approached the camp, and James nodded to Andrews, who was talking to Ann and Tom, then walked behind the wagon to check on Eric. Unsure of what to do and, not wanting to look awkward, Lily began to build a fire.

"Billy," James called roughly, "could you fetch some water."

Lily nodded. She grabbed the two buckets in the back of the wagon and headed for the shore. "Head up stream, I saw a pool, see if it's any good for fishing."

Walking through the woods, she was initially glad to be away but nervous about being alone. Lily found the pool her brother had been referring to, it did look good for fishing. She returned with the buckets of water and grabbed some hooks and line. The men had jacked up the wagon and were replacing a spoke on the wheel. Ann had put coffee on the fire and Tom had his head over a map with the Lieutenant Colonel. She turned to head back for the pool when Eric stood as they greased the axle with tar and put the wheel back in place.

"You thinking about doing some fishing?" He asked her casually. She nodded and he added. "I think I'll join you, are the hooks in the back?" She nodded again.

No one seemed to notice her silence and Lily was relieved. Eric followed her along the trail but said nothing until they were out of earshot. "Are you doing alright?" He asked.

"I'm fine." She whispered back. "But I'll be glad when they go."

"Me too. I've met Andrews on a few occasions and I don't want him to recognize me." Lily thought that might be the case.

"Is he dangerous?" She asked. While the soldiers made her nervous, she knew that it was just a small faction that followed Colonel Kingsley and participated in his criminal acts.

"Yes." Was all Eric said and Lily felt her insides tighten. She consoled herself that things seemed to be going well and that, with any luck, the soldiers would soon head north. She wondered, however, if they would be back and if the lost girl was, in fact, herself.

She looked at Eric and he patted her on the shoulder. It was a brotherly gesture and Lily knew he had to keep it that way in case someone was watching. Since she had to play the part of boy, she may as well enjoy it. They reached the pool and Lily smiled at her fiance. "Care to make a wager?" She gave him a crooked smile and Eric raised one eyebrow.

"I'm listening." He cocked his head to one side.

"If I catch more fish than you..." she paused thinking of a worthwhile wager. "I get to sleep in your bed role with you for one night." She whispered so only he could hear.

"And if I win?" He asked cocking his eyebrow once again.

"I won't. I'll do as James asks and won't cause any more trouble for you." Lily laughed quietly, not wanting to be overheard.

"It sounds like either way, I lose." He smiled the gorgeous smile that made her toes curl and the hair at the back of her neck stand up. "But you're on."

She returned his smile then cast her hook out into the deep pool and began to twitch the line, pulling it slowly. Immediately she got a hit. She smiled as she jerked the line, sinking the hook deep into the fish's mouth then pulling him in.

"I've been had!" Eric chuckled softly but soon was bringing in a fish of his own. After an hour, they had caught seven fish total, Lily three and Eric four. It had been fun, but she was slightly disappointed that she had lost. It was totally worth the hour of quiet conversation they had shared. It was amazing she could have such a wonderful time under the shadow of so much danger.

"I had no idea you were that good!" Eric said clearly impressed.

"Wait till you see me clean them." She smiled.

"I don't believe it." He stated softly.

"Well, hopefully, it leaves little question with the Lieutenant Colonel and the other soldiers that I am what I say I am, or what Tom says I am." Lily shrugged.

"It would sell me, if I didn't already know what was under those clothes." He gave her a devilish grin and she returned with a withering look. If she hadn't had several fish hanging from her hands, she would have smacked him. But, it was just as well. Boys didn't go around smacking their elders.

She and Eric returned to camp and set on the bank of the river, silently cleaning, then deboning the fish. She had done a great deal of fishing growing up in an ocean town and she made quick work of her fish. Once they had removed the skin, Ann came over and collected the fish to toss in a frying pan.

"Billy, would you be a dear and see if you can find me some chives to toss in with this fish?" Ann smiled and winked at her.

"Yes ma'm." Lily returned softly and set back down the trail. They all seemed determined to keep her out of the camp. That was fine with her.

She headed back towards the fishing pool, hoping to find some chives there. She was thinking that she would spend some time sitting by the pool, rather than hunting through the woods. As she stepped out of the clearing, she found one of the soldiers taking a bath in the pool. She felt her face flame up and turned to leave when he noticed her.

"Hey kid, you think you got some soap I could use?" He called to her.

"Sure." She said back, her heart hammering in her chest. He was turned partially away from her but she saw far more of him than she really wanted to and she had to go back and see him again! The whole situation made her extremely uncomfortable.

Within ten minutes, she was back at the camp. Ann smiled at her "Back already?"

She shook her head no. "One of the men needs some soap." She reached for the soap but the Lieutenant Colonel stopped her.

"You've given us enough of your hospitality. I'm sure he can do without soap. Just go tell him I said so." Lily nodded but her insides churned. That would require her to say more words than she had uttered the entire day. She didn't want to give herself away now.

James stepped in. "Billy, why don't you go get Ann her chives, I think I saw some downstream. I would be happy to bring your man some soap." James grabbed the soap and Lily headed in the opposite direction but she could feel the eyes of Lieutenant Colonel Andrews on her back.

Chapter 20

After having fed the soldiers and fixing the wheel, the two groups parted ways, with the soldiers heading north and the rescue mission south. Everyone was on edge and while Ann's presence had been a blessing today, Lily was frustrated that she could ask no questions about where they were or what the plan was. She wished she had asked more back at the hotel but she had only been concerned with resting and being under the protection of her family again. She bit her lip.

At least she was back on her horse and not next to Ann again. While she preferred riding in the wagon, she didn't think she could make polite conversation anymore. Besides, she had finally adjusted to riding a horse like a man, and it was no longer uncomfortable.

The group rode until the dusk had long settled into darkness and then finally stopped to rest. Everyone in the group was tense, the day had worn them all thin and Lily decided it would be best to eat a few bites and go to sleep. She tossed her sleeping roll next to Eric's and felt James glaring at her back. She ignored it and lay down, closing her eyes. She was not sure why James was upset with her this time but she was in no mood to deal with him tonight.

Eric lay down next to her but didn't speak or reach out to her. As she had promised to be good, she didn't either. Ann had already climbed into the back of the wagon, and she would have loved to provoke James, but a bet was a bet and she had lost. More and more these days, she felt anger and resentment building inside her and she wanted to vent it. She knew how much trouble this had all caused her brother but she had been through a great deal of strife on his behalf and she had not been so unreasonable. She thought again of her beautiful mother, so full of personality and passion. When she was little, her father had always remarked that she was the spitting image of her mother only with his hair color. She had always had a temper and gotten into her fair share of mischief. Lily thought back to some of the things she had done to try to keep up with her brothers and laughed to herself. When her parents died, she had shut down. Built walls that kept everyone out and her emotions in. It was easier for James, easier for her. But with all the feelings she had for Eric and what she had been through, she felt those walls crumbling, she felt her anger rising, her temper soaring.

Finally, after the camp had long since gotten quiet, she heard Eric whisper "Lily, you have to go to sleep."

"I can't." She groaned back. "Today was..." She didn't have to say it, he already knew. She realized another emotion that was feeding into her frustration, desire. She wanted to feel Eric, to touch him and be touched. It was curling up inside her, consuming her, feeding the flames of emotion.

She scooted over towards him and wrapped an arm around his shoulders, then nuzzled his neck. Maybe they could slip away.

"Lily, you promised." Eric gritted out.

"Everyone is asleep, we could just..." He picked up her hand and moved it off of him.

"Tom is keeping watch and he will notice. Go to sleep." Eric turned away from her and Lily wasn't sure if she wanted to cry or to spit but she knew that white hot fury was coursing through her veins.

She could do nothing and so what seemed like hours later, she finally fell asleep but she slept restlessly and dawn came agonizingly early. If it was possible, she woke in a worse mood than when she had fallen asleep.

James seemed to have suffered a similar fate and no one

spoke over breakfast, the tension was palpable. They packed up and headed out early, Lily was sure that the group was trying to put as much distance between themselves and the soldiers as possible. She said little as the miles passed and tried to focus on the beautiful scenery around them, but her anger was too fierce to allow her to enjoy it. They finally stopped for a late lunch. Ann went to get firewood and asked Lily to help her. Lily trailed behind her, not really wanting to help but unable to say no. It was exhausting trying to act like someone other than yourself. Ann turned suddenly. "Billy, can I talk to you for a second?"

Lily started and looked up in surprise. She didn't know what to say. She only nodded. Ann hesitated then continued. "Are you the girl they were looking for yesterday?"

Lily stared at the other woman completely unsure of what to say. She knew James would not want Ann to know but Lily didn't know what else she could tell the other woman? "What do you mean?" Lily finally stuttered out.

Ann sighed. "You don't walk, talk, look or act like a boy. Sometimes you are better at it than others, you did fine yesterday but it's obvious, having spent so much time with you that you are no male. Are you the kidnapped girl?"

"If you're wondering if I am being held hostage; the answer is no. James and Tom are my brothers." Lily hesitated, she hadn't answered the questions but maybe she was addressing Ann's fears.

Ann nodded. "But why are soldiers looking for you?"

Back to that, Lily thought, biting her lip. She couldn't say anymore without admitting she was female but Ann already knew. "I was kidnapped by a Colonel. He... he wanted to marry me but I escaped. Now, we are trying to get back home. I'm sorry that you have been dragged into this."

Ann waived her hand. "Truthfully, this is far better than the circumstances I was in. My husband became ill and died shortly after we moved to Bucksport. We had come to enter into the fishing business but I had to use what little money we had saved to live and the money had run out. I had few options, none of them good."

"I'd love to hear the whole story sometime." Lily smiled at the other woman. Ann returned the grin.

"I think we had better talk about your story first. The Lieutenant Colonel said that you had run away from home and been picked up by a group of men. He claimed you were related to the Colonel, the one who wanted to marry you I guess. He must really want to marry you if he is sending out his subordinates to find you." Ann looked at her.

"The Colonel is not a nice man. He is involved in a great deal of illegal activity. I am sure anyone who is helping him is involved with him." Lily wanted Ann to understand the danger but the other woman misunderstood.

"I won't help them, I..." Ann started but Lily stopped her.

"Ann, I just want you to know the danger you are in." Lily stated firmly.

"Oh, I understand. Thank you." Ann nodded.

The two women went back to gathering firewood and Lily whispered to Ann. "Don't let on that you know yet. James will not be happy."

"He's angry with you isn't he?" Ann asked.

Lily nodded and shrugged. "He'll get over it." She said but she was beginning to wonder.

They returned to camp and James glared at her, eyes narrowed. Lily hoped she had done the right thing by confiding in Ann.

They ended up throwing the firewood in the wagon for dinner that night and quickly hit the trail again. Lily spoke little, which was not unusual, and it gave her time to think. The more she thought about what she told Ann, the more worried she had become that she had done the wrong thing. Ann had seemed so confident about her knowledge that it seemed Lily had little choice but perhaps she should have held out. She was absolutely sure that she did not want to talk to James about it. Relations were tense enough between them. She considered talking to Eric but she was hurt and still angry about his rejection last night. When Lily had been kidnapped, she told herself no matter what Eric was willing to give, she would take it. She did not want to be married to anyone else. It wasn't that she had changed her mind, she hadn't. It was just that she was beginning to truly understand what it would mean to love someone so much more than they loved you. To want things that the other would be unwilling to give. She would always be aching for more and she wondered if she would always be feeling anger and resentment. It didn't seem like a good situation for either of them. The thought of not marrying Eric made her heart ache but the thought of watching her heart broken over and over again made her pulse with pain. Lily still hadn't decided what the best course was.

That left her with her original problem. She wasn't ready to talk to Eric about anything and she wasn't going to discuss it with James so that only left Tom. He was always the easiest to confide in. He was not the parental figure that James was but he usually offered a less decisive course of action. It was the only course she could take now however.

They stopped for the evening at dusk and hurriedly built a fire. When Tom went to get water, Lily offered to help. He accepted with a nod. Her brother looked more tired than she could ever remember seeing him and once they cleared camp she touched his arm. "Are you alright?" She whispered.

"Just tired and anxious to get home." He smiled weakly. "I'll be glad when we get to Portland."

She hesitated. "Is that where Ann leaves us?"

"Yes, if her family is there. James is going to look with her while we head home. If she can't find anyone, I imagine she will come to Boston with us or go to our house in Maine. James hasn't decided yet."

An immense relief washed through Lily. Ann was already part of the fold. "Oh that is wonderful! I was so worried I had made a terrible mistake but..."

"Wait, what mistake?" Tom stopped walking and turned to stare at her.

"Well, Ann said that she knew I wasn't a boy and..." Lily was interrupted abrubtly.

"What! She knows. Lily, how could you? After just seeing Andrews, how could you tell her? It was so irresponsible." Tom started heading in the opposite direction of the river, back to the camp.

"Tom, where are you going, we haven't gotten water? Why do you have to immediately tell James? He is going to..." Tom quickened the pace and she had to stop talking to keep up.

Tom practically ran into camp. Lily had clearly underestimated his reaction. He stopped in front of James and Lily skidded to a stop behind him. "Ann knows." Was all he blurted out.

"How?" James stood fury evident in his stance.

Lily looked around. Ann was nowhere to be seen. She wasn't sure if that was good or bad. "She asked. She wanted to know if I was the kidnapped girl. She already knew I was female."

"Dammit Lily!" James practically roared. "Why do you insist on making this as difficult as possible? It's like you want to be kidnapped again. Why do you continue to take the worst possible path? You have been nothing but trouble. What is wrong with you?"

Lily felt her own anger that she had been pushing down inside bubble to the surface. "What is wrong with me? What is wrong with you? Why do you insist on being angry with me for things that are completely out of my control? I can't help the kidnapping, or unjust rumors started by a malicious man or the fact that you have forced me to find a husband in a ridiculously short amount of time. Nor can I control what Ann has figured out! I am doing the best I can, can you say the same?"

James looked ready to spit. "I have done everything for you. I left school, got married, ran the business to take care of you and now this is how you repay me?"

"When are you going to stop blaming me for things I can't control. I have tried to be the best I could for you. I tried to be as easy and helpful as possible but it's never enough. Well, I release you of your duty. Go live your life, stop trying to help me. You're making us both miserable!" The words ripped from her mouth a mere second before James' hand came down hard across her cheek. She fell backwards landing on her rear. Lily was completely stunned. Her brother had never hit her and she didn't process it for a fraction of a second which was the time it took for Eric to tackle James to the ground, pummeling him with his fists. James wasn't about to give up and began to fight with all he was worth. Lily dimly saw Ann and Tom standing to the side, transfixed before she got up and ran.

She didn't know where she was going and wasn't even aware of what direction she was traveling until she found herself on the river bank. Lily stared at the water for a few minutes then threw her hat on the ground, ripped her bandana off and started unlacing her shoes. She yanked her shirt and pants off and finally unbound her breasts, leaving it in a pile on the ground. She stepped into the waist deep water and immediately let her head sink under. The water cleared her head and she touched her cheek, feeling the warmth of where her brother had smacked her. The motion let out the flood of emotions that she had damned up and tears began to leak out of her eyes followed by racking sobs. Lily leaned her upper body on a rock and let her emotions pour out of her. She couldn't remember when she had felt more desperate. All her doubts about her marriage came bubbling to the surface. James resentment of her only added to the knot in her stomach. She desperately needed to find her way.

The fight did not last long. Eric had pinned James when a voice from across the clearing had casually asked. "Is this a bad time?"

Both men jumped up and Eric gruffly asked "Who are you?"

"I'm Michael Abrams, currently known as Tracker, but the better question is shouldn't you go after Lily?"

Tracker smiled as he began approaching the group.

They collectively started and Eric began scanning the woods for her path.

"Towards the river." Tracker gestured in the direction she had headed and Eric took off after her.

It didn't take him long to cover the distance and he easily found her pile of clothes. Eric heard her sobs and began to take his own clothes off.

She wasn't aware that someone had joined her in the

water until a hand lightly touched her shoulder. A scream escaped her lips as she turned to see Eric. "You frightened me."

"Sorry about that. Are you alright?" He touched her hair.

"Fine." She turned her face away trying not to look at his beautiful physique. It would only distract her from the real issues.

Eric put his hand under her chin and turned it back towards him. "What's wrong?" Lily knew that he wasn't talking about James.

She ignored his intent. "Am I ruining everything?"

"I have gotten you into a great deal of this trouble and I am trying not to get you into anymore but you are not exactly making it easier for me."

"Is that why you pushed me away yesterday?" She asked, her hurt evident.

"I'm sorry. I was trying to pacify your brother but I'm sure I have just undone all my hard work. I should have just done it my way." Eric smiled wickedly.

She felt her breath coming in shorter gasps. "Do you think it would have turned out better?" Lily asked.

"I don't know, but we're about to find out." He reached his arms around her back and pulled their bodies together. Lily gasped. She had never felt a man's skin against her own and it felt deliciously wonderful. She wiggled ever so slightly and the friction of their skin along with the slipperiness of the water sent shivers shooting through her body.

"Lily," Eric said through clenched teeth. "I am only human and this has been a long time coming. You are incredibly beautiful and even harder to resist. I want to be gentle..."

She responded by kissing him with all the passion she had been storing up. It bubbled out of her and as their lips met and tasted each other over and over, her hands were all over his body feeling his back, his buttocks, his neck and chest. He felt amazing. His muscles rippled under her touch adding to her own pleasure and desire.

He broke the kiss and began trailing kisses down her

neck, sending wave after wave of sensation through her. As he kissed down her chest she groaned and arched her back, thrusting her breast up and begging him with her body to take it in his mouth. Eric obliged her, and another groan ripped from her mouth. His hand traveled across her buttocks then reached between her legs lightly touching her. A gasping moan escaped her and he increased the pressure. She was writhing underneath his touch as desire built inside her filling her every pore. She wanted more although she was unsure of what that was.

Eric lifted her up out of the water, supporting her weight with his arms as she wrapped her legs around him. He lay her down in the grass on the river bank. Lily's legs and arms were still locked around him as she pressed closer to his body. She lifted her face to his for another kiss and they stayed locked together for a few moments more before she felt him reach down again and spread her apart, thrusting quickly inside her. She felt another groan rip from her chest but this one was of pain rather than pleasure.

He stilled his movements and lightly kissed her lips. "Are you alright?" He asked softly as he nibbled at her neck.

She nodded, not wanting him to stop but not trusting her voice yet to speak. She was so glad to be in this moment finally, to belong to him and no one else. Finally she calmed enough to say "Don't stop."

It was all the encouragement he needed and he was again moving inside her. She had lost the passion but his smell and feel filled her senses and as her pain lessened the friction began to, again, stimulate her body. She could feel herself building towards something and she ground her body closer to his, moving with him, wanting more. The feelings inside her became so intense that she cried out and felt herself tumbling over the edge of her lust.

Eric let out a groan his body shaking with his release. Lily clung to him, not wanting the moment to end. He wrapped his arms even tighter around her and shifted them both so that they were lying on their sides facing each other. He snuggled her into him and nuzzled her neck.

"I...I wasn't expecting that." Lily laughed softly.

"Which part?" He smiled into her neck.

"All of it but I guess the end the most." He laughed and kissed her lips.

"I wasn't either." Eric kissed the tip of Lily's nose.

"But what do you mean, you were married, I am sure there were many other..."
Eric interrupted her.

"This was special, you are special." Eric looked into her eyes.

"Oh." Lillian felt herself blushing deeply. "What makes it special for you?" She couldn't help but ask.

He laughed. "Well, I have never been with a virgin before..." She gasped and he nodded. "Caitlin, although she told me that she was, was not, not that it would have mattered to me. It is a person's actions after marriage that are important to me but as most of society doesn't agree, she felt the need to lie."

She nodded. She hadn't given it a great deal of thought, as a woman she had always assumed she would wait till marriage. It hadn't worked out that way but she knew Eric would make an honest woman of her soon enough.

"But, I don't know that I have ever wanted a woman as much as I have wanted you. It has been... difficult." Eric smiled ruefully.

Lily felt her jaw drop. "What?" Was all she could think to say then she recovered herself. "You have been pushing me away since we met until, well, yesterday. How could that be true?"

Eric chuckled and nuzzled into her neck. "You smell like lilacs or roses. Not too sweet, intoxicating." He stopped to nuzzle her ear. "I dream about it."

She giggled and pushed him away slightly. "What are you talking about?"

Eric sighed. "I should have told you about this before but there hasn't been time. I promised you that I would tell you about my first marriage."

Lily bit her lip. She had been so curious about his first marriage but now that he was offering the information, she wasn't sure she wanted to know. What if he told her how much he still loved his first wife? What if he said something that implicated him in her death?

"Caitlin was larger than life. When I first met her, I had been in society for several years and I admit, I was bored. She was a breath of fresh air. Funny, smart, beautiful and extremely exciting." He paused. Lily had stopped looking at him and was now staring off into the darkness, it was as painful as she feared.

He lifted her chin and kissed her lips. "Just listen. We had a whirl wind romance and were quickly engaged. My mother hated her, but I had expected that. My mother is extremely practical. The first year of our marriage was as exciting as our courtship had been. We attended parties, balls, social engagements of every kind. I, however, started to grow tired of the late nights. I had been neglecting my business and I began to wish for a quieter life. For a while, I convinced Caitlin to stay in with me. Read, talk, spend some time really getting to know each other. What I found out was that Caitlin was not well suited for that kind of life. She did not share many of my interests and seemed only to come to life when surrounded by a crowd. She was discontent, even angry with me. I tried to strike a balance with her but I never seemed to do enough. Then, she became pregnant. She was furious at first. This was not the life she wanted, tied to the home by a young child. I was stunned, why had we gotten married if not to eventually have a family?" Eric stopped. Now he was staring off into the distance. Lily wrapped her arms around him tighter, wanting to comfort him.

His hand traveled down her back, holding her closer. "I think, we made the right decision having this conversation without clothes." He kissed her eyes, then her lips as she gasped and swatted at him. "Anyway. I didn't know what to do. We seemed to want such disparate things from life. I told myself we would have the baby and then figure things out. Caitlin grew more and more resentful as the pregnancy progressed and the gap between us widened. When Toby was born, she wanted nothing to do with him. Once she had recovered, she begged me to take her out, bring her places. At first I acquiesced, wanting to make her happy, but I had a business to run and a child to take care of. She started going out more and more alone and then not coming home at all. I had long since realized that I had made a mistake marrying Caitlin. A marriage is not built on excitement alone. The rumors started then, of affairs. Before Toby, I would have thrown her out without a second thought but I wanted my son to know his mother. Finally, when she came home, I issued an ultimatum. She was to cease the affairs and stay at home or our marriage was over. She agreed and for a time we were more stable." He kissed Lily again and smiled. "Then, something happened."

"What?" Lily was totally transfixed.

He smiled at her. "I met this beautiful honey haired girl."

She stared at him. He couldn't mean their first meeting? "You're not talking about me?"

"I am. I remember meeting you for the first time, you were just a girl. It must have been your first season." She nodded. "Even then you smelled amazing. And those eyes stared at me, so beautiful and innocent. My reaction to you was written all over my face. Caitlin was furious. We fought horribly. I had done nothing, but she knew that you were not a girl who I would have a brief affair with but would marry. She thought I was going to replace her. I told her I had no intention of doing anything of the sort but she felt betrayed anyway. She left shortly after that and started an affair with Colonel Kingsley."

Lily gasped! Caitlin had had an affair with the Colonel. Eric rubbed her cheek and continued. "She wanted to punish me. Kingsley had tried to bully me into doing business with him. He wasn't successful and he was angry with me. Still is, I believe. He is a man who is used to getting his way. Caitlin thought he was the best choice for her affair. Our marriage was over in every way but in the eyes of the law. She became the Colonel's ward. She had little or no money of her own. I'm not proud of cutting her loose but I couldn't continue to support her when she lived with another man."

"You don't have to explain. You didn't have any other choice." Lily stroked his hair.

He sighed. "I don't know. Making her dependent on

170

the Colonel is a move I will always regret. He is not, as you know, a kind man. He was abusive to her, cruel. He took his anger at me out on her. Finally, in desperation she came to me begging me for help. I agreed to set her up in an apartment. She stayed at the house for a few nights but left, to see her sister, she said. She died that night in a carriage accident although the circumstances have always been suspicious. I have no proof that it was Kingsley but I would bet money that he was responsible. I saw him a few months later. I confronted him about his affair with Caitlin and her death. He said 'what do you care, now you are free to marry your little blond.' Clearly Caitlin had told him what drove her away. He smiled. 'I hear she is an heiress, is she as pretty as they say?'

"What did you do?" Lily felt her heart beating wildly.

Eric chuckled. "I broke his nose. Best punch of my life." He snuggled her close.

"Eric, why did you think I needed to know this before we got married?" Lily couldn't believe he had reacted to her the way she had to him on their first meeting or that it had so impacted his marriage.

"Don't you see, Lily? This has always been about me. Kingsley wants the land, he wants the beautiful wife but he would not have picked you if it wasn't for me. Caitlin's description of your innocence, my infatuation and his anger with me has made you an irresistible prize. He would not be taking such big risks otherwise. He is using Kathryn against me and he tried to turn Caitlin against me as well. She told me that he seemed to have a loathing for me. You are another punishment for me." Eric looked at her, touching her cheek.

Lily shook her head. "This is not your fault, it's his. You can't blame yourself for his actions."

"When we were at the inn you asked me if I wanted to back out of the marriage because you brought too much trouble. Now I offer you the same."

Lily kissed him long and slow, so happy to be with him. He smiled at her in the way that made her whole body tingle. She snuggled into him.

He kissed her one more time "We should think about

171

heading back. Your brothers must be worried. We've been gone a long time."

They got up and began to get dressed Lily's mind full of all that she had heard. A doubt crept into her mind. He had called her the marrying kind and he said that he wanted her but he hadn't married her. In fact, he had gone out of his way to not marry her. It could only mean one thing. While he wanted her he didn't love her. She was the marrying kind so he hadn't acted but once he had to marry her, he gave in to his desire. It explained all his actions.

Walking back towards the camp, Eric held her hand and it calmed her building fears. She had always known he didn't love her, it was just more difficult after what they had just done. If he wanted her, they were married, and built a family, perhaps in time he would grow to love her. She almost smiled to herself. 'Keep telling yourself that Lily, you might wish it true.'

They entered the camp and Lily realized that she hadn't asked Eric how he had found her so quickly or what had happened between him and James. She immediately saw James. He was sitting next to the fire. His clothes were filthy and torn and he had a cut under one eye.

"Eric, did you do that to him?" She turned to look at him.

"Only some of it." He was looking across the fire to someone else.

"I see you're in good hands." Tracker's voice rang across the camp as he stepped out of the shadows.

Lily ran the few steps and gave Tracker a hug. It seemed natural, she had spent several days riding on his horse with him, sleeping next to him. He felt like her family. James stood up suddenly and Eric closed the two steps between them, grabbing Tracker by the collar while wrapping his arm around Lily and pulling her away.

"Eric, stop." Lily almost laughed and a small giggle escaped.

"What are you giggling about?" James almost roared.

"Are we back to that?" Lily's exasperated tone shushed

172

James in a second.

He rubbed his neck with his hand. "Lily, I've been a real ass. It's not you. You're right. You've done more than I could have asked. It's me, I've failed you. I should have protected you."

She hugged her brother. "You've done a wonderful job."

"And what about this one?" Eric nearly growled.

"You can let him go Eric." Lily gave him a small push. Eric slowly released his collar but he looked like he was about to commit murder.

"It's alright Lily." Tracker said easily. "He has a right to keep his lady away from strange men who go around kidnapping young women."

Lily rolled her eyes. "I've told them the whole story. They know that you are the one who saved me and that you were a perfect gentlemen.

Tracker looked over at Eric. "Besides, it's obvious she only has eyes for one man."

"That so." It was Eric's turn to rub the back of neck with his hand.

"Actually, several of the men could tell you that she says your name in her sleep." It was Tracker's turn to laugh.

"Tracker!" Lily blushed, mortified.

Eric responded by reaching over and grabbing Lily up into a hug. She tucked her head into his chest and he stroked her hair, which Lillian had left unbraided. She realized her hat was still by the river.

Ann stepped forward, "It's nice to meet you Lily." Lily gave Ann a small hug which Ann returned. As the other woman backed away Lily noticed Ann giving Tracker a sly glance. Lily smiled to herself. Ann was still a young woman and quite pretty. She had dark hair and eyes that gave her an exotic look.

Eric let her go and Lily turned to the rest of the group. James said nothing, he was clearly on his best behavior, so she turned to Tracker. "Not that I'm not happy to see you but why did you come?"

Tracker smiled. "I told you that my real name was

Michael and it will be again soon. Kingsley has a large shipment coming in for which I was able to get inventory lists. When he does not pay any of the taxes or tariffs, we will be able to arrest him."

"Is that the worst of his crimes?" Eric asked. They all knew that tax evasion was relatively common.

Tracker shook his head. "There are several other charges that we have been gathering evidence on, prostitution, murder, theft and warrants have been issued. Tax evasion is the easiest to prosecute. I am delivering the last of the evidence and with luck we will arrest the Colonel and Lily will be safe."

"How likely is it?" Eric asked, his mouth thinning.

"Truthfully, not very. Maine is a vast state and there are lots of places to hide. Even if he is not arrested, he may be too busy hiding to be much of a bother to you or..." Tracker paused.

"He may make it his last mission." Eric finished.

"You know him." Tracker stated.

Eric nodded. "He will want to take us down before he goes."

Tracker nodded. "I'm afraid it might be so. But that is a problem for another day. The reason I have taken a several hour detour is that you have another problem."

Lily felt her spine stiffen with fear.

"I ran into Lieutenant Colonel Andrews on the way to deliver my evidence. I told him, of course, that I was also looking for Lillian, trying to cover all areas. I tried to tell him that we thought you might be dead but he doesn't believe it. You leaving Bucksport in the middle of the night has made him suspicious. And while he doesn't yet know who you are he has also grown suspicious of your group. He can't put his finger on why but he has met no more travelers and wants to speak to you again." Tracker paused.

"What do we do?" James sounded more tired than Lily could ever remember hearing him.

"We ditch the wagon and make a break for Portland. If we leave early, we could be there by nightfall." Eric said grimly.

Tracker nodded. "They will easily catch up to you if you don't and that could be extremely dangerous. Finding the empty wagon will certainly tip them off but hopefully you can hide in Portland."

"We have a ship, waiting in port there." Eric told the other man.

"Ah, than that is definitely the way to go." Tracker affirmed.

"What about my aunt? I was hoping to find my family or at least one person from my family in Portland." Ann asked the question quietly but Lily could hear the tension in her voice.

"We will split up. Morph our group again." James turned to Ann. "I will stay in Portland with you while Tom, Eric and Lily return to Boston."

"I have another ship, The Divine, that will be arriving in Portland in three days to unload. James, you can return on that boat. There may not be another for several days so make sure that you are on it."

"Ann." Lily turned to the other woman. "If you don't find your family, please consider coming to stay with us." Eric nodded beside her.

"We can certainly make room for you in our home and help you find an income of your own or a suitable husband, whichever is your desire."

Ann nodded, smiling at the couple. "Thank you. You have no idea how much comfort it brings me to know that I will not be left out on the street. I am beginning to wonder if I was meant to meet you."

Lily returned her smile, "I think perhaps you were."

Tracker turned to Eric. "If I am unsuccessful at capturing Colonel Kinglsey, I would beg you to allow me to come help you in Boston. I think it may serve both of our purposes."

Eric nodded. "That would be most appreciated." Eric gave Tracker the names of several ships he might look for passage on then went to his satchel to find paper and pen to scroll notes for James and Tracker to receive passage.

Tracker followed, handing Eric a small pouch. Eric tucked into his satchel as he pulled pen and paper out. Lily wondered what it could be.

"Well. Let's get some sleep. Tomorrow is going to be a

busy day." James stood, tucking his papers into his bag.

Lily lay down on her bed roll but Eric immediately pulled her into his arms. With a smile on her face, she fell instantly asleep.

Chapter 21

The group woke early, ate little, and climbed into their saddles. They had taken everything they needed, and could fit on their horses, with them and left the wagon for another traveler to use.

Tracker departed, heading west, while the rest of the group moved due south with the sun rising on their left shoulders. James took the lead with Lily and Ann behind him and Eric and Tom at the back of the group. The two men seemed to be talking often, but Lily could catch little of what they said.

They did not stop until midafternoon and the pace was a great deal quicker than Lily was used to riding by herself. Every muscle in her body ached and she would have loved to stop. Only the demons behind them drove her forward when Eric called everyone back on their horses after only twenty minutes. If Ann were uncomfortable, she said little and she gave Lily strength. She did tell Lily some about her life in Maine, her family and her husband. Lily found the conversation extremely enjoyable. It kept her mind off the journey, Ann was a good storyteller and she found she liked the other woman a great deal.

"Ann, I hope you find some family in Maine but I will miss you if you don't come to Boston. But even if you don't, I would like to visit. Once this is all behind us, Eric is planning on buying a home in Kennebunk for us to use part of the year. It would be wonderful to see you."

"I would like that." Ann paused. "Truly, though, I am not sure who will be waiting for me in Portland. My parents died some years ago and my uncle is a bit of a wanderer. My aunt raised me and her health was failing when I left a year and a half ago. I hated to leave her, but Jake had found a good opportunity north and we were trying to make a life. I was planning on coming back for her when Jake died. I should have just come home then but Jake had a stake in a boat and I was trying to recoup that money or make some profit in the boat but I didn't get very far. Much of it was done with a handshake and not on paper." Ann's mouth was drawn and Lily could see how painful the experience had been for her.

"I am so sorry." Lily comforted her as best she could.

The day dragged on and finally towards nightfall, they could see signs that they were nearing their destination. The path they had been traveling on became a road and outlying settlements could be seen. They stopped at a stream to water the horses before heading into town. Portland was on a peninsula and could only be accessed by one strip of land in and out. They were stopped at the threshold.

Lily was dipping her hands into the cool water, grateful for a drink. It had been a long hot day on the trail. Lifting her hands to her mouth, she heard the distant sound of what she first thought was thunder.

She could see James scanning the horizon. He jumped on his horse and headed back the way they had come.

"Lily." Eric was already mounting his horse and Ann and Tom followed suit. Lily turned to him and Eric pulled her on his horse as she heard James shout.

"Go." Without a moment's pause, Eric kicked the animal into action. Lily could tell immediately that this horse was a beast of quality. Even after riding all day it took off with amazing speed. It must have been from Eric's personal stable. She looked back, but already she could not see Tom or Ann. She hoped that they were alright.

The two of them rode into town with amazing speed, heading for the docks. Eric must have been familiar with the town, as he weaved his way through streets and alleys. "Are they going to be alright?" She shouted over his shoulder.

"Fine." Eric didn't need to ask who she was talking about. He knew it was Tom, James and Ann. "They headed south, only we came into town."

Lily immediately realized what this meant. Their pursuers might follow the others instead of her and Eric. With night approaching, it would be easy to hide. Or Andrews and his men could be following them and, hopefully, they would be safely on a ship before they were caught. It was a good plan but Lily could not believe that James had allowed it.

Over the clatter of their own horse, Lily could hear the thunderous hooves of horses behind them. She turned to look and could see several men in uniform pursuing them. It suddenly occurred to her that there was a third option. They could catch her and Eric and being military, no one would question their right to capture her. Suddenly, Eric turned a corner and in front of her the sails of several ships billowed out in the wind. The tide had risen and ships were leaving the harbor.

Eric pressed the horse faster and called out to the men on one of the ships. There was a second's pause and then a swarm of sailors came dramatically down the sides of the boat, sliding on ropes and skidding down the gang plank and launched themselves down the peer towards them. Several held pistols in their hands as well as long swords. Lily felt almost as afraid of them as she did the men behind her but Eric reared up the horse and tossed a man the reins,

"Take care of her, see that she makes it to the stables of James Carter in Kennebunk." The man nodded and jumping on the horses back took off into the night. Eric started pulling her through the men towards the boat when a hand clamped down on her arm. She cried out and turned to see a soldier, still on horseback, gripping her by the upper arm. He gave her a good yank but Eric held firm. The man growled and yanked harder. Lily felt like she was going to be ripped in two when one of the sailor's fists came down like an anvil on the soldiers forearm. Lily felt the strength of it, like steel, shoot through her own arm.

The soldier cried out, almost falling off his horse, and immediately let go of Lily. Eric gave her a good tug and they were in the thick of the crowd of sailors.

Andrews voice pierced the night. "Why so hostile Sam? Or is it Sampson?" Lily looked at the other man. He was a handsome enough man but somehow when he spoke, he lost all of his attractiveness. "I should have recognized you before but I guess I didn't really ever look at you, only your gorgeous wife."

The group of sailors moved toward the gang plank, taking Lily and Eric with them.

Eric did not respond but Andrews called again. "Do I at least get to meet the lovely lady? I'm curious to see the woman who has sparked such love and devotion. I will admit, Sampson, you seem to have a way with beautiful women."

They moved up the plank and Eric turned to the Lieutenant Colonel.

"This was never about Miss Carter and you know it." Eric gave her hand to the man who had struck the soldier and the sailor began propelling her across the deck and towards the captain's quarters. He was a large, burly fellow and he honestly frightened her, but she trusted Eric.

"True, true, but still I hear she is a beauty. Was she with you the entire time? Come back down and we can discuss this." Andrews must be stalling.

"Thanks, but I would rather you came up. I have some questions of my own." Eric stood firm, knowing full well that the sailors had intimidated the soldiers into the passive stance they were now in. Andrews would never step onto the deck.

Lily could hear no more of the conversation as the door to the captain's door closed behind her. She could, however, hear ropes and rigging being pulled and sails, unfurling as they got ready to set sail. She would breathe easier when they left the harbor.

Eric came into the room a few minutes later, he was carrying two buckets of water. Two sailors came in behind him carrying buckets as well. She could have cried with joy at the thought of taking a bath. "We're leaving the harbor. While the

Colonel has several shipping schooners as well, I don't think he'll lay chase by sea. Unless he is running for his own life or leaving the country. But we'll keep an eye out."

"Do you think James and Tom will be safe?" Lily felt the knot of fear tighten again at the thought of them.

"They'll be fine. Kingsley already knows our destination so Tom and James are of little use. Besides, your brother is in his home territory. He also knows plenty of sailors. It'll be very easy for him to disappear."

Lily nodded. Eris was right. Kennebunk was less than a day's ride from Portland. One of many friends along the way could easily hide them. A tub was brought in and all of the water emptied into it. It looked delicious after the long day on the trail. The sailors left, closing door and Eric walked over to her.

"Alone at last." He smiled then kissed her lips. Lily, about to protest, began to lose herself in the kiss. He had that effect on her. She could feel him unbuttoning her shirt and slipping it off her shoulders. A small part of her told her that they should wait, that it wasn't good to continue down this path. She had wanted Eric to take her virginity. After what had happened with Slim, she didn't want to wait and take the chance that she could be kidnapped again. But it didn't seem right to do it again without being married. She had another problem, however, and that was being with him hadn't lessoned her desire for him, it seemed to have, in fact, made it stronger! Eric cupped one of her breasts stroking the nipple ever so slightly and she felt herself arch backwards and moan. Her arms wrapped around his neck. His hands slid down to her waist and then to the button on her pants.

"Wait." She struggled out, trying to catch her breath. He quickly undid her button but he laughed softly.

"I thought you would want to take the first bath." Lily pulled her head back to look at him and Eric was laughing as he looked back down at her. "Worried I was going to compromise you again, huh? I thought this was what you wanted?"

He was making fun of her! "I said I wanted you to be the first man I was with." She shot back. "How much longer till our wedding?" She struggled out. He was rubbing her nipples again and kissing her neck

"Maybe an hour." He said as he took one of her nipples in his mouth. She gasped at the pleasure of it, completely losing her train of thought. She felt him cup her buttocks and realized that she was somehow, completely naked, while he stood fully dressed. She felt a twinge of embarrassment then the reality of his words sunk in.

"An hour? What do you mean? Our wedding isn't for another..." She paused, unsure of how many days it had been since she left Boston.

He laughed again and lightly kissed her lips. "I am inclined to agree that it would be better to be married before we have any more relations, but as we are about to spend a few weeks on this ship together, I don't see how I could keep my hands off you for that long." He started kissing her neck again and she struggled to think. The only thing that kept her focused was that he seemed to be enjoying torturing her.

"But James..." Lily started to protest.

"He knows. This was the alternate plan if our original plan was foiled. He was not pleased, but at least you will be married and safe for now." Eric rubbed her cheek and then stroked her hair. "I'm sorry that your family won't be here to see the service."

She shrugged, "What about your family? You know so much about mine and I so little about yours."

"Well, my father became ill and died when I was nine, I think I mentioned to you that my mother raised me and my two younger brothers." Eric wrapped his arms around her again and picked her up.

She nodded. She knew how difficult it was to lose a parent. "It must have been difficult for you. Your poor mother." Lily rubbed her cheek against his.

"It was a long time ago and my mother is tough as nails. She did just fine. Although, I tried her patience a great deal which she is always reminding me of." He set her back down on her feet. "Now in the bath with you. You have a wedding to get ready for."

"Do I get to meet her? Does she know you are getting

married?" Lily was suddenly curious.

"Yes and yes, although the longer we have, the happier we will be." He winked at her as he too began to undress.

Eric helped her wash up and then he, himself, did. She dressed her hair, wearing nothing but a chemise that Eric had left out on the bed. She was beginning to wonder if she was going to have to be married in the men's clothes she had worn on the trail. Built into the wall, were several closed shelves and what looked like a wardrobe. Eric went to it and pulled out some clothes for himself then began dressing.

"Eric, that's a lovely shirt." She smiled at him, hoping to drop a hint. She would settle for a set of clean men's clothes.

"Thank you." He smiled back. "I must say you look stunning yourself."

"Eric!" He chuckled and pulled out a pale blue muslin gown. It was beautiful. He quickly helped her lace up her corset and pull on her petticoats. She put on the dress and Eric buttoned her up. She glanced in the mirror. Her face looked thinner than normal but it was so nice to see herself in a dress again.

"Such a shame to put all these clothes on!" She swatted at him as he returned to dressing himself.

"Thank you for the dress. It's beautiful." Lily smiled at the man about to be her husband with her whole heart.

"You are beautiful." He kissed her forehead.

"Where did you get it?" Lily asked curious to know how he had gotten a dress just her size onto the boat.

He chuckled. "I knew Captain White would be in Boston Harbor the day after we left. I left a note to be delivered that told him to wait in Portland and get some dresses. I left a quick description and measurements for the dressmaker." Eric put on his jacket, he looked extremely handsome.

"How did you know to send him to Portland? I never asked." Lily's brow furrowed.

"Tracker left us a note. We decided to follow on horse but leave a ship in Portland in case the note was authentic and not a red herring. It is a frequent stop for this ship and so did not draw any unnecessary attention."

Lily tested her sore muscles and smiled ruefully. "It's too bad we couldn't have just taken a ship from Bucksport."

Eric nodded. "James checked into it. The harbor was heavily guarded." He took her hand. "Are you ready?"

She nodded, suddenly incredibly nervous.

"Are you alright?" Eric took her other hand. "I'm sorry if I'm rushing you. I just want you to be safe."

"No, I'm wonderful. This is wonderful. I just wasn't expecting to get married today. Usually, a person wakes up in the morning knowing that is their wedding day." She laughed, despite herself and it helped ease the tension.

"It's not the dream wedding, I know. I wish it could be different." Eric grimaced but Lily shook her head. He left her side and pulled out the small satchel that Tracker had given him. He opened the bag and pulled out her diamond necklace, earrings and ring.

Lily gasped at the sight of them. Eric fastened the necklace around her neck. It warmed her heart to have her mother's jewelry on for her wedding. "Eric, thank you for all of this. I know it hasn't been easy and I don't know how many men would have given up on me, and my brother, but you didn't and I can't thank you enough. This is exactly what I wanted." He leaned down and rested his forehead on hers and they stood together that way for a few seconds. Of all they had shared, this was one of the most intimate and special moments of their relationship.

As the last rays of sun peeked over the horizon, Lily stood in front of Eric as Captain Jack White performed the ceremony that made them man and wife. The sailors of the ship stood in attendance, and they stood solemnly, if not awkwardly, as the couple said their vows. Lily had to smile, because although she had spent her life amongst sailors, she had never seen them called to battle before tonight. They had looked so fierce to her for a few moments but now seemed so bashful.

"I now pronounce you man and wife." Captain White's rich baritone carried over the rush of the sea. Eric leaned down and kissed his wife on the lips. She heard several of the men clear their throats and a few snickers as well.

"Now, if you will follow me, we have a small reception ready for you, as much as an hour will permit." Captain White pointed back towards his quarters and the men of the ship began to disperse.

"Won't the rest of the crew be joining us?" Lily asked.

"They are not the best company for ladies and we have only had time to prepare so much food that would constitute a reception." The Captain grimaced slightly.

"Oh, I'm sure we could share what little there is and combine it with whatever the men were to have for the evening. They saved our lives, it seems that we should celebrate with them." Lily smiled at the captain as a few of them men stopped to see how the conversation would end.

"I agree, Captain White, although thank you for your consideration." Eric gave her a small squeeze.

The Captain gave them a genuine smile then called the men back. Tables were set out on the deck and food was piled up for everyone to share. Lily and Eric sat at the head of the table while the Captain sat at the other end. The men ate heartily, and while quiet at first, they gradually began to relax.

They told many harrowing tales of life on the sea. Storms and pirates dominated the stories and Lily found herself gasping and laughing with the rest of the men. The evening grew later and later and despite herself, she finally let out an ear splitting yawn.

"I think perhaps it is time for you to get to bed." Eric leaned over and whispered in her ear.

"Oh, I'm alright. It has just been a long day I suppose. But we don't have to go to sleep yet." Lily felt relaxed for the first time in what seemed like months.

Eric leaned down and whispered in her ear. "I have no intention of sleeping yet."

Lily felt herself blush to her roots. Eric excused them to the sound of a great deal of cat calls and cheers. She grew even more embarrassed.

Lily entered the captain's quarters first. He had retired

them to the couple, Eric came immediately behind her. He firmly closed the door behind them and then pulled her back against his chest, kissing the back of her neck, sending shivers throughout her body. He reached for the buttons on her dress and gave them tug, sending several buttons flying.

"That is my wedding dress!" Lily chastised her husband.

"I'll get it fixed later." Eric pulled the dress from her shoulders and it landed in a pile on the floor.

"Please tell me I have something else to wear." Lily giggled as he kissed her neck again.

"Hmmm, I am not sure, maybe you will have to go naked." Eric was unlacing her corset.

She pulled away from him. "I will not, and speaking of naked, I don't want to be if you're not."

He smiled at her and started taking off his clothes. She was amazed by how comfortable he seemed. He took off his shirt, and Lily stared at his bare chest. His shoulders were incredibly broad with a well-muscled chest that tapered down to a narrow waist. She felt the urge to run her hands up and down it.

She stepped back into his arms and did just that. In no time the rest of their clothes landed in a heap on the floor.

Eric picked her up and carried her to the bed. He entered her quickly but this time, there was no pain, only an intense pleasure. She held his body close as they climbed together finally climaxing in unison.

She lay in the circle of his arms, drowsy and content. Eric kissed her hair and stroked her arm. "Why did we wait so long?" She murmured as she drifted to sleep.

"I honestly can't remember." Eric smiled into her hair as she fell sleep.

Lily woke late the next morning feeling drowsy and content. She rolled over to touch Eric and realized the bed was empty. She sat up trying to figure out where he was when she clearly heard his voice outside of the door.

"I need you to watch over her while I am gone." Eric sounded mildly worried as he spoke the words.

"I ain't no nurse maid for Christ sake, I'm a sailor!" She heard someone respond.

"If we are attacked, I need someone to protect her, you're the man I trust the most to do it." Eric sounded firm and the other man's lack of response seemed to be his affirmation.

Eric reentered the room and smiled at his wife as he came over to kiss her. "Where are you going?" She asked the concern evident in her voice.

He laughed. "It's a ship, I can only go so far. But, I need to speak with the captain about plans for the trip."

Lily smiled to. "You said we would be on the ship for a couple of weeks, we are not going straight to Boston?"

Shaking his head, Eric stroked her hair. "I thought we might take a break and a honeymoon of sorts. It might be nice to feel like we are not under attack for a few weeks."

"Then why do I have the guard?" Eric chuckled at her observance.

"I just want to keep you safe. A precaution, Kurt is a bit gruff but no one can protect you as fiercely as him." He kissed her forehead and stood up to leave.

Lily lay back down on the bed stretching and arching her back. "Are you sure you have to leave now? What about breakfast?" She asked innocently enough but Eric could see right through her and he smiled devilishly as he picked her up out of the bed with only a sheet covering her.

He kissed her long and hard and she found herself panting for more. "There is nothing I would like to do more than stay for breakfast." He paused smiling at her. "But it turns out that keeping you safe is a full time job."

He laid her back down on the bed and gave her one last kiss. "I will see you later Mrs. Sampson."

Lily lay in bed a little while longer then got out to wash up and dress. Her stomach was beginning to grumble and she would have to hunt down some food. She stepped out of her door and realized that the man, Kurt, that had been set as her guard was none other than the man who pummeled the soldier the night before. He gave her a long look but said nothing.

Lily cleared her throat. "I didn't thank you properly for what you did for me yesterday. If there is anything I can do..."

Kurt cut her off. "You can stay out of trouble and make my job as easy as possible."

She nodded, unsure of what to say. His tone and demeanor annoyed her but she had asked and now she would acquiesce to his request. It shouldn't be that difficult anyway. How much trouble could she get into on a boat?

"Perhaps you could show me to the galley. I could use a little something to eat." He nodded and turned, walking off without saying a word. She had no choice but to follow.

When they arrived in the tiny kitchen area, Lily could see that it was a mess. The crew of fifteen men were all fed from this one part of the boat.

"There's some grub over there." The cook pointed towards some vittles on the stove. They were less than appetizing, but Lily scooped some out for herself anyway. She returned to the deck to eat, glad for the fresh sea breeze and the beautiful view. Lily wondered what she was going to do with her day. She was not used to being idle and it made her restless. As she stood there, she watched some sailors pulling down a sail.

"It's got a rip in it again." She heard one call.

"Dammit, another one. I hate sewing those damned things up." The other spat over the side of the ship.

"Excuse me." Lily suddenly made a decision. If she were going to be on this ship, she may as well make herself useful. "I'll sew it for you." Kurt, who had been leaning against the rail, stood up suddenly to give her a sharp look. She wasn't sure if this was his idea of staying out of trouble, but she didn't see what the harm was.

"We couldn't ask you to do that. It's our job and you're..." He paused then lowered his voice. "the boss's wife." He finished.

Lillian had to smile at that. "Don't be silly. I'm just standing here, I may as well be useful. If you will show me the stitch you use, I would be happy to do it."

One of the men found her a chair to sit in the shade while the other got out the needle and thread. It was a big tear and was going to take her a while to stitch properly but it felt nice to do something. If her hands weren't busy, she would have had a great deal more time for idle thought.

When she had finished, Kurt fetched the men to take the sail. Lily decided to head back to the kitchen. After days of not eating a great deal, she found herself famished again.

When she got to the kitchen, she found the cook hard at work. He had clearly finished plucking some geese and was trying to cook some dish. He looked fit to be tied.

"How's it going?" Lily quietly asked.

He threw his hands in the air. "With Sampson on the boat..." He paused. "Sorry ma'm. Your husband is a good owner, better than most, but with him on the boat, the captain has ordered all this extra food and wants all these complicated dishes. I got these geese I gotta cook up and strawberries I'm supposed to make into some dessert."

"How many pie pans have you got?" Lily asked.

"I don't know, maybe seven." He pointed over to a corner.

"Do you have any rhubarb?" She asked.

"Yeah, how'da know?" Cook looked perplexed.

"Not from Maine, are you?" she smiled and grabbed some lard and flour.

He shook his head and started clearing a space for her.

It took her three and a half hours but at the end she had seven beautiful, strawberry rhubarb pies. She had to admit, they looked good enough to eat.

Kurt had been standing silently in the doorway for most of the time while she and the cook chatted away. She had learned all the gossip on almost every crew member and the captain. She hadn't seen Kurt eat anything but he was staring fixedly at the pies. She took the small ball of remaining dough and the little of the filling left and popped it in the oven. Feeling the blast of heat, reminded her of how hot and sweaty she was, spending the afternoon in front of a hot stove.

"Kurt, would it be possible to have a bath brought to the room. I'm a mess."

"Yes ma'am. I'll be back in just a minute." He left.

"He actually speaks." Lily muttered more to herself but she heard Cook chuckle.

"He does but that was the politest sentence I may've ever heard him utter. Not much for being friendly but he's tougher than most and loyal to the bone. He'd give his life for you because you're the boss's wife." Cook nodded his head to emphasize his words and Lily pondered them. She couldn't have spent the day with two more opposite men. Cook seemed to say whatever came into his head while Kurt barely spoke.

"He's been grumpier than normal lately though." Cook waved a knife to emphasize his point.

"Why is that?" Lily asked genuinely curious about the man.

"Sailor a few months ago, got in a tiff with Kurt, took a knife to his pillow. Kurt loved that thing, don't know why. Anyway Kurt thrashed the guy to a bloody pulp. The guy, can't remember his name, left shortly after." Cook shrugged.

Lily wondered what the significance of the pillow was. A lost love? "Would you mind is I used the goose feathers tomorrow?" She asked Cook.

"Sure, take em. And thanks for your help today. I couldn't have done it without you and it sure was nice to have company."

"It was my pleasure, thanks for sharing your kitchen." She reached down and pulled her mini pie out of the oven. Kurt walked back into the kitchen.

"Your bath is ready." He turned to lead her back to the room.

"Wait." She turned and slid the pie onto a plate. "This is for you." She handed him the plate. "You haven't eaten all day." She smiled and left the plate in his hands as she walked back to her room.

She quietly heard him utter. "Thank you."

Chapter 22

After a bath, Lily dressed her hair and put one of the dresses Eric had gotten for her own. She felt so much better and was growing excited as the evening approached. Eric walked in looking tired. He gave her a genuine smile and then he sat on the bed to strip off some of his clothes. She sat down next to him. "How was your day?"

Instead of answering, he wrapped his arms around her and kissed her. "Better now." He kissed her again until she was breathless. "How about you?"

"Very good thank you." She smiled and he looked slightly surprised.

"You weren't too bored?" Eric turned to look at her face to read her expression.

"Oh no. I kept myself busy." She answered evasively. She didn't want him to tell her that she had to stay in the room or that she shouldn't be doing work.

"Doing what?" He asked, not letting it go.

"Some sewing and a little cooking." He looked at her with one eyebrow raised but said nothing else as he began to bathe and dress.

They had dinner with the Captain, First Officer, and Kurt and the conversation was slightly stilted. She hadn't heard any hint as to what they had planned that day and there seemed to be little else to talk about. They exhausted commenting on the weather, the sea, and the Coast of New England. She was extremely relieved when dinner was finished. She was hoping to speak with Eric privately about what plans they had made that day.

Lily sat quietly as two of the pies were brought in by Cook, the rest were for the crew. The Captain looked extremely surprised and turned to Cook. "Impressive!"

"Don't get used to it." Cook said looking slightly offended. "I didn't bake 'em, she did."

"You baked two pies today?" Eric raised an eyebrow.

"She didn't bake two pies." The Cook slapped the two pies on the table and Lily tried to catch his eye to tell him to stop but he wasn't paying attention. "She baked like eight of 'em, which the men ate every bite of, you'd think I never cook 'em anything. And she sewed a sail today, you'd think Venus had stepped on the boat the way they're singing her praises."

The Captain cleared his throat. "Thank you Cook, that will be all." Lily was looking in her lap suddenly embarrassed by the praise and slightly nervous as to what Eric and Captain White would think of her getting involved in daily ship life.

Cook nodded then turned back, "Come back tomorrow, if you want." He smiled and winked at her then left.

"You were busy today." Eric looked at his wife, sounding slightly amused.

"I hope it's alright. I'm not very good at sitting idly and there seems to be so much work to do." She looked from the Captain to her husband, hoping to get some clue by the look on their faces.

"It can't hurt that you're winning over the crew." The Captain nodded, looking longingly at the pie.

"Next time, please check with me first." Eric smiled slightly then turned to Captain White. "Shall we?"

Everyone ate in silence and Lily felt herself growing more nervous. Were they that angry with her? Finally, his pie all gone, Eric spoke. "Where did you learn to cook like that?"

Her face broke into a huge smile, lighting up her entire face. "I mentioned, I'm not good at sitting idly. I spent a great deal of time during my childhood under the cook's feet or following the maids around. My mother encouraged it. She said it's good for a mistress to understand the jobs of her staff and I'm sure she preferred it to me trying to follow my brothers around." She smiled again and heard the men around her chuckle.

"Are you planning on cooking again tomorrow?" Captain White asked looking slightly hopeful.

"I don't know. The cook looked a little put out. Besides, I have a sewing project in mind, that I can do without getting in the way of the crew." Eric nodded as she finished.

Kurt had remained silent and was on his third piece of pie. Finally he spoke. "I haven't had pie like this in twenty years. At least not since this afternoon."

"You cooked extra pie for Kurt? Where was my pie this afternoon?" Eric said looking, not put out, but pleased.

She laughed in response and he gave her a small kiss on the cheek which made her blush.

They soon left and returned to their room. As soon as they were back in the room, Eric began to kiss her neck.

She laughed and pushed him lightly away. "Tell me what happened today."

"You mean like, a little cooking and sewing?" He gave her a one sided smile.

She laughed again. "Sorry about that, I didn't know how you would react. My mother was always full of mischief, I seem to be growing more like her by the day."

"It's alright. Captain White is very good at strategy and we are trying to form plans for every scenario. We want to have a shell in place that will combat almost any set of circumstances." Lily sat on the bed. Even after a day, she had begun to relax and feel safer. The reality of her situation, however, came crashing back to her.

Eric sat down on the bed next to her and wrapped his arms around her. "I am going to keep you safe. I have a cousin who is a duke. If we have to, we'll head to England. There is nothing like a castle to keep you safe."

Lily chuckled despite herself and she felt her spirits lift a little. He kissed her forehead and pulled her into his lap. "I really mean it. I am not going to let anything happen to you."

She nestled close to him. "You told me that your work really suffered when you first married Caitlin. I'm afraid I am even worse!"

He laughed and gave her a squeeze. "You're worth it."

Lily woke the next morning, feeling like she had never slept so well in her life. The sun was already high in the sky and Eric had left. She got up and dressed and headed to the galley for some breakfast and the start of her next project. She grabbed some shirts that they had used on the trail and brought them with her for her next project.

She greeted Cook and was glad that he didn't seem to be holding a grudge. Lily boiled the shirts then took the large bag of feathers. She hung the shirts up to dry then found a shady spot on the deck and began the tedious process of going through the feathers. She had to find only the softest and most flexible feathers to use as stuffing and discard the larger ones. It took her most of the morning but by the time she was done, she had enough feathers for a decent sized pillow.

Just as Lillian was about to leave for lunch, two of the sailors rushed up to her, one bleeding from his upper arm. "M'am, can ya stitch him, he's bleedin' real bad!"

She stood up from her chair looking at Kurt, who had been keeping silent guard. "Can you find me some thread?"

He nodded once and disappeared, coming back with a bag of sewing supplies. She looked at him. "Captain got it when he heard there'd be a lady on the boat."

Lily nodded, cut some thread and quickly thread the needle. The sailor was bleeding heavily and time was of the essence. Her hand shook a little but she took a deep breath to calm herself then began to stitch him up as best she could. Lily tried to keep the stitches tight without hurting the man too much. When she had finally finished, she tore some strips from the shirts she had just cleaned and wrapped the man's arm.

"Thank ya kindly m'am." He was looking a little pale. She sat him down in her chair, then sent the other sailor to get some food for his friend.

"You just sit and relax. He'll be back in a minute." She

194

patted his good arm. "Can I get you a drink of water?" She asked, unsure of what to do.

"He'll be fine after a good night's sleep." Kurt said, but his voice was gentle. She nodded, still patting the sailor's arm as she waited for the other man to return with some food.

After she had sent the man off to rest, Lillian sat stuffing the feathers into the bag she had made from what was left of the shirts. She thought about starting the embroidery on the last seam but decided that her nerves were too shaken up. She was horrible enough at embroidery without adding in extra distraction. She stood at the rail, Kurt beside her, watching the sun set.

"It's so beautiful." She sighed.

"It's been a long time since I sat and watched the sun set." He added as much to himself as to her.

"Tomorrow, if you have something you want to do, I can just take my embroidery with me. It will take me a while." She added, knowing how difficult it must be to stand behind her all day.

"It's alright, this is practically a vacation. You talked a lot with the cook but you don't seem to need conversation. It's kind of nice to just stand and think my thoughts." Kurt paused for a minute then added. "You're awfully kind to the men. Lots of women of your station wouldn't be so nice to common sailors."

She laughed and he looked slightly offended so she added. "I am not laughing at you. My family has had very little money the last few years and I spend of a great deal of time doing chores that these sailors would turn their nose up to."

Kurt laughed too. "Ain't nothin' wrong with that. But I see your point." They watched the sun set for a few more minutes in silence then Kurt added. "I didn't care for the last Missus much and I was expecting to not like you either, bein' so beautiful and all, I'm glad Mr. Sampson found a woman of quality, who is not afraid of a little work."

Lily thanked him, knowing that it was praise of the

highest quality, coming from a man who rarely shared his feelings.

"What are you two chatting about?" Eric came up behind them, placing his arm around his wife.

"I was just telling your new wife that I admire her work ethic and her character." With that Kurt turned and left.

"What on Earth did you do to him in two days? That is more words of praise then I have heard him utter in fifteen years." Eric stood with his mouth slightly open, watching Kurt retreat.

"I don't know." Lily responded, slightly mystified. She tried to think of what she had done. "I stitched up a sailor today who cut his arm. Baked some pies. Sewed a sail. Oh, I am making a pillow." She shrugged. It didn't seem to add up.

"Well, I'll have to ask him tomorrow. For now, we are off to our room for dinner and bed." He gave a crooked smile and the two headed for another night of bliss.

Chapter 23

The days on the ship passed quickly as The Anna Marie made deliveries down and then up the east coast of America. Lily kept herself busy making her pillow. She wished several times that Elise was there to help her and frequently took breaks by helping Cook out in the kitchen, although she tried hard to just assist him rather than making any dishes as high profile as the pies. The men noticed the difference in the food anyway and there was talk among them that they should make a few additional stops before returning to Boston so as to delay the trip.

They had stopped in New York, Eric grumbling about his family finding him. He seemed to breathe easier once they left but Lily felt herself growing more apprehensive as they approached the Boston Harbor. She didn't want their time on the boat to end. Not only was she frightened about her kidnappers finding her again but she had a growing fear about rejoining society. Before they had left, Eric had been so distant. Since they had been away, they had grown closer and had established a relationship that Lily was coming to depend on. She wondered which couple they would be when they returned. She did not even know if he planned to announce their wedding or pretend they were simply engaged. Would she live with her husband or go back with her brother? It was time to talk to Eric but it was not a conversation she relished.

As evening approached, Lily felt herself growing more

apprehensive and Kurt noticed her nervousness.

"What's stuck in your craw?" He finally asked as they watched the sun go down.

"I..." she paused unsure if she should confide in her husband's guard. She had grown to like Kurt but his loyalties were not to her.

"Nervous about headin' into Boston?" Kurt asked and she nodded. "Can I ask you a question?" She nodded again. In the two weeks she had been on the boat, Kurt had not asked her to volunteer a single piece of information. "How did you convince Sampson to marry you? I woulda thought that he would never marry another woman again, after that she-devil. I mean, I can see why he picked you, you're a cut above, but even with all your qualities, I didn't think it was a hurdle he'd ever clear."

Lily stood open mouthed. She knew that it had been a rocky road for Eric but she hadn't put it together that he might have been scared off of marriage. A comment he had made about feeling too strongly about her to court her drifted back into the fore-front of her mind. Could Eric have avoided her because he was frightened?

"I don't know Kurt, to be honest, for a while he seemed to avoid me like the plague. At least, most of the time." Kurt chuckled, he knew what she meant. She remembered Eric stealing kisses when no one was looking. "But when Colonel Kingsley tried to make me his wife, I think it changed Eric's mind."

"Well, provided we all get out of this unscathed, you'll have to thank the Colonel." Kurt chuckled and Lily suddenly burst out laughing. She hadn't thought of it that way but Kurt had a point.

"What is so funny? In fifteen years, I don't think Kurt has ever made me laugh like that. Should I be worried about you two?" Eric came up behind them laughing as well.

Lily gave her husband an angelic grin. Kurt excused himself and she turned to Eric.

"I wanted to talk to you before we docked." She asked, screwing up her courage. "When we arrive in Boston are we married or engaged?"

Eric smiled slightly, kissing her temple. "If you think, I am going to let you go back to your brother's house, while I sleep in bed alone, you are mistaken. Actually, I think I'll move some or all of your family in temporarily to have as many men on hand as I can."

She smiled, suddenly feeling better about their relationship and what she could expect when they returned. It didn't seem as though things would return to the way they had been before her kidnapping. She had another question, though, that had been nagging at the back of her mind?

"What were you talking to Kathryn about when I was kidnapped?" She looked into his faced as it darkened considerably.

"You, of course. She said I was a fool to remarry and that you would bring me nothing but trouble. I wouldn't have listened to what she had to say except she told me that she had information about Kingsley's plan and that she could help me protect you. I should have known that it was a trap. But both sisters have a gift when it comes to lying but I wanted to keep you safe and..." He stopped squeezing her. "It was miscalculation that almost cost me you."

"Eric, you can't keep blaming yourself. It was out of your control." She stood on tiptoe and kissed his cheek. "I have one more question," she took a deep breath and one of Eric's eyebrows arched at the buildup. "Why didn't you want to court me?" The hurt was evident in her voice, although she had tried to keep it out. She felt like she understood but for some reason it was important to hear an explanation from him.

Eric stepped back from her and leaned against the rail and Lily wished she could take the question back. "I know I told you that Caitlin had a great deal of public affairs. I didn't discuss the emotional manipulation, the lies, the deceit that went with my marriage. I promised myself that I would never play another woman's fool. I planned to remarry again, only to provide a mother for Toby. I wanted someone I could remain emotionally detached from. From the first moment I met you, it was obvious you were different from Caitlin. And every time I saw you, you proved how different you were but I just couldn't bring myself to trust my feelings again. I knew I couldn't remain detached from you."

He stood up and hugged her again. She wrapped her arms around him, glad that she asked. "Why did you change your mind?"

"Well, you are difficult to resist. Those eyes, those lips and god, the honey hair, I already told you that I dream about the way you smell. And all those men were swarming around you and I kept thinking, she is going to be someone else's wife, he is going to hold her every night and she is going to have his children and there I will be with a woman I don't care about."

"You thought about me?" She smiled her whole face lighting up. "I thought for sure you didn't care about me at all."

"How could you think that? Of course, the Colonel's interference pushed things along. I am not sure how long it would have taken me otherwise. Although after our night in the study, I was pretty close to caving. Then I really knew what I was missing. Every time I could get you alone, I couldn't keep my hands off of you." Eric squeezed her again. "Still can't."

She laughed too. "But you never called. I assumed you weren't interested. And here I spent five years daydreaming about you."

"You did, huh." He looked down at her, his eyes darkening with desire and she felt her own pulse quicken. "I think it is time for us to head to our room Mrs. Sampson." Lily smiled back at her husband, her heart full. It was satisfying to know that he had always wanted her. One of these days, she would get the courage up to tell him how much she loved him. In the meantime, this was enough. As they turned to leave, the lookout sharply called.

"Ship on the starboard bow."

Kurt reappeared in an instant and Eric kissed her hard on the lips then let go of her as Kurt took her arm. "Be safe. Listen to Kurt." He turned to join the Captain. She wanted to call out that she loved him, that she would always love him, but words failed her and Kurt was steadily propelling her below deck. As they entered the cargo area, Kurt began to whisper instructions to her.

"We're hiding you in a cargo crate. There are supplies in there, air holes and a chamber pot. If anyone comes down to the cargo area, do not put your eye up to the hole, they'll see ya. Stay at least a foot back. Do not move. Keep your mouth covered with your hand, it'll keep ya from accidentally screaming. Whatever happens, do not give yourself away. You'll defeat the whole purpose of hidin' ya. I'm gonna close you in. Whatever you do, don't let em know where ya are."

"Do you think the ship is dangerous?" Lily was growing more worried.

"Well could be just another vessel but they have clearly set an intercept course." Steering her behind a crate, Kurt placed her inside a good sized box, and then began nailing it closed. "Remember what I said. No matter what happens, don't give yourself away."

Kurt finished nailing the box closed then whispered, "I'll be right over there." With that, he walked away and Lily sat in the dark crate. She made a mental note to start asking her husband more questions and let him distract her less. She would like to be prepared for these situations when they arose rather than surprised.

They sat for what seemed like hours but suddenly, she heard voices drifting down towards her. She could only see a small portion of Kurt's knee out of one of the holes in the front of the box but she could hear everything.

"You're not fooling me Sampson. I know she is on this boat and we can search it, if you don't turn her over." Lily distinctly heard Colonel Kingsley's voice.

Eric paused then said casually, "She isn't on the boat. She left with her brother. Could be anywhere by now."

"You are lying and we will turn this boat upside down to find her if we have to." The Colonel almost yelled.

"We don't let pirates raid our ship." She heard Kurt's voice taunt the Colonel. The Colonel turned and sneered where Kurt was sitting.

Eric stopped directly in her line of sight and she covered

her eyes as Kurt directed. "Where is your warrant? Last time I checked you couldn't just take cargo or people off a ship without one." Eric shrugged, looking unconcerned.

Colonel Kingsley turned back to Eric. "Still have your muscle around I see. I won't need a warrant when I tell the general you are hiding English soldiers on this ship."

"But what will he say when he hears of all your outstanding warrants?" Eric smirked and the Colonel suddenly drew a gun and pointed it at Eric's chest. Lily gasped into her hand and was suddenly thankful of Kurt's direction to cover it. She briefly considered pounding on the crate to distract Kingsley but remembered Kurt's instructions. How could she just sit in this crate and watch her husband be shot? Eric, meanwhile looked unconcerned and hadn't even flinched. Kurt suddenly stepped into her view with a gun at Kingsley's back.

"I wouldn't fire if I were you." Kurt said in a low growl.

She heard several other hammers on other guns click back and she knew that everyone she couldn't see had also drawn their guns. What she didn't know was who was there and which side they were on.

"I told ya she's alive." Lily clearly heard Slim's voice and her blood ran ice cold. "Tracker's responsible, he probably hid her."

Another familiar voice rang in her ears. "She wasn't with them when I met them on the trail. Maybe Tracker helped her meet up with them later." Lieutenant Colonel Andrews added, sounding slightly nervous. Clearly, he was trying to cover his mistake.

Eric smirked. "If you want to know how she escaped. You should talk to your man Slim. He knows all about it."

"Bastard!" Slim roared charging at Eric. Another sailor's fist clocked Slim in the jaw, sending him crashing to the floor.

A small smile broke out on Lily's face. But Kingsley suddenly glanced at her crate and she stopped cold, closing her eyes, so that they couldn't be seen. She didn't even breath.

"Maybe I should pay a visit to James then." The Colonel turned suddenly and several set of feet followed.

She heard Andrews say. "I still haven't seen her."

Eric turned and followed, and only Kurt remained. He waited several minutes then she heard him whisper, "Just a few more minutes."

She closed her eyes and waited until she heard footsteps return then suddenly, Kurt was prying the side off of her crate.

"Thank God you're alright. I was so frightened." Lily threw her arms around her husband as soon as she was free.

He wrapped his arms around her, burying his face in her hair. "You did wonderfully but it's not over I'm afraid. We are in a race to the harbor now. I have to warn your brother that Kingsley is on his way and I have to find a way to safely get you off this boat." He gently stroked a curl that had fallen around her face.

"Do I have to wear men's clothes again?" She wrinkled her nose and both men chuckled despite the situation.

"I haven't decided yet. But whatever it is, you probably will not like it." He kissed her one more time then started propelling her towards the deck. "Let's go talk to Captain White."

They emerged out on deck to find the crew busy at work. The other ship was almost a speck on the horizon and Lily began to worry about her brother. Captain White could see the anxiety on her face. "Don't worry. We'll catch him."

"The larger problem is how we are going to get you off the ship." Eric grimaced but Lily was glad to finally be part of the dialogue.

"We could take her off in the crate." Kurt suggested.

"Or put her in sailor's clothes." The Captain added.

"They will be expecting both and both leave Lily too vulnerable." Eric ran his hand through his hair.

An idea suddenly struck Lily. "What if we make it look like you are smuggling me off in a crate but really you and I slip off the boat while they are removing the crate?"

"A diversion!" Captain White nodded his approval.

"We would simply blend into the crowd." Lily was becoming excited about her plan.

"I don't know." Eric frowned. "If they find us out, we have little protection."

"I'll follow ya." Kurt added. "Just to make sure you make it safely."

They flushed out the plan and the crew began to make preparations for the rouse. A man was being dispatched to the Carter's home to bring the family to Eric's house. While it would be easier for Eric and Lily to go to her family, it was agreed that Eric's house was both larger and more easily defended with a larger staff.

As the couple walked back to their room, Lily felt her apprehension growing. There were so many variables, any of which could go wrong. She had so many things that she wanted to say to her husband but she was afraid.

Eric closed the door behind them and Lily turned to face him. "Eric, I want to say something..."

Eric stopped her. "We only have an hour then we'll be in the harbor. Let's save the difficult conversation for when we are tucked into our home."

She smiled at the thought of it being their home. "I don't want to have a difficult conversation! Well it's a little difficult for me but..."

He interrupted her again. Wrapping his arms around her, he kissed her hard. She felt her body responding to his passion and he began to undo her buttons. "We have to change you anyway." He smiled as he kissed her and her dress fell into a heap on the floor. She couldn't explain why but the events of the evening had sparked a passion inside her, a need to be a little reckless.

She had wanted to tell him how much she loved him but she decided that perhaps she would show him first. Lily stepped away from him sitting on the bed she held out each foot for him to unbutton her shoes. Then, smiling, she reached under her petticoat and pulled her pantaloons off. Lily put her foot onto the bed and slipped one stocking off then the other. She gave him a playful push as she loosened her petticoat and slipped it off. She could see his eyes darkening with every piece of clothing that she took off. After two weeks of being his wife, she had lost a great deal of her bashfulness and she wanted to show off. She did a little spin in nothing but her corset as Eric stripped off his shirt and undid his pants, following Lily with his eyes.

He reached for her but she danced just out of his reach and the game of cat and mouse added an extra sway to her hips and pout to her mouth. She smiled coyly.

"Lily." Eric growled her name. "Come here."

Lily giggled and danced just out of his reach again. She wasn't sure why, but she wanted him to chase her a little. It made her feel desirable. She turned away from him then turned her face back towards him. "Come get me."

He growled deep in his throat as he lunged for her, wrapping his arms around her waist. Their bodies melded together as he began to kiss the back of her neck while running his hands from her neck to her thigh and then back again. Shortly, she was breathless and she felt her legs sliding open to allow him to enter. He quickly did just that, placing one hand on her breast and the other between her legs. She moaned, unable to control herself it felt so intense.

As Eric quickened the pace, Lily felt herself climbing and she leaned back against her husband for support. He groaned into her ear and she reached back to wrap her arms around his neck. "I love you." She had been thinking the words, but didn't realize she had said them out loud until she heard herself. She felt herself climax as Eric roared in her ear.

Eric quickly pulled out of her and picked her up, carrying her to the bed. He settled onto them onto the bed and wrapped her in his arms.

Lily was suddenly feeling incredibly shy about the way she acted but more so about what she had said. She said nothing and neither did Eric as the silence between them lengthened. Was it better to ignore it or explain her feelings? She was deep in the thought when she heard the soft but distinct sound of snoring. Eric had fallen asleep!

"Eric. Are you asleep?" She gave him a small shake.

"Mmmm." He snuggled her closer.

"Wake up. We have to get dressed and leave soon."

Here she was agonizing over her words and he had fallen asleep!

"I'm awake." Eric murmured when a knock came at the door.

"Fifteen minutes." Kurt's voice cut through the silence and Eric jerked awake.

He gave her a lopsided smile. "Sorry about that, I haven't been getting much sleep. Some little vixen has been keeping me awake." He nuzzled her neck. "You were amazing."

She blushed and pushed him away. Jumping off the bed, she went to the wardrobe to pull out a skirt and blouse. They had agreed that more modest clothes would help them to better blend in.

Eric came up behind her. "Are you alright?"

Nodding, she continued to get dressed.

"Are you upset that we didn't have that conversation?" Eric rubbed her back as he asked.

"No, I'm fine." Was all she could mumble. She didn't sound fine even to her own ears.

"Nervous?" He tried again. Lily had to appreciate him trying to figure out what was wrong but she couldn't believe that he didn't know. She had told him that she loved him and he had not responded, had never told her that he loved her. It stunned her to realize that he was her whole world.

"If something happens to me, I just want you to know that I am happy with the time that we had. It has been amazing and..." Lily stopped when Eric grabbed her by the shoulders and spun her around.

"Nothing is going to happen to you, I won't let it." He was squeezing her arms rather tightly.

"Eric, you're hurting me." Lily cringed and recognition dawned on his face as he let her go and wrapped her into a hug.

"Sorry Sweetheart. Once I have you safely in my house, surrounded by your family, I will breathe a little easier." Eric gave her a gentle squeeze then helped her finish dressing.

Chapter 24

They met the crew, out on deck as the boat stealthily glided into the harbor. It was midnight and the water front was dead quiet. Lily felt the butterflies rising up in her stomach and she hoped that her plan was a good one. Maybe Colonel Kingsley wouldn't even try to stop her but then again, he had boarded their ship when he himself was a wanted man.

The men moved silently off the boat, retrieving, and then loading several of the smaller crates into dinghies. Lily and Eric lay down next to a few crates in the bottom of one of the small boats as two sailors silently rowed to shore. It was cramped but Lily held still. Kurt was two boats behind them. They had intentionally separated to draw attention away from them. The boats pulled up to the peer and a wagon was backed up to the edge of the shore. As crates were being unloaded, Lily and Eric crept behind the pile of crates. Four men began to move two of the larger crates and the couple crept between them and inched down the peer. They climbed under the wagon as the crates were loaded in. The sailors went back to get the rest of the crates. Lily could feel her heart hammering in her chest.

Eric squeezed her hand. "Don't worry. They won't attack until the wagon is out of sight of the ship. Kingsley won't want to risk it."

Finally the wagon began to slowly move and Lily and Eric crawled along underneath it. Lily could feel her legs cramping but she grit her teeth. Shortly, the group entered into an alleyway and Eric motioned to her that it was time. They slipped out from under the wagon and the sailors adjusted their movements to make them as invisible as possible. They slipped in between two buildings. The plan was to let the wagon continue on as they found a path to another street. They would stay in the shadows until they could find a cab for hire. They moved further back between the buildings a noise made them both stop cold.

"Halt. You are under orders from the United States Military." It became immediately clear that the soldiers were not talking to them but to the sailors transporting the empty crates. "What have you got in those crates?"

"Special delivery. It has to arrive first thing in the morning. We just arrived." One of the sailors responded. Lily saw a shadow moving towards them and she tugged on Eric's arm but he squeezed her gently and she quickly realized that it was Kurt.

The three of them moved deeper between the building as Lily could hear the soldiers begin searching the crates. She did not hear the Colonel and at first she was relieved.

"No Kingsley." Kurt added grimly, confirming her thoughts.

"Do you think he's waiting for us or off the to the Carter's?" Eric asked, sounding equally grim.

"He could have fled. I don't know if word has spread that he is a wanted man but it will soon." Kurt didn't sound like he believed it. They came out from the alley onto another street and crept in the shadows for several blocks. It was extremely late and there were no hansoms about.

As the night grew later, Lily felt herself growing more and more exhausted. They had been walking for forty five minutes. Her only saving grace was that they had seen very few people and had been able to duck into cover whenever they did.

"How much longer do you think we will have to walk?" Lily asked, trying not to sound too exhausted.

"Maybe half an hour." Eric was scanning the street in front of them when he suddenly pulled her into the shadows.

Kurt stepped behind a tree when Lily heard what the two men already had noticed, a wagon approaching.

It was led by two soldiers on horseback and Lily didn't need to see the occupant to know that it was the Colonel. He was heading directly for Eric's home and she knew that he would be setting up an ambush. Her shoulders slumped. "What do we do?"

Eric waited until he could hear no more then they continued walking. "We keep our eyes and ears open." Eric quickened their pace and Lily felt her heart hammering in her chest. She worked as hard as she could to keep up but she could feel her strength weakening and she was slowing their pace. Eric picked her up and slung her on his back without breaking stride, in fact, they seemed to be going faster. She smiled into his hair and hung on.

They turned onto Beacon Hill from a side road, 200 feet from Eric's front door. Even she could see the men in the shadows across from the house. What surprised her however was how many lights were on in the home. Kurt melted into the shadows and Lily and Eric crouched down, between two neighboring homes. They sat down and Eric pulled her into his lap. She leaned against him and closed her eyes. Despite the danger, she could already feel herself drifting off. He stroked her hair. "Kurt is going to try to find a way in. He knows all the doors in the house. But otherwise we will wait them out." He whispered in her ear.

She nodded, glad to just be in his arms. She had just drifted off when a loud bang cut through the night. She jerked awake. From their limited view, she could see nothing but she could hear another wagon rolling down the street. Kurt's voice boomed out the front door. "You're loitering. If you don't leave, we will be forced to call the police."

A soldier responded. "We have reason to believe that you are hiding English soldiers on the premises."

The wagon that Lily heard rolled by them and she could clearly make out the faces of the sailors from the Anna Marie. Eric pulled her up, and the two dashed to the crew members, hoping onto the wagon. The wagon continued on but before it could reach the drive the Colonel's men halted its path. Lily's heart pounded in her chest as she saw Colonel Kingsley and Lieutenant Colonel Andrews step into view behind the men.

She was surrounded by men but she could see Andrews and Kingsley searching for her. Eric held her tighter. "Step aside. You're blockin' the street." One of the sailors called.

Kingsley smirked, his eyes had finally found her. "Well hello Miss Carter. It's lovely to see you again. As always, you are a difficult woman to track down."

Lily said nothing and she looked down as Andrews studied her face. It was Eric who spoke, not to the Colonel but to Kurt. "Have you sent for the police?"

"Yes sir." Was all Kurt said as he moved down the driveway with several men behind him.

"I want to know the game." The Colonel had not taken his eyes off of her. "Is it still Miss Carter or have you become Mrs. Sampson?"

Lily still did not respond but looked back at her husband instead. "You'll have to wait until tomorrow to find out." Eric casually answered. The soldiers had not moved and Lily could see that they would come to blows soon.

"Do you want to end this now Kingsley?" Eric looked at the other man levelly. Kurt and what looked like seven other men, holding guns of some sort, reached the end of the drive. The soldiers were flanked on two sides.

"You are prepared, Sampson, I'll give you that. I think you have the advantage here." Kingsley had barely taken his eyes off of her and she felt herself growing restless under his gaze.

"It's nice to finally meet you, Miss Carter." Lieutenant Colonel Andrews had also fixed his eyes on her and she shrunk back into Eric. Tracker had taught her not to speak to her attackers and she thought it was appropriate now, it might only provoke them.

"She ain't normally this quiet. She's kind of a yapper. Most women are I guess." Slim spit and shrugged. It was the first time Lily had had a chance to see and be seen by Slim and she felt the bile rise in her throat. If she had a gun in her hand she knew what she would do with it.

It was then that she broke her silence. "You should keep better company Colonel. It can't be good to have men who double cross you in your employ."

A cold smile touched the Colonel's lips. "I should like to hear more about it, perhaps you could tell me sometime."

"Slim can tell you himself. I hear it isn't the first time." She turned her gaze toward Slim who had gone pale.

"But it would be so much more interesting coming from you." Eric's arm came down over her shoulder and wrapped around her torso while she held onto his arm. She rubbed her hand up his arm and gave it a squeeze. His other hand touched her cheek and she leaned into it.

It was Eric who then responded. "If you would excuse us Colonel. It is late. As fun as this is, perhaps we should continue it some other time."

Andrews was staring intently at her and he took a half step closer. She wondered if he had made the connection between her and Billy.

"Another time." Kingsley nodded and the wagon began to back away as the soldiers melted into the night.

Kurt approached them then the group proceeded up the driveway. Eric hopped off the wagon and Kurt began to furiously whisper in his ear. She saw Eric's shoulder's drop and she began to worry, first about her own safety then about her families. Finally, she could no longer stand it. "What is it?"

Eric grimaced as he looked at her. "My mother is here."

"Oh." For a brief moment she was relieved that it was not serious. She looked down at herself, however, and realized that she was dressed in a very plain clothes and had been awake all night. Eric had told her that his mother was extremely tough and that she had not liked Caitlin. What would the sister of a duke think of the woman her son had married on a boat after a kidnapping? This was horrible.

Eric helped her down from the wagon and held her hand as they approached the door. The look on her face said it all and even Eric chuckled slightly. "Is it as bad as I think?" She asked softly.

"Worse." He grimaced then smiled. "Don't worry.

She'll love you."

Lily knew that he was lying and she braced herself as they entered through the front door. It was a strange feeling. She had only been here once before but it was technically her home. The entry was quiet and she felt herself breathe a sigh of relief. Perhaps she had been granted a reprieve until the morning.

At the top of the stairs, two people appeared. A younger man, who looked strikingly like Eric, and an older woman, who even in her night dress, appeared extremely regal.

"Hello Mother. Kyle. It is wonderful to see you both. To what do I owe this pleasure?" Eric held her right hand in his and wrapped his arm around her waist.

"What the devil is going on?" His mother's voice pierced the entry hall as she began to descend the stairs.

"What do you mean Mother?" Eric looked at his mother levelly.

"I get a letter no more than three sentences long that you are engaged and getting married at the end of the summer and I arrive to find you gallivanting all over the East Coast with a parcel of soldiers to greet you, explain yourself?" She stopped on the last step so that her eyes were level with her sons.

"Mother, I would like you to meet Mrs. Lillian Carter Sampson, my wife." Eric nodded towards her. "Lily, this is my mother, Mrs. Victoria Sampson."

"How do you do, Mrs. Sampson?" Lily curtsied, feeling herself blush under the woman's scrutiny.

The other woman did not respond but turned back to her son. "Well?"

"Mother, I am a grown man I owe you no explanation." And Eric began to steer them both down the hall. They entered what was clearly his office and his mother was forced to follow. Eric poured himself a drink, then sat in his chair, motioning for Lily to take a chair just off to his right. She obliged. Mrs. Sampson stood in the doorway for a moment. She appeared to be surveying the situation then she too crossed the room and sat in a chair directly in front of the desk. Kyle followed behind them sitting as well and finally, Kurt brought up the rear, standing in the back of the room. Mrs. Sampson turned to see who else had entered the room and for the first time addressed someone other than Eric.

"Wonderful as always Kurt. Were you on board with my son?" Kurt nodded. "Will you be heading back to the boat this evening?" Mrs. Sampson stared directly at the man. While Eric had moved them into his office, his mother still controlled the conversation.

"No ma'am. I reckon I'll be staying on dry land for a bit anyhow." Kurt, never one to mince words, did not do so now.

"Why is that?" One of Mrs. Sampson's eyebrows arched up but Kurt only nodded towards Eric.

"What do you want to know Mother?" Eric sighed and took a large swallow of his drink.

"Who is this girl? Why have you had a wedding that defies all social convention? Why did you not do me the courtesy of explaining any of it before?" Her lips pursed and Eric sighed again.

Eric ignored her questions. "First mother, Lily's family will be arriving shortly and I beg you not to voice your concerns about our marriage. James is disgruntled enough with me..."

"Disgruntled with you, whatever for? Any woman would be extremely lucky to marry into my family. Who is James?"

"James Carter is Lily's brother and guardian, and he feels, not without good reason, that I am to blame for many of Lily's current difficulties. He is also extremely unhappy with the time line, that was my choice, and feels that his sister would have been better married to someone else."

"I see. You have mentioned 'current difficulties.' Is a child on the way?" Mrs. Sampson pursed her lips.

"Any child will be nine months after our marriage Mother." Eric leaned forward looking angry.

"Then why would you marry such a woman..." Eric banged his hand on the desk.

"Mother, Lily is from a very respected family and I am lucky to have her hand over her many other suitors. The accelerated timeline is due to the interference of Colonel

Kingsley."

First surprise then an inkling of understanding crossed her face. "What does he want with a respectable girl?" Lily noted that Mrs. Sampson's word choice about her had changed dramatically.

"To marry her, of course. " Eric paused taking a deep breath. "Lily, on top of her many virtues, is an heiress. Her mother was Regina Lafeyette."

Mrs. Sampson looked abruptly at her then back at her son.

For the first time, Kyle spoke. "Who was that?"

Eric nodded at Lily. "My mother came from the Lafayette family of Boston and New York. She defied her father's wishes and married my father but she still retained much of her dowry. My father already had a successful business so some pieces of it he retained for my brothers and myself."

"Wait." Kyle's eyebrows shot up. "The Lafayette family?"

"What is your dowry?" Mrs. Sampson asked but her voice had softened.

"A piece of land on the harbor." Lily answered directly.

"And why did her brother agree to allow you to marry her so quickly?" Lily was shocked at Mrs. Sampson's change in attitude.

"He is not happy about it. The Colonel forced my hand by first degrading her reputation with rumors then, when I stepped in, attempting to kidnap her."

"He is a man who will use any means necessary." Mrs. Sampson nodded. "Why didn't you explain any of this before?"

"There has not been much time. I actually have a letter I wrote to you a short time ago with specific details and instructions. Perhaps tomorrow you can read it to fill in any other gaps. For now, Mother, we are exhausted and tomorrow, I have much to do." She nodded and stood, Lily did the same but she was beginning to feel light headed from the complete lack of sleep. Eric looked over at her and reached for her, tucking her next to him. She closed her eyes, wishing to collapse into bed. She pried her eyelids open to see Mrs. Sampson giving them a long look.

"Goodnight." Was all she said, then turned and left the room.

Kyle turned to his brother. "How did you do that?"

Eric merely smiled as the butler entered, amazingly in complete uniform, and announced that the Carters had arrived.

Chapter 25

Lily woke late the next morning, feeling completely exhausted still. She could have slept for another three hours but she knew that everyone else was awake and that they wanted to speak with her.

After a bath and being dressed, she felt slightly better but a knot of dread filled her at the thought of facing Mrs. Sampson and James at the same table.

She entered the dining room to find most of the family already through eating. The company seemed surprisingly cordial. Even James and Kurt seemed deep in conversation. Elise jumped up from the table and Lily felt her heart soar. The two women embraced.

"Thank goodness you are alright." Elise held her close.

"I missed you. How is Tom?" Lily felt herself drawing strength from her sister-in-law.

"Better. He and Danielle should be here shortly but we have scarcely seen them since he and James returned." Elise smiled and winked and Lily understood completely.

Ann stepped around from the table and Lily motioned her over, embracing the other woman as well. "I am so sorry that you couldn't find your aunt." Lily held her hand sympathetically.

"Thank you." Ann whispered. "I am lucky, though. At least I found you and your family."

"I am sorry to interrupt." Eric cleared his throat. "Lily

would you accompany me to my office."

Lily nodded and fell in line behind Eric, hopeful to have a few minutes alone with her husband. They had collapsed into bed last night and Eric had obviously gotten up a good deal earlier than her. She was disappointed, however, when first Kurt, then James, and finally Eric's mother fell in line behind them. Her shoulders drooped. This couldn't be good.

The group stepped into the office and Lily was struck by the magnificence of the room. While not overly large, there were subtle touches everywhere that spoke of the wealth of the owner. For some reason, it made Lily's mood more melancholy. She preferred the small room they had shared on the ship that was simple and intimate. She worried that here, the gap between them would be as large as it was before they had left.

Eric leaned against the desk and took Lilian's hand, drawing her up beside him. Kurt stood in the corner, while James and Mrs. Sampson sat in the wing back chairs on the other side of the desk.

"How was your honeymoon?" James smiled tightly, clearly on his best behavior.

"Very nice thank you." She smiled tensely back.

"I must say dear, you look lovely this morning. We must take you shopping for some additional clothes." Mrs. Sampson was also on her best behavior if she was offering to take her shopping. This was not the conversation she had expected.

"Precisely what we are here to talk about." Eric turned to her. "Kurt will be attending to you, much as he did on the ship, about the house. The police have been notified the Colonel is an outlaw and, although his ship has left the harbor, I assuming that this is not over. I don't think he will give up now. You are to go nowhere unescorted and keep trips as limited as possible. We will be attending a few social engagements to announce our marriage and put to rest any rumors about it. You shopping with my mother..."

Mrs. Sampson interrupted. "It would be good for us to be seen out together. It is a show of solidarity."

"I agree. We just have to make sure you are safe. In

addition, James has provided us with a story for the public. You left to visit your favorite aunt. Her dying wish was to see you married so we decided to marry in Maine before her death."

Lily nodded. She was feeling amazingly hungry and tired but she tried to focus. "When will we be shopping?" If they said today, she might cry. She was not sure that she was up for such a busy day.

"In a few days." Eric squeezed her hand as she went limp with relief. "I have a great deal to do today but your family is staying for a few days. My mother will help you settle into the house." He kissed her forehead and turned to sit behind his desk as James pulled his chair closer. She had been dismissed. She walked out the door and glanced back to see James and Eric poring over some papers. Kurt fell in line behind her and she returned to the dining room where she ate breakfast. Elise and Ann chatted and she did her best to participate. At least, she thought with a sigh, Elise could help her finish the embroidery on her pillow.

The day passed in a blur, ending with a large dinner. Lily excused herself shortly after to go to bed. She felt she needed to try to catch up on sleep. Her exhaustion seemed to be affecting her entire outlook. She had barely spoken to Eric and the large crowd of people seemed to command his attention. She felt disconnected and alone. She lay down on the bed to collect herself before undressing and fell sound asleep.

She had no idea how much time had passed when she felt someone roughly shaking her. "Lily wake up."

She lifted her head trying to figure out where she was and why Eric was shaking her. "What'sa matter, where'm I?" Her voice sounded slurred even to her. She was trying to clear the cobwebs in her mind but she couldn't.

"You're home." Eric's face was only inches from hers and she looked around confused. "At my house." he corrected.

"Oh." She tried to reason out his concern. "Why are you shaking me?"

"You are sprawled out on the bed completely dressed. Your maid attempted to wake you and you were unresponsive."

Eric looked angry.

"I'm just tired." She lay back down but Eric pulled her up and began unbuttoning her gown.

"I know you went to bed late but you slept until almost noon and you went to bed at 8:30. Are you feeling ill?" Eric had worked at the rest of the layers of her clothes. He pulled a night gown over her head and she began unpinning her hair. He started pulling pins out when there was a knock at the door.

"Is everything alright?" Kyle called.

"Fine." Eric said tersely.

Kyle poked his head in the door and Eric scowled at him as he pulled another pin out of her hair. "What was the problem?" Lily heard James call.

"For heaven's sake! I was just tired, I fell asleep. It has been an exhausting month!" She stood up. "Kyle, I am sure you are lovely but I do not need any more brothering. I am almost smothered as it is. I can't even go to bed apparently." Lily felt herself growing more and more annoyed.

She sat back down and began to rip the brush through her hair. James walked into the room and kissed the top of her head. "I love you." He turned and walked back out.

"No lectures?" Lily felt her anger dissipating but it had been a trying day and she wasn't ready to let it go.

"I don't think I need to do anymore lecturing, I will leave it to your husband. Besides, I think he is doing enough worrying for the both of us."

James and Kyle left and she turned to Eric. "How is it going to be?" She was exhausted and she couldn't mince words or pretend.

"What are you talking about?" Eric was clearly not in the best mood either.

"Before we left, I mean before I was kidnapped, we barely spoke or looked at each other, you didn't seem to like me very much. Are we going back to that?" She turned to look at him.

"How could you think that? Everything I am doing, including having our entire families in my hair, I am doing for you! I am only trying to keep you safe!" Eric gave her a black look.

Feeling instantly guilty, Lillian stood and wrapped her arms around her husband. "I'm sorry. I am feeling tired and irritable and I missed you today."

Eric smiled, his beautiful smile and whispered, "I missed you too." He scooped her up in his arms and carried her to bed. They made love intensely and desperately. Lily snuggled into her husband afterward and once again fell soundly asleep.

Two weeks passed in much the same routine. Lily was worried that she was getting ill. The stress of the past few months seemed to have finally caught up with her. With so much family around, she and Eric rarely spent any time together. She slept late, went to bed early, and ate ravenously. She was sure that she must have put all the weight on that she had lost.

The family was attending a ball that evening, one of the last of the summer, and Eric had asked her to try to make it down for breakfast so that he could talk to everyone about their plan for the evening. While the Colonel had fled the city, Lieutenant Colonel Andrews had stayed behind, and Eric feared it was to once again capture her. They had attended a limited number of social events to announce their marriage and publicly have the support of their families but each affair had been exhausting for Lillian and she was not looking forward to tonight.

She entered the dining room, as everyone was taking their seats, still feeling sleepy. Eric rose to kiss her forehead. As his lips passed overhead she inhaled the distinct odor of eggs Florentine that was placed at the end of the table. She felt the nausea rise in her chest. Her whole body went suddenly hot then cold. She covered her mouth and nose. She was sure she was turning absolutely green. Eric pulled back from her, a look of concern passing over his face.

"Lily, what is wrong?" His brow furrowed as he looked at her but all she could gasp was.

"Bucket!" As she doubled over.

James grabbed an empty bowl and stuck it under her face as Eric supported her torso and she emptied the contents of her stomach. She heard the groans and gasps behind her but she couldn't care.

Finally, Lily was done. Eric grabbed a napkin and swabbed her face. She felt immediately better but dared not smell. "Take the eggs away!" She gasped through her mouth, holding her nose.

"Are you alright, what's the matter?" Eric was scowling but everyone else at the table seemed to be smiling.

"Don't you know?" Mrs. Sampson smiled angelically at her son and Elise had tucked her head down to giggle. What was going on?

A servant started carrying the eggs away but Kyle stopped him. "We're not going to waste perfectly good eggs are we?"

Eric gave his brother a black look. "Take them away!" He held her close but she could feel him smiling on top of her head.

"Why is this so funny?" It was her turn to look less than amused.

"How are you feeling now?" Eric asked.

She looked at the table of food and her mouth began to water. "Hungry." Was all she could say when the whole room burst into laughter. Only Toby seemed to share her ignorance.

"Is Lily alright?" He asked a look of concern on his face.

"She's fine." Eric patted his son on the head. "You are going to have a little brother or sister."

Lily looked at her husband, completely stunned, as the pieces fell into place in her mind. He stroked her cheek and then whispered into her ear. "You had better go eat!"

She smiled back and headed down the table to dig in.

After the family had finished eating, they discussed that night's ball. While Eric would spend most of the evening with Lily, one of the three brothers would always be with them, in case Eric had to step away. In addition, two women would go with Lily whenever she needed to use the powder room. They would take several carriages, all looking alike, so that it would be difficult to tell which one Lily and Eric were in.

The family dispersed to begin their daily activities. Lily sat with Elise to finally finish the embroidery on her pillow. After lunch, she was feeling sleepy but now that Lily knew why she had been so tired, she decided to take Toby for a walk, instead of retiring to her room. Kurt looked relieved. He was clearly tired of standing outside her room all afternoon.

They spent a pleasant afternoon identifying flowers in the garden. Lily taught Toby the Latin names of several of the plants. He was a charming boy to be with and she found herself laughing a great deal. Finally, he was called in by his nanny and Lily sat on a nearby bench, exhausted.

Her eyes began to close and she thought she had better go inside and lay down. Suddenly she felt a hand on her shoulder and her eyes snapped open.

Mrs. Sampson was standing above her. "Are you alright?"

Lily smiled weakly, "Just sleepy."

"You should lie down before tonight." Lily nodded as her mother-in-law sat down next to her.

They sat in silence for a few minutes "Neither of my other sons are married. Kyle seems to despise the idea and Nate is completely indifferent. I was excited when Eric first told me he was marrying, but I didn't see eye to eye with Caitlin. I always thought she was more interested in Sampson money than Eric. You will have to forgive me for the way I acted the first night I met you. I was afraid that you were cut from the same cloth. It is obvious that you are not and that both my son and grandson love you."

Lily did not know what to say. It was very gratifying to hear but she wasn't sure that Mrs. Sampson was right. "Thank you. I appreciate your kind words and support. I...I love them more than anything." She answered honestly and Mrs. Sampson squeezed her hand before she departed.

The sun began to set in the sky but Lily sat pondering Mrs. Sampson's words. She wanted so badly to believe that Eric loved her, that she was as important to him as he was to her. She had lost track of time when another figure approached. In the sun, she would have sworn it was Eric. The broad set of his shoulders, the particular way that he moved. She smiled with her whole heart and stood to greet her husband.

"No wonder my brother is so crazy about you, that is quite a smile." Lily instantly realized her mistake. It was Kyle, not Eric, who approached. She sat down again, blushing with embarrassment.

"I'm sorry, I thought you were Eric." She floundered, unsure of what to say.

"No harm in smiling, although I knew you must have thought I was him. I have to warn you, Nate looks even more like him than I do." Kyle smiled an amazing smile of his own.

"I don't believe it!" Lillian laughed. "I must be careful who I smile at." Kyle chuckled in return.

"I'm glad that you and my brother are so happy. After Caitlin, I thought he might give up. It's nice to see him in love again." Kyle stretched out relaxed but Lily felt her whole body tense. This was the second family who had mentioned love.

"I thought your mother told me that you're opposed to love or is it just marriage?" Lily was not usually so forthright and she bit her lip at her words but Kyle only laughed.

"My mother would think so but I am not opposed to either. I'm just waiting for the right girl. When I meet her, I'm sure I'll act as crazy as my brother." Kyle glanced at her but stopped to stare and she realized that she must looked pained. "What's wrong?"

"I just... I didn't think our marriage... why do you think he's in love?" Lily finally just asked the question directly.

"Why, do you not feel that way?" Kyle sat up looking stunned.

"Of course I do, I just didn't think..." her voice trailed off.

Kyle suddenly rolled his eyes. "The man can't keep his hands or his eyes off you. He's been up and down the eastern seaboard to protect you, he spends every waking hour attempting to keep you safe, if he were any more in love, I think he might keel over and die. Why wouldn't you think he was in love?"

"He seemed to court everyone but me, he only married

me to save my reputation, and apparently for my dowry and he has never said it." She wasn't sure if it was pregnancy that had her answering so honestly, but she couldn't seem to stop herself from saying exactly what was on her mind.

Kyle laughed long and hard until tears ran down his face and Lily began to get annoyed. She stood to leave but Kyle pulled her down. "Wait, I'm sorry. I'm sure that Eric is having a difficult time sharing his feelings because of his first wife but sometimes I am amazed at how absurd he can be. I am sure, once all of this is behind you, that he will be very open about his feelings. But you have to know that they are there."

Lily said goodbye to Kyle, her head full of what he had said. Kurt escorted her inside. It was time to get ready for the ball. When they reached her room, she turned to Kurt. "Wait." She went into her room, Eric was waiting for her.

"There you are. I expected to find you sleeping." He smiled at her and she returned the smile but she held up her finger for him to wait for a moment. She grabbed the pillow she had finally finished and turned back to the door. Kurt was waiting on the other side.

She had tied a satin ribbon around it and, frankly, she was proud of the embroidery she had done. It was a complicated stitch and it had taken her a long time.

"Kurt, I wanted to thank you for helping me. This is for you." She held out the pillow for him but he didn't take it, he just looked at it a minute and Lily began to worry that he wouldn't accept it at all.

"How did you know about my sister's pillow?" Kurt's face was contorted in pain and Lily bit her lip, she had made a mistake.

"I didn't know, I just knew someone had destroyed a pillow of yours, I thought you would like a replacement. I'm sorry if I've offended you... I didn't mean..." Kurt cut her off by reaching his hands out and touching the embroidery.

"She made it for me before I set off on my first trip to sea. There never was a sweeter girl than her. She took after my mum I guess, but I don't remember her much. She died when I was little. My pap was the meanest man you ever met, and

224

Annabelle was the only light in my life for a long time. I never understood how someone so mean could have such a sweet child. I wouldn't have left her but my pap kicked me out, told me he weren't supporting me no more. I promised I'd come back for her as soon as I had a little money. I kept my promise but I was too late. When I came back six months later she was already dead. My pap said she got sick but I know he killed her and my mum too. The pillow was all I had left of her."

"Kurt I am so sorry. I shouldn't have tried to replace it." Lily felt awful.

"No, don't be sorry. It was real nice of you and I could never have just bought a pillow. Leaving her was one of the worst mistakes of my life, it would nice to get a pillow for doing something good." He smiled. "Don't go dyin' on me now. I don't want to carry this pillow around for the next twenty years in your memory."

Lily swallowed the lump in her throat. She hoped it wasn't a bad omen that she had given Kurt the pillow. She went back into the room and Eric was standing in one spot, staring at her. He reached for her and pulled her into his arms. "I can't lose you. Maybe we shouldn't go tonight."

"Eric, I just want you to know, that whatever else happens, I love you and I am so glad we've had this time..." He interrupted her before she could finish.

"Nothing is happening to you, I won't let it." He gave her a squeeze then let her go as a soft knock came at the door. Her maid had arrived to help her get ready for the ball.

The entourage of carriages pulled out of the Sampson home and made their way the short distance to the home of Senator Graham. Lily was to claim that she had hurt her ankle so as not to dance with any one and never be parted from her family. She understood the need but Lily rather liked dancing and was sure this was going to be a tedious night. They entered the ball room and worked their way through the crowd.

It was mid-August and the heat of the night, coupled with the mass of people made it incredibly hot. Lily felt herself getting dizzy and nauseous and prayed that she would not be sick in the middle of a crowded room. She was beginning to think that Eric had been right about not going. She turned to tell him so when a figure squeezed his way through the crowd and grabbed her arm.

"So nice to see you again Mrs. Sampson. It has been too long." Lieutenant Colonel Andrews smiled, his eyes running up and down her in a way that made her extremely uncomfortable. "You are even more beautiful than I had expected."

Eric's hand clamped over the Lieutenant Colonel's. "What do you want?" His voice came out in a low growl.

"Just to ask your wife to dance." Andrews smiled.

"Lily is not dancing tonight, she has hurt her ankle." Eric leaned closer to the other man. "Besides, I don't let her dance with kidnappers."

"You have me all wrong. I thought I was saving the Colonel's niece, if I had known what a criminal he was." Andrews shrugged his shoulders as if to emphasize his innocence.

James had come up on her other side and she heard him snort. "Please, no one is buying it!"

The crowd was extremely thick pressing all of them together. While they were surrounded by people, no one was listening or had any idea what was going on.

"Precisely. Now, if you will excuse us." Eric lifted his hand off her arm and spun her to his other side. The Lieutenant Colonel nodded with a smirk then melted into the crowd but Lily knew that was not the last they would be seeing of him.

Lily and Eric made a quick circle of the party, speaking with a few people and nodding to several other acquaintances. Amazingly, it took almost two hours to complete and Lily was exhausted by the end. Everyone was tense and Lily breathed a sigh of relief when they left the ball.

"Thank god that is over!" Lily climbed into the carriage and plopped herself onto a seat.

Eric chuckled at her statement then slid next to her. "I hope it is. I am trying to figure out what the Lieutenant Colonel's end game was in approaching us but I don't know what it is yet. I'm afraid what might happen next."

Lily sat up straighter, a knot of fear twisting in her stomach. It was a short ride home and she felt the tension building until they finally reached the drive to their home. Eric seemed to relax somewhat until they approached the front door to see it wide open. Lily swallowed a gasp as Eric hissed to her.

"Stay in the carriage!" He jumped out and bolted up the front steps into the foyer. James followed close behind, Kyle and Tom directly after James.

Kurt, climbed into the open door and drew a pistol, shutting the door behind him. "Don't worry. I'm just gonna stay with ya until Mr. Sampson gives the okay."

She nodded as they sat and waited for what was only a few minutes but felt like hours. Finally Eric returned looking pale and visibly shaken. "Toby is gone."

"What!" She gasped, feeling the color drain from her face.

"He's been kidnapped. Two of the servants are dead and three more were bound and gagged. They headed north, James says the trail is extremely clear, they didn't try to hide it like with you, they want us to follow." Eric shuddered and Lily wrapped her arms around him.

"Go." She nodded as she said the words.

"But, I can't leave you unprotected, James is going to..." He stopped his face contorted with pain.

"Kurt will stay with me, I'll be fine, you go." Kurt nodded but Eric shook his head.

"What if this was the plan. We all chase after Toby and they take you. I have to think clearly here." Eric raked his fingers through his hair.

"Eric. Toby is more important. Kurt and I can take care of me. You have to go. Remember... I love you." She kissed him and he held her for a moment.

"I love you too." He kissed her again than practically ran for the stables.

She sat stunned for a few seconds before Kurt gently nudged her, "We should get inside."

She followed behind him but her thoughts were filled with her husband. She had waited so long to hear those words but now she realized she would trade them for a second to have Toby and Eric back safely. Her stomach knotted in fear.

Lily entered the house followed by Elise and Eric's mother and she saw firsthand the destruction that had been caused. The butler, normally so composed, was still being untied on the floor while furniture had been destroyed and paintings torn down from the walls in the foyer. Lily wondered if any other rooms had been vandalized.

Lily turned to Elise. "Kindly make some tea for everyone. We need to put this place back together before Eric and Toby return." She could say one thing. For the first time since entering Eric's home, she felt like she had a purpose here.

They spent an hour, removing broken furniture and paintings and sweeping up the mess. It looked better, although replacement furnishings would have to be found. Lily turned to the housekeeper. "Are there any other rooms?"

The housekeeper nodded. "The library is the worst and Mr. Sampson's study."

Lily felt her shoulders droop but straightened her spine.

Mrs. Sampson cleared her throat. "Perhaps we should change into something more suitable."

Lily looked down and realized they were still wearing their ball gowns. She chuckled. "Good idea. We will meet back down here in half an hour." And she started up the stairs and toward her room, Kurt behind her.

Kurt entered the room first and searched it before allowing her to enter. "I'll be just outside, and I plan on leaving the door open a crack. Hope that's alright?"

She nodded and Kurt stepped out as a servant stepped in to help her undress. She put on a simple day dress that was much more practical for cleaning and moving furniture. She reached into her top drawer and pulled out a small knife, tucking it into the sleeve of her gown. Lily sat down to have her hair undone and braided when a movement caught her eye in the corner of the mirror. She motioned for the woman to stop. Lily turned to see what had moved when a hand shot out and covered her mouth while the maid disappeared from view. She reached to pull the hand away when another arm closed around her like a vice, knocking the chair over. Her capture swung her around and she could see the open window where he must have entered and relief washed through her. Kurt would hear the noise and come to her aid. But as he spun her the rest of the way around, she saw Kurt being wrestled to the floor and tied up by three men. A sick dread filled her stomach and all she could think was not again.

Chapter 26

She stopped fighting. It was futile and it used up her energy. This time Lily was going to be smart. She knew that Tracker was not behind her and she was not safe. The question was who was her captor. Kurt looked at her and she tried to say with her eyes that she was calm. He seemed to read her message.

"Twice in one night, what a treat Miss Carter." Lily clearly recognized the voice of the Lieutenant Colonel and she felt herself grow more relaxed. She was relieved that it was not Colonel Kingsley. His reference to her maiden name was not lost on her but she hoped that with Andrews she might be able to get some information. She smiled under the hand that was covering her mouth and forced her body to relax.

"I'm going to uncover your mouth, you can scream but no one is coming to your aid." She nodded as the arm holding her torso shifted so that he had both of arms trapped under his one. "You and you may go." He nodded to two of the men who exited out the door. Lily assumed that they were to subdue any servants who came to investigate. There remained only the Lieutenant Colonel and one other soldier.

The hand holding her mouth slowly lifted and he stroked her cheek then began to touch her hair. She took a deep breath to try and keep relaxed, she wanted to shiver with revulsion but she forced it down. It was time to play her part.

"How nice to see you again, Lieutenant Colonel Andrews. To what do I owe the pleasure?" Lily turned her head slightly and gave him the most winning smile she had. She thought of her mother and Amelia and the flirtation lessons that Elise had given her. She batted her eyelashes and Andrews gave her a lopsided grin.

"Well, Ma'am I'm here to take you to your husband. Your new husband that is." He shrugged, drinking her in with his eyes. She had seen Andrews looking at her before. She thought at first that he was just curious but she realized that he very attracted to either her or her inheritance. Most likely it was both, but she was going to play it to her advantage.

"You don't strike me as a cruel man, why would you do this to me?" She looked at him with pleading eyes, begging him to be her savior and he smiled in return.

"Unfortunately, we need your property to operate our business and bring it to the next level." Andrews frowned slightly.

"But does it have to be him? He frightens me." She squeezed his arm for effect. She glanced at Kurt and he nodded his accent, ever so slightly. He agreed with her plan.

"I tried to convince him that I was the better choice but he wanted to marry you and I..." He stopped talking, frowning.

"But you are so much younger, more handsome, more suitable as a husband. Why let the Colonel decide? Shouldn't we make the decision?" She smiled again and he touched her cheek. She could see his head leaning towards hers. She closed her eyes and pictured Eric. She was doing this for him and for Toby.

His lips felt revolting but she forced herself to kiss back with enthusiasm and she felt his breath quickening. He turned her around, crushing her to his body and Lily felt the fear rising in her chest but she forced it back down. She had to do this.

He lifted up his head. She could see the uncertainty in his eyes and she smiled again wrapping her arms around his neck. "I don't want to marry him, I want you."

He seemed to make a decision because he kissed her again and then lifted his head. "We'll have to kill him."

Lily felt panic rise in her chest. Was he talking about Eric or Toby. "Who?" Her confusion and fear showed momentarily and he frowned.

"The Colonel, of course!" He looked uncertain again, and he was staring at her suspiciously. Lily tried to cover her tracks.

"Slim too." She smiled hoping he wasn't changing his mind. "He'll try to kill both of us as soon as our backs our turned."

Andrews returned her smile and nodded. Lily breathed a sigh of relief. "We'll pretend that I am dropping you off to him but we'll ambush him instead. I don't need him anymore, I can run the business myself."

This next part she had to do very delicately. She didn't want to arouse any suspicion. "How many men does the Colonel have with him?"

Andrews thought for a moment. "A fair number but I am hoping that your husband takes care of several of them before we arrive. Is he trying to recover his son?"

Lily was unsure if she should divulge Eric's plans but she glanced quickly at Kurt who gave a small nod yes.

"Yes. He is." Lily kept her voice calm but it was inside she was shaking with fear.

"Excellent. Two birds, one stone." Lily felt herself go pale but she kept her head down and said nothing. She didn't have to ask what he meant, he was planning on killing Eric. He didn't notice her reaction because he was gathering a few of her things from around the room.

"I have a bag in the closet. Should I get it?" She asked smiling sweetly. He gave her a long look, clearly he did not completely trust her, then shook his head.

"Allow me." He smiled and entered the closet. She took two steps toward him, which also put Kurt by her feet. The other soldier was watching his commanding officer and Lily slipped the knife from in her sleeve and bent ever so slightly to put it in Kurt's reach. They had tied his hands in front of him and in a flash the small knife disappeared into his hands. Lily could already see him working at the knots.

Andrews came out of the closet and Lily herself began gathering a few articles that she tossed hastily in the bag. It didn't matter what she brought. Lily only wanted to give Kurt the opportunity to cut himself loose and follow. She knew that it was safer if she stayed at home, but she was in it now and she had to help her husband and her son.

"Ready?" Andrews smiled. Lily nodded hesitantly. Her plan was working but she felt a sudden knot of fear at what she was about to do. She pushed down the fear, took Andrews hand and he led her to the window.

It was amazing; maybe five soldiers materialized and began filing down the ladder from her window. It was more difficult for her, with her petticoat on but Andrews seemed to wait patiently. She hoped Kurt had cut his knots.

They quickly left Eric's property and crept down some side streets until they reached the horses. Once she looked back and could have sworn she saw someone following but then the shadow was gone again. Lily bit her lip. She hoped she wasn't alone.

Andrews helped her onto a horse then climbed behind her, snuggling her into him. She felt nothing but revulsion but allowed herself to be moved into him. "We are going to be king and queen of a great empire. Kingsley has been holding me back. With your dowry and my knowledge, we will make a fortune!" It was clear why she was so easily able to persuade him to turn on his partner. He had already wanted to do it. Andrews hoped that Eric killed Kingsley but Lily's hope was that Andrews and Kingsley destroyed each other before her husband got involved. She said a prayer for herself and Toby as they left the city limits. She hoped she could find Toby and protect him.

After half an hour Andrews pulled up in a clearing. She let out a sigh of relief. She was not sure she could stand anymore of his self-grandeur. He had talked of nothing besides how successful he was going to be and how good he was going to look with her on his arm. It was astounding one man could be so in love with himself.

"I have to talk to my men, they must be aware of the change in plans. Don't worry about Lieutenant Surrey, he is my closest aid and can be trusted." He must be talking about the man who had stayed in her room and knew the plan. She nodded, unconcerned. It didn't matter to her as she hoped this whole charade would be over soon. The Lieutenant Colonel sat her on a rock, by the edge of the clearing and began preparing his men. Lily wondered how willingly these men participated in crime. Andrews claimed that Kingsley had forced them to do something illegal and was now attempting to have them take the blame. She could hear the men becoming stirred up. One thing was for sure, Andrews was an effective liar. She was completely absorbed in what he was telling them when she felt a small tug on her sleeve. She turned startled and saw the face of Tracker smiling up at her, finger held to his lips for her to be quiet.

"How did you find me!" She whispered as quietly as she could.

"Turn your head and face forward." Tracker whispered back.

"I discovered Kingsley's camp this afternoon; you're not that far away. I overheard the plan to kidnap you using Toby as bait to lure Eric away. I didn't have time to stop the kidnappings but I was able to call in reinforcements to capture Kingsley and Andrews. I just hope they make it in time. As soon as they are not looking I will hide you and..."

"I am going." Lily mumbled so that Tracker could hear her but, hopefully, Andrews couldn't see her talking. "Andrews thinks I want to marry him and he plans on taking out the Colonel. If your reinforcements are not in time, Eric will need help." Lily's jaw was set at a determined tilt and Tracker said nothing.

"Someone else is following you." He added.

"Kurt. He's a friend."

"Swarthy looking sailor?" Tracker asked, double checking that they were talking about the same person. Lily nodded. "Good, I will ride on and see if I can help your husband. He's going to need it. Good luck." Then he was gone.

Lily sat up a little straighter, bolstered by the fact that both Tracker and Kurt were there to help.

Andrews walked back from the group of men smiling in a satisfied way. He held out his hand to pull her up and then pulled her into his arms kissing her neck. She smiled through gritted teeth as he led her to his horse.

"This is going to be an amazing night." He inhaled deeply.

"I agree." Lily responded sincerely. She was not sure how it would turn out but she had the feeling that tonight, this would finally come to an end.

The group rode for another half an hour when they heard the distinct voices of a camp set up nearby. Lily could smell fresh water and assumed that they had set up camp near a pond or lake. She wondered if Eric were already here and if he had tried to recover Toby. She guessed that he had not since the camp seemed so calm. She hoped that Tracker had warned him of her plan. It would be easier for him if he knew.

Andrews leaned in and whispered. "I have to turn you over the Colonel initially. It will keep you out of harm's way and allow me to move freely against him."

Lily nodded but the knot of fear tightened in her stomach. She wondered briefly who was going to double cross who tonight. Was Andrews just playing her now. She had to do something.

She turned in the saddle and kissed him with everything she had. She pretended he was Eric and he had just pronounced his love. When she pulled away his eyes still looked slightly glazed and the men around them were looking uncomfortably at them, a few with suspicion in their eyes but she couldn't worry about that now. She had to make sure she had Lieutenant Colonel Andrews on her side.

"I just don't want you to forget me while we're apart. Promise you won't." She smiled as sweetly as she could. He returned her smile, looking slightly drunk.

"I won't." He looked at her lips clearly thinking of kissing her again.

"How will I know when to rejoin you?" She asked.

"I will come for you when I have disposed of my, competition. You must stay where it is safe." He stroked her cheek but she tried not to be sick as she thought of Andrews trying to kill Eric.

"But what if someone else tries to capture me, Slim or someone else. How will I protect myself?" She wrapped her arms around his neck and tried to smile persuasively.

He seemed to think for a moment then nodded his head. "You are right. But could you really shoot someone?" Andrews slipped a small revolver in her hand. She tucked it into the bosom of her dress and nodded.

"Unfortunately, I have had to do it before." He could hear the sincerity in her voice and smiled again.

"We are going to be a great pair." And he kicked his horse into a trot to head into the camp.

Lily felt her heart beating wildly but she tried to remain calm. It was important to keep observing and to pay attention to the people around her. Immediately she recognized the Colonel and Slim with a few other men. She didn't have to fake shrinking into Lieutenant Colonel Andrews. He was her protection at the moment, small as it may be. He squeezed her arm and she reminded herself to look around.

There must have been thirty men milling about and Lily wondered if they were all loyal to the Colonel or if some of them were under Andrews. Lily hoped it was the latter, otherwise the odds were not good.

Colonel Kingsley looked up at their approach and smiled a cold smile that sent chills down her spine. "At last." He said as he held up a hand to her to help Lily off the horse.

She took it hesitantly and Andrews let her go. As soon as her feet hit the ground he held up his other hand and struck her hard across the cheek. Without thinking she let out a cry and stumbled back. Slim cackled and Lily couldn't keep the hate and loathing out of her eyes as she stared at the man who had tried to kill her.

"That was for making me wait so long. If you are with child there will be further reprimand and the child will never survive the first day." Lily's eyes shifted to Kingsley but she couldn't keep the fear out of her eyes. How could he be so cruel?

236

"Now, my dear," he grabbed her roughly by arm. "I want the truth about how you escaped."

Lily took a deep breath. Tracker was not under Kingsley's employ but she did not want to implicate him. Slim on the other hand, she had no trouble sharing his part.

"Slim intended, I believe, to rape and kill me. He thought you would never find out and that everyone would assume I had escaped and gone into hiding." The Colonel turned to look at Slim as the smile slowly left his face.

"It's a damned lie! You know it was Tracker who let her go free." He was too emphatic though and the sincerity of her story shone through.

"How did he get you out of the camp?" The Colonel stared at her with hard eyes that made her mouth go dry. She swallowed, the truth would be best, as much as she could tell.

"My guard fell asleep. I walked out." He stared intently at her but she met his gaze, despite her fear.

"Tracker fell asleep?" The Colonel's eyes narrowed.

"No it was Rings. Tracker left." She shrugged, finally breaking eye contact.

"Where?" The Colonel's eyes narrowed and his face leaned closer to hers until their noses were almost touching.

"I don't know." She did know but she was afraid to implicate him.

"She's lyin. He was always jabberin' her ear off!" Slim sounded panicked and the Colonel grabbed her chin forcing her eyes to again meet his. His grip was hard and she knew that she would have bruises.

"Did he tell you?" She forced herself not to cry out at the pain.

"He said the less he told me the better off I would be." Lily spoke the truth, Tracker did say that to her and the Colonel seemed to believe her because he released her chin but not her arm.

The Colonel looked at Slim, thought for a second, and then motioned to a man nearby. He wasn't in uniform but was in ragged clothing. He had a blank expression on his face that was difficult to read. Lily couldn't tell if was skilled at remaining impartial or just not very bright. He was huge, at least 250 pounds and tall. A chill moved up her spine at the sight of him moving towards her. "Sven, kill him."

"No hold on, just cause some good for nuthin' girl says..." Slim was backing away but the man reached out, grabbed him by the arm, then the head and just like that snapped Slim's neck. He crumpled to the ground, dead.

Lily could not contain the cry that escaped her lips and she clamped a free hand over her mouth to keep from sobbing. She had never seen death so close and, as much as she hated Slim, it was revolting and frightening.

"Now," He roughly pulled her to look in his face again. "I have waited a long time for you and I wanted a virgin for a wife but I will be content if you are not with child. A doctor will be examining you shortly. Pray, that you are not carrying Sampson's brat!" He roughly let her go and Lily fell to the ground.

She looked briefly at Andrews, wondering if he would step in at any point or if he had lost his nerve. Kingsley had always frightened her and, apparently, before today he had been on his best behavior. Perhaps he frightened his partner as well. Andrews face was unreadable and he did not glance at her at all. Lily wondered if he was just trying to keep the Colonel from becoming suspicious or if he had changed his mind.

"Take her to my tent." He motioned to Sven who frightened Lily even more than the Colonel, he could kill her by sheer accident. She shook her head and a slow smile spread over his face. Lily had been right. The man was slow. Slow and mean were a bad combination.

Andrews swung down from his horse. "I'll escort her." And he reached his hand down to pull her up from the ground.

Kingsley's face went absolutely black. "Are you questioning me?"

"We are partners, and I am protecting one of our assets. If she is dead before you can marry her, this will all have been for nothing. You don't give a beast fine china!" Andrews did not flinch and Lily thought that he was either incredibly brave, foolish, or he knew something about Kingsley that she did not.

"You are right, of course. I am forgetting how unaccustomed to female company Sven is." The Colonel's expression had not changed and he glared at her, then Andrews, but allowed the other man to escort her.

Andrews did not look at her but mumbled. "We do not have much time. Your first husband's advances are of little concern to me but Kingsley will positively ruin you for anyone else."

Lily swallowed hard sure that his words were the absolute truth. He brought her in the tent, kissed her briefly, then turned to leave. She turned to survey the room. There was a desk piled high with papers on one side and a narrow cot on the other. As desperate as her situation was, she was exhausted. She desperately wanted to stretch out on it and fall asleep. As Andrews opened the tent flap, she heard his voice.

"If you were planning on walking over to the tent, why didn't you escort her yourself?"

"I find I am not all that interested in her company. Are you?" The Colonel returned.

Andrews ignored the question. "If you are not interested in her company then why marry her? Generally men spend at least some time with their wives."

"There are things I am interested in, which will keep me content for a while. Don't pretend that you would be any better. We all know how your relationships end."

"They were not ladies, they were whores!" Andrews was clearly getting upset.

"It doesn't matter, we stick to the plan and don't you forget it." Kingsley must have left because Lily heard nothing else.

She gave a shudder and said a silent prayer that someone rescued her before she had to face either of those men again. She looked around the tent again. She was only in the front half of the tent. It was divided into two sections. She could hear a faint crying coming from the other side. Lily peaked through the flap to see a small figure huddled on another cot.

"Hello." She said softly. She did not want anyone to hear her and stop her.

The little figure turned over and Lily clearly recognized the face of Toby, bruised as it was. "Toby!" she rushed over to the bed and picked the little boy up in her arms.

"Lily is that you?" He mumbled back. He looked disoriented and she wondered if he had had anything to eat or drink.

"Yes, sweetheart. I'm here." He snuggled into her.

"Where's Daddy?" Lily could hear the tears in his voice and she wanted to cry to. This was too much for a little boy.

"He's coming soon." She said as she held Toby. He quickly fell asleep in her arms. Despite the danger, she felt an overwhelming love for her new family. She didn't know when Andrews or Kingsley might be back but she couldn't leave Toby alone. She lay down with him in her arms and fell asleep.

It felt like only minutes had passed when someone shook her awake and she swallowed a scream. She had been dreaming of the doctor who was supposed to examine her. He had been attempting to force her to miscarry. It had been a horrifying dream.

Her blurry eyes worked to refocus to see the person in front of her and she nearly cried when she saw the face of Kurt.

"Thank goodness!" She gasped but he put his hand to his lips.

"I took out a guard to get in here but there are at least four more. I was trying to figure out why they would put you and Toby together but I guess it is to keep you well guarded. Come on, let's go."

"I have to stay Kurt. If Andrews kills Kingsley then Eric won't have to. I can't risk losing him." Lily shifted Toby's weight onto Kurt.

"What if Kingsley kills Andrews? What then?" Kurt's face was hard. He clearly did not approve.

"It is still one less person for Eric to fight and I don't think the Colonel will hurt me, yet." She looked away. She didn't quite believe her own words.

"And what about the baby?" Kurt stared at her but she couldn't make eye contact.

Their conversation was abruptly interrupted when they both heard the front flap of the tent being lifted. Lily felt her heart leap into her chest but she knew what she had to do. "Go. Tracker knows I'm here, he's gone to Eric."

This seemed to pacify Kurt who nodded but turned and whispered. "Remember your promise."

Lily bit her lip. She had promised to stay alive and Kurt was right, it was a deadly game. She didn't have time to think now. She opened the partition to see who was waiting on the other side.

Andrews stood looking at the cot, clearly perplexed she wasn't there. She smiled ready for the next round. "Back so soon?"

"What were you doing back there?" Andrews looked genuinely puzzled.

"Was I not supposed to go back there? I heard crying, I went to see who it was then I put the child back to sleep." She was careful not to use Toby's name. She didn't want to remind Andrews again of her intimate relationship with Eric.

"That's right, you are his step mother. I can assure you I have no former children." Andrews walked up to her, pulling her into his arms and kissing her long and hard. It didn't seem to matter to him whether she kissed back so she stood passively. "I have taken care of the doctor, he will not come tonight. I am to move you to another tent so that Kingsley can use his own. Tonight is the last night we will have to pretend that you will marry him. Tonight, I will rid of us of our...problem."

Lily wondered if she should ask more but decided against it so she merely nodded. If Lieutenant Colonel Andrews failed, she would want to know as little as possible. She looked briefly back at the tent and wondered if she should have listened to Kurt. If Kurt could get in to take Toby, why hadn't Eric? Maybe Kurt was more able to sneak in being alone. She was glad, at least, that Toby had been able to leave.

"What are you thinking about?" Andrews' eyes narrowed, he was clearly suspicious of her again as, she thought to herself, he should be.

"I'm just worried for you, that's all." Lily gave him her

best smile and he returned it, obviously pacified.

"Don't be. I have known Kingsley for a long time, I know exactly how and when to strike. Now, let's get you to your tent." Andrews held out his arm and Lily took it. She was still amazed that she could so easily deceive this man. He seemed well spoken and intelligent but clearly his ego got in the way of his better judgment. Lily was afraid that her assassination plan may be another example of this character flaw. She was afraid that Colonel Kingsley may be far more difficult to kill than Andrews planned.

Andrews escorted her the short distance to her new tent. As they stepped into the tent, he leaned down and whispered into her ear. "Good night, my love." He left whistling and Lily turned to survey her tent. It was smaller, dirtier and even less appealing than Colonel Kingsley's had been. She sat on the cot unsure of what to do.

The night lengthened and without meaning to, Lily slipped into sleep. In her sleep she heard yelling and shouting and she turned restlessly, wanting to rid herself of the terrible dreams that plagued her. Suddenly and hand grabbed her around the neck and yanked her out of her bed and out of sleep. The yells had been no dream.

The Colonel grabbed her by the hair and pulled her out of the tent. Still half asleep, Lily stumbled and he righted her by pulling harder on her hair. She cried out but tried to keep going. "You put him up to this, Bitch!" She struggled to understand his words until she saw Lieutenant Colonel Andrews lying on the ground in a pool of blood struggling to get up. His breathing was labored and Lily let out a cry. Colonel Kingsley shoved her towards the dying man and she knelt down on the ground next to him. Her hands shook as she reached down to touch him.

"Andrews?" She said softly. She drew her hand back unsure of where he was bleeding from.

"I had to try." His breathing was labored and he paused. "So much to gain." He paused again and she tentatively patted his head to give him some comfort.

A sick dread filled her stomach as the Colonel pulled her

back up. "The boy is gone. You are all the leverage I have left."
He sneered in her face. He seemed to dislike her as much as she
him. Then he turned to the woods.

"Sampson, I need her alive. I know you know that, but
that doesn't mean I can't inflict horrible pain. Show yourself,
let's get this over with, or you will have to hear as I torture your
wife."

Lily felt her insides lurch at the same time the Colonel
started pulling her towards a stump. He stretched her hand out
on the top and held it there as Lily tried to yank herself free. She
heard herself whimper despite her attempts to keep quiet.

"Do you want to hear what it feels like to lose your hand
one finger at a time?" Out of the corner of her eye, Lily saw
Sven approach with a hatchet in his hand. She tried to pull
harder and she bit her lip to keep from screaming. Kingsley gave
a maniacal laugh that echoed around her.

"Come on out, Sampson. She's almost out of time!"
Kingsley laughed again and Sven, now in front of them, raised
the hatchet over his head. Lily couldn't help it, she let out a cry
and pulled frantically under the Colonel's vice like grip. She
heard Sven's dull laugh as he leaned back for more power. "Only
one finger now!" Kingsley's voice rose with excitement and Lily
allowed a sob to escape her lips. With sickening slow motion,
Lily saw the hatchet falling towards her hand. She held her
breath, waiting for the pain.

Suddenly, the hatchet, traveling in a perfect arch,
stopped its descent then fell to the ground as a loud bang ripped
through the air. Lily's head jerked up to see Sven fall to the
ground dead. Lily stared in disbelief, then saw the bullet wound
in his temple. Twenty feet in front of them Eric stood with
James and Mark behind him and ten other soldiers. They must
have been the reinforcements Tracker had sent for. Lily let out
another sob, this one in relief.

She tried to pull away and run but Colonel Kingsley was
holding on to her with all the strength he had and she didn't even
budge.

"You killed one of my best men." The Colonel growled.
"You're trying to kill me and marry my wife." Eric

cocked one eyebrow, as he reloaded his pistol.

"Fair enough. Frankly, she is nothing but trouble. She has turned several of my associates against me, including my partner." Kingsley nodded his head toward Andrews, still struggling to breath.

"Are you sure that's Lillian's fault?" Eric seemed perfectly calm and Lily felt herself relaxing slightly, her head clearing.

The Colonel waved his hand, dismissing the Eric's comment. "You don't hope to beat me and save your wife with that small group do you?"

"No, I have plenty more men waiting in the wings but as you asked me to step out, I brought a small amount of reinforcements."

Lily felt Colonel Kingsley twitch slightly and she began to feel more nervous. Would he kill her out of spite if he thought there was no way he could win? She feared the answer was yes.

"Bargain for your freedom." She mumbled to him. She saw Eric frown but she didn't know if Eric was aware how much Kingsley disliked her or how unstable he was becoming.

He yanked her hair again. "I don't need help from you!" He whipped her to the ground by her hair and Lily felt like every strand was being pulled out of her head. The force of it sent her flying six feet from him and she allowed herself to role, to gain some more distance between them. Her proximity to Kingsley must have been the only thing holding back the attack because as soon as she was clear, guns started firing all around her and the air was quickly filled with smoke. She stayed close to the ground and headed for the woods but it wasn't an easy journey. She looked back twice to see if she could see her brother or Eric but couldn't find either. Twice a man dropped in front of her, hit by a bullet and, as they were all wearing the same uniforms, she had no idea whose side they were on.

The firing of guns and the screams were deafening. If she weren't so afraid, she would have cried. She said a prayer that Toby wasn't there and that Toby and Kurt were alright. Now she could hear the clash of metal on metal and knew that some of the men must have drawn swords. The smoke began to clear and she could see that she had almost made it to the cover of the woods. Lily doubled her efforts. She was just crawling into the cover of the underbrush when a hand grabbed her ankle and started pulling her out. This time, she wasn't going to be a victim. Kingsley was behind her and she used her free foot to kick him as hard in the face as she could. His nose began to instantly spurt blood and she felt some small measure of satisfaction after all the bruises he had caused her. She reached to her left and grabbed a large branch, an inch and half thick and three feet long. She got up on her feet ready to defend herself.

The Colonel stood and lunged for her but she jumped out of the way and came down with stick across his back. Clearly the exertion of the fight had tired him and Lily played her advantage by moving several feet away onto the edge of the woods. She looked quickly around but saw only a few groups fighting here and there, several men were strewn on the ground but she assumed many were being chased through the woods. Where was Eric?

"Know this. If you do not leave with me and marry me, I am going to make you suffer until I kill you slowly and painfully." Kingsley practically snarled at her and despite herself a small laugh bubbled out of her mouth. It's not that she didn't believe him, she did. His offer was so ridiculous that it was no choice at all.

Kingsley, however, did not appreciate her reaction and pulled a knife from his belt. Her stick suddenly felt a great deal smaller but she held it tightly.

"Feeling confident are you?" He sneered. "Your husband is most likely dead, along with your brother, and no one is coming to save you."

She felt the color drain from her face and the stick in her hand dropped a few inches. Lily raised it up. "Then I choose death. I would rather die a slow and painful death than be married to you."

"Oh, I think it will be both. I am not going through all this without first getting your inheritance. Originally I planned to settle down but now, I will discard of you at the first possible convenience." He smiled a very cold cruel smile but Lily set her jaw.

"Then you are doing me a favor. I would much rather be dead than settled down with a vile man like you." He was moving slowly closer and Lily realized that she needed to come up with a plan. Fight, run, or stall, she had to do something. She backed up a few more feet.

"You can't keep backing up, my dear, eventually I will catch you." The Colonel took two more steps, further closing the gap and Lily felt her heart hammering in her chest.

Suddenly she felt a hand at her back and she jumped to the side, unaware of whom it was. She swung the stick with all her might but Eric ducked just in time.

"Eric!" Tears stung her eyes, she was so relieved to see him and she wanted to throw her arms around him but he gently touched her cheek then tucked her behind him.

"Sampson, not dead yet huh?" The knife in the Colonel's hand shifted but Eric didn't move.

"If I'm going down, you're coming with me." Eric sounded extremely casual while Lily's heart was hammering a mile a minute.

His relaxed attitude was clearly making Kingsley more nervous and Lily realized that Eric was strategically placing the Colonel at a disadvantage.

She was feeling more confident when four men joined the Colonel's advance. She recognized Bags but none of the other men. None of them were in uniform and she guessed that these were his real smugglers and thieves. Lillian held her stick higher but she could feel herself trembling. From out of the woods, however, she clearly saw the silhouettes of James and Mark in the dim morning light. Just behind them, the swarthy figure of Kurt lumbered, as if on deck, directly towards her. Her heart soared.

The Colonel paused for just a moment then covered the last few steps in a run. "Kill them all! Leave the girl." And he tried to jab his knife into Eric's stomach. Eric was ready for the attack however and side stepped the move, making a sweep with his own knife at the Colonel's side who just stumbled out of the

246

way. The two men squared off again, as Bags and another man made a move towards her while the other two engaged James and Mark.

Kurt knocked one of them off balance but Bags swung at him, just skimming his arm with the knife and leaving a shallow gash. Kurt seemed not to notice as she shoved Bags to the ground and the other man attacked again. Kurt spun him around and sent him head first into a large boulder were he crumpled to the ground but Bags saw his opportunity and stuck his knife into Kurt's side. She heard Kurt's grunt of pain but he grabbed the knife and Bag's hand and Lily took the opportunity to come around Kurt and hit Bags over the head with her stick using every ounce of energy she had. He fell to his knees where Kurt then grabbed the stick from her hand and hit him hard upside the head. The man crumpled to the ground.

"Kurt, are you alright?" Her hands trembled as she helped him to the ground.

"I'll be fine, you stick close to me." She nodded, then turned to see the Colonel miss again as she lunged for Eric. Eric was clearly besting Kingsley and it was only a matter of time before Eric would win. James and Mark were slowly subduing their opponents as well when Lily saw the flash of metal from Colonel Kingsley's belt.

"Let's get this over with." Eric stood poised like a panther, ready to jump, as Kingsley took aim. Suddenly a figure streaked across the field, knocking Kingsley off balance, sending the bullet off in another direction. In an instant, Lily recognized Tracker. She heard his groan and stood, looking to see where Kingsley had stabbed him.

"Traitor!" The Colonel yelled as he raised the knife again but another gun went off. This time, however, it was Eric who fired and he didn't miss. Kingsley dropped to the ground, dead.

Lily ran to her husband and Tracker. Tears of joy and worry flooded her eyes at the same time. Eric wrapped her up in her arms. Holding her tight for one second before he set her down and they both went running for Tracker. He was holding his leg, a deep gash oozing blood.

"Eric get a fire going, needle and thread, boiling water. I need to get Tracker and Kurt stitched up." Lily began ripping strips from her dress. She looked up to see James approaching, the other two men had run as soon as Kingsley had died.

"Thank you James." She wrapped her arms around her brother and he returned the hug. "Help me get some fabric from my dress." He nodded and began working on her petticoats as Mark joined to help.

Lily wrapped Tracker's leg tight to stop the bleeding then went to stitch Kurt. She knew his wound had to be sewn up soon, it was to the body. She bathed the wound then sewed it as quickly and neatly as she could.

"I'd be worried if I hadn't already seen you do this." Kurt gave her a weak smile.

"With two brothers, she stitched loads of cuts." James patted Kurt's arm.

She worked quickly washing wounds stitching both men then moved on to other soldiers who had been wounded. They quickly set up a medical tent of sorts in Colonel Kingsley's tent. Eric and the others began clearing the bodies and assessing the damage. She had worked for a few hours when she turned to Eric. "Where is Toby? And Tom?" Panic filled her voice.

"Not to worry. Tom returned with Toby. Which is what I need to do with you." He folded her in her arms. As he spoke, a caravan of soldiers arrived. Tracker gingerly got up and went to greet them. Lily saw the stripes of a general as Tracker motioned towards the bodies of Colonel Kingsley and Lieutenant Colonel Andrews. Was this who Tracker had really been working for? She was too tired to think anymore. She leaned into her husband ready to go home and go to sleep. A small smile touched her lips as she realized that the nightmare was over.

The next day passed in a blur. Lily and Eric had to tell their story to General Wilson who had been leading an investigation against Colonel Kingsley for the past few years, trying to have him removed from service and jailed. Lily, finally collapsed into bed with Eric on one side of her and Toby on the other.

She awoke the next morning, famished. She got quietly out of bed, not wanting to disturb Eric. A brief look in the mirror told her that it had all been real. Her face was bruised and battered and there were several more bruises on her body. Eric winced as he came up behind her.

"I am so sorry you had to go through all of this." He winced again as he touched a particularly bad bruise under her eye. She turned to him, he too had several bruises and scrapes covering his body.

She smiled and touched his cheek. "I'm just glad we're both still alive."

He returned her smile. "Me too." He grimaced again looking at a few more bruises. "How is the baby?"

She smiled. "Everything seems fine. The doctor seemed to think that everything was still going well. But I can tell you one thing. Baby is hungry and so am I."

Eric laughed. "Then let's get you down to breakfast!"

Lily had expected an air of jubilation when she entered the dining room but instead everyone was very hushed. She got several hugs but very few words. She was initially worried that everyone was put off by her bruised and battered face but finally she couldn't take the silence. "What is wrong?" She finally asked the general assembly.

No one spoke for a second and then Elise finally took her hand. "Kurt's not doing so well. The doctor isn't sure he's going to make it."

Lily felt herself go pale and she took an unsteady breath. She turned to Eric who looked equally shaken up. He nodded to her and she stood from the table and left the room heading for Kurt's quarters.

She knocked briefly then was told to come in by the doctor. Eric followed behind her and squeezed her hand.

"What is wrong?" She addressed the young doctor, a different man than had treated her wounds.

"He lost a great deal of blood. He has spiked a high fever that I am trying to control but it seems to continue rising. If I can't get it down, he will perish."

Lily bit her lip then reached over and held Kurt's hand. It was extremely warm and Lily felt her brow crease. "Kurt, this can't be the end. You haven't told me any of your best sea stories. Besides, neither Eric nor I have a father who is going to give Toby and our baby piggyback rides? We need you!" She knew she sounded like a fool but her words came from her heart and she realized that Kurt had become like family, much like a father figure to her. She didn't want to lose another man like that in her life.

She sat by his bed all that day, holding his hand, telling him stories, talking about plans for the baby. She took all her meals there and Toby came and sat for a while with her. When night fell, his fever seemed to worsen and Lily had a cot brought into the room. She was bone tired but she couldn't leave him now. If it was his time, she wanted to be there with him. Finally, she drifted off to sleep but her dreams were restless and fretful. At four in the morning she woke to the distinct croak of Kurt's voice.

"Water." he mumbled through dry lips.

Lily quickly got up sprinted over to the bed. Shakily, she poured water into a glass then held it to his lips. He took a long drink then fell back to sleep. Lily felt his head. He was much cooler. She sighed in relief, and returned to her cot. If he needed anything, she would be here.

She woke a few hours later when the doctor arrived to check on his patient. After speaking with the doctor, Lily decided to return to her room. The worst was over for Kurt. With his fever down, the doctor was extremely hopeful Kurt would recover.

As she was walking back, she stopped to check on Tracker. She knocked softly on the door and peeked her head in. Ann was sitting next to him, holding his hand and brushing the hair back from his face. Lily smiled and closed the door. She was so glad that two people who had seemed so alone had found each other.

Lily softly opened the door to her room to find Eric asleep in bed. She crawled in next to him and curled up against her husband. He wrapped her in his arms. "How's Kurt?"

"Better." She smiled again glad to be in her husband's arms.

"I could sleep for a week." She snuggled in closer.

"Right now?" He nuzzled her ear as his hand ran up her side.

She laughed softly. "I suppose sleep can wait, I seem to have plenty of time for it now!"

"That is one of the things I love about you." He started to kiss her but Lily pulled away.

"Do you really?" She looked into his eyes and he touched the bruise under her eye.

"How can you not know that I am madly in love with you. I think I have been since the first time I met you all those years ago. I wasn't ready to love again and honestly, you were too young. You wouldn't have been able to handle my feelings for you." He kissed her again and this time she returned his kiss.

"But even when I returned to Boston this spring, you pushed me away!" There was a small pout to her lips that showed her hurt.

"I'm sorry love, I just knew I could never remain detached from you. After Caitlin it was so difficult to allow myself to love again. I was afraid of getting hurt. But now I know it is totally worth it. You are worth it." He kissed a third time and this time she did not protest or ask questions but let her husband fill her with love.

Epilogue

Lily sat in the carriage with the nurse and her baby daughter. She smiled at the sleeping child, her heart full of love. Eric opened the door and helped Toby in. The boy was carrying two large bouquets of flowers. One he handed to her with a kiss.

"Those are for you Mommy." He smiled and hugged her again. Toby had gradually started calling her mommy as the baby grew bigger in her belly. Now it seemed completely natural to them all.

Eric winked and kissed her cheek as he snuggled her into his side. She smiled at her husband so glad to be with him and her family.

"Who are the other flowers for?" Lily chuckled to herself, she knew the answer of course.

"Kurt. He might like them for his room in Maine." Toby nodded to emphasize his point and Lily had to laugh. Kurt had spent the summer at sea and was returning to Maine with them to spend the fall.

"I'm sure he will love them." Lily hugged her son and snuggled in for the ride.

They reached the harbor quickly and all of their trunks were loaded onto the boat for the journey. They were making the trip to attend Tracker and Ann's wedding but would stay to visit family for a few months. Because of the birth of her daughter she had missed Mark and Amelia's wedding and was glad they had an extended stay to celebrate with her family and friends.

Tracker had just finished his final tour with the military and was going to work for her brother. James was in desperate need of more help with so many contracts to fill.

Kurt swaggered onto the deck and hailed Toby who went running up the plank to greet his friend. Toby gave Kurt his flowers, who grimaced slightly, but accepted them all the same.

Lily held her daughter as Eric helped them both up the plank.

"Well, I'll be. Last time I saw you, you could barely move and here you are lookin' as fit as a filly in her first season!" Kurt must be extremely happy to see them. He never talked that much.

"I have someone to introduce you to." She uncovered the babies face. "Meet Annabelle Marie Sampson." She gently placed the baby in Kurt's arms.

"You named her after my sister?" She could hear the slight choke in his voice as Eric wrapped his arm around her waist.

"It seemed like the perfect choice." She smiled and Kurt nodded his head.

"The sea ain't what it used to be." Somehow Lily doubted the sea had changed but she waited to hear what Kurt would say. "I been thinkin' about spendin' more time on dry land."

Lily and Eric both laughed and Lily knew the Annabelle was going to be spoiled rotten.

Titles Available From
Charles Towne
Publishing

True Heroes by Miles Gann

Caleb Whitmor was born with unusual talents. From day one, he has been obsessed with the details that most people in the world couldn't see, and capable of feats that most people could never dream possible. The question facing his unlimited potential is simple: what side of good and evil will he take? Even as he must decide that answer, his rare gifts fight for control from within his own mind, and it is up to a shy girl named Alice to show him the love that could point him towards the righteous path. Now Caleb must fight every battle from all sides, as the world around him screams for a true hero to save everyone.

NOW AVAILABLE ON KINDLE AND AT AMAZON.COM

The Amazing Pitsville and The Beggar's Invisible Railways
by Gabe Redel

When McGavin gets knocked from the clouds, he crashes into the amazing land of a humble lumberjack, a weeping butterfly, and a high-strung, grub eating, goofy fuzzball named Beagle. There, in Pitsville, he finds a wife and begins to learn how to be everything he is not, until Kemp The Beggar conjures up a plan to steal Pitsville and exile its people into his own evil alternate world. McGavin and team find help from a lazy critter and a careless Army tank driver to take down The Beggar by learning the secret of The Invisible Railways, befriending powerful enemies, and convincing a world of stolen people that their only way home is through the belly of a raging volcano.

NOW AVAILABLE ON KINDLE, AT AMAZON.COM, AND RETAILERS NATIONWIDE.

Crooked River by M.P. Murphy

Captain Gilmore, a baron of Cleveland industry, is appalled by the negative press his two daughters have brought on the family, so when the youngest is caught up in a blackmail scandal he does everything he can to keep it out of the local tabloids, including hiring former FBI agent Jack Francis to track down the blackmailer. With a passion for bourbon and women, Francis dives headfirst into a case that soon turns into a murder investigation with a disappearing body. Knowing that he may be in over his head Jack calls on the help of his former partner at the Bureau to give him a hand, only to discover it was agent Colin Sommers who had recommended him to the Captain in the first place. Soon Jack is looking over his shoulder and questioning loyalties as he tries to retrieve the blackmail evidence and stop a killer from striking again.

NOW AVAILABLE ON KINDLE AND AT AMAZON.COM

More titles and book information available at

www.charlestownepublishing.com

Made in the USA
Lexington, KY
10 December 2012